What makes Cody Matthews so obnoxious?

Joan smiled at what she'd written across the top of the paper. She was pleased with the harsh directness of her words and wondered if she'd need a second sheet. There were so many things not to like about the man.

Ten minutes later she had a sizable compilation of sins. Feeling in control once more, she scanned the list she'd made.

Overbearing arrogance
Ego the size of a planet
Poor taste in clothes—especially belt buckles
Beautiful bedroom eyes
Lascivious nat—

Wait a minute! *Beautiful bedroom eyes*? Where had that come from? Those eyes didn't belong on her list.

Annoyed, she stood up and filled the teakettle. Waiting for the whistle, she leaned against the doorjamb and stared at the list on the table.

All right, so he did have great eyes. She'd give him that one. But they didn't make up for all his bad qualities.

No. Number four on her list was simply a slip of the pen.

Dear Reader,

Growing up in my house, I remember thinking that my poor father was at a real disadvantage. Females outnumbered him three to one. Even our pets were female.

But Dad was a real trouper. The father/daughter relationship he shared with my sister and me was pretty special. Even though I suspect he would have preferred to be watching golf on TV or out fishing, he still found time to be a guest at our backyard tea parties, a customer at our imaginary shoe store and the first one to sample our latest triumph from the Easy Bake oven.

As I was creating Cody Matthews, my hero for this book, I envisioned him sharing that same kind of bond with his own daughter, Sarah. But what would he do, I wondered, if something happened to change that bond? Something he didn't understand or have any clue how to handle? Suppose his daughter went from being an angelic daddy's girl to the devil in blue jeans, all in a matter of weeks.

That's one of the dilemmas facing Cody in this book. And that's where Joan Paxton comes in. Even the greatest father in the world needs help now and then, especially if he's a single parent. Only one problem—Cody is just as stubborn as his daughter. He'd rather wrestle a bull than admit he can't handle his own child!

Poor Joan. She's the one who can bring the Matthews family back from the brink of disaster, but she's got her work cut out for her. I hope you enjoy reading just how she accomplishes bringing Cody and Sarah back together, and most of all, how she finds love along the way.

Ann Evans

That Man Matthews

Ann Evans

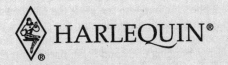

HARLEQUIN®

TORONTO • NEW YORK • LONDON
AMSTERDAM • PARIS • SYDNEY • HAMBURG
STOCKHOLM • ATHENS • TOKYO • MILAN • MADRID
PRAGUE • WARSAW • BUDAPEST • AUCKLAND

ISBN 0-373-70957-9

THAT MAN MATTHEWS

This edition published by arrangement with Harlequin Books S.A.

® and TM are trademarks of the publisher. Trademarks indicated with
® are registered in the United States Patent and Trademark Office, the
Canadian Trade Marks Office and in other countries.

Visit us at www.eHarlequin.com

Printed in U.S.A.

This book, a story about fathers,
has to be dedicated to one of the best dads
I know—my brother-in-law, William Wilson Marsh.

CHAPTER ONE

CODY MATTHEWS took one look at Merlita Soledad's broad, dark features and immediately recognized trouble ahead.

His live-in Mexican housekeeper was normally a pleasant apple dumpling of a woman, a whirlwind of efficiency when it came to keeping the ranch house organized. She had a generous heart, a bone-crushing hug and an ancient recipe for the best darned chilies *rellenos* in south Texas. But when she was angry, she had a tendency to mangle the English language, and right now she was grinding it up like a steak in a blender.

"You try it, *jefe*," she demanded, her arms planted across her chest, her nostrils flared wide. "You tell me how you like."

"Lita, if I don't leave soon, I'm gonna be late for the afternoon flight to Washington." He tried to give the woman back the plate and fork she'd thrust into his hands when she'd invaded his study. "You know I love your cocoa cake. I'll be home tomorrow night. Save a piece for me."

"No," Merlita said with a firm shake of her head. Her arms tightened, and he caught his first glimpse of the kitchen paring knife she held between her capable fingers. "You taste my cake. It's important. You, too, Señor Walt."

Cody didn't think it wise to argue with a woman who held a knife. He glanced at his father. Walt Matthews cradled a similar plate of the sweet chocolate dessert, but from the crinkle bisecting his forehead, it was clear he didn't have a clue what was bothering Merlita, either.

With an uncertain smile Cody settled back, hooking one leg over the side of his desk. If the woman was desperate for a compliment, he'd have no trouble giving it, and then he could be away from Luna D'Oro and off to the airport.

He stuck his fork into the wedge of chocolate and scooped a generous helping into his mouth. "Mmm..." he began. "Still my favorite dess..."

The words trailed away as he stopped chewing. *Whoa! Sam Houston's underwear, something was mighty wrong with this batch!*

He cast a suspicious look at his plate. The cinnamon and chocolate couldn't disguise the fact that the cake was just plain awful. He wanted to spit the mouthful in the trash can next to his desk. But Merlita's dark eyes were throwing off sparks now, and he didn't dare.

Again he looked to his father for help. Pa had taken a small bite from his own dish. Cody could see he was having trouble swallowing.

"It's...uh...a little different from your usual, isn't it?" Cody ventured.

"*Sí.*"

"Trying a new recipe?" his father asked when he finally appeared to get his tongue under control.

"No," Merlita said, looking indignant. "Emperor Maximilian ate my great-great-great grandmother's cake in the Spanish court of kings. I do not change her recipe. But how you like it?"

"Might be a tad overcooked," Cody suggested, clearing his throat and wishing he had something to wash the taste out of his mouth. "Or maybe the mixing bowl didn't get cleaned well enough. Some soapsuds—"

"*Tu eres loco?* I don't cook in dirty bowls!" Merlita exclaimed in horrified tones. She waved away his words with a broad sweep of the hand that held the paring knife. "It's the salt. *Dos.* Two cups."

"Oh." Cody and Walter exchanged looks. Neither of them had a clue what went into the making of Mexican cake. Or what to say now. Cody settled on evasion. "Seems like a lot of salt."

"That's because it should be sugar. Someone switches the labels on the jars in my cupboard. A funny joker with yellow hair."

"Oh. I see." Cody straightened, suddenly understanding. He set the plate down on the only exposed corner of his desktop. Sarah! He should have known. Wasn't it always Sarah these days? "Lita, darlin', I—"

"You promised, *jefe,*" Merlita reminded him, making her point with the tip of the knife. "No more, you say. You say you straighten her out but good. You are *el jefe grande* around here, but you are not a man of your word."

"I *did* talk to her. But I'll talk to her again—"

"You do more than talk now. This is times three she makes jokes on me. The rubber bug in my guacamole. The bubbling soap pouring out of my washing machine. I can take no more. *Comprende?* She does not stop? *Via con dios, jefe.* I go home to Mexico." The woman's eyes narrowed threateningly. "And I take my *rellenos* recipe with me."

With a clatter of annoyance, the housekeeper scooped up the plates and forks and left the study. She muttered a litany of Spanish complaints all the way to the kitchen.

Cody turned back to his desk, searching through the mess of paperwork for his plane ticket. He smiled at his father, whose faded-blue gaze gleamed with knowing concern. "Don't say it, Pa," Cody warned. He didn't have time right now for a lecture about things he already knew.

"I didn't say a word," Walt Matthews protested.

"No, but you're thinking it."

"It's still a free country, ain't it? Man's got a right to think whatever he wants." Leaning heavily on one of the metal crutches that helped him get around, Walt came slowly to join him at the desk. "But I'm not one to stick my nose in where it ain't welcome."

Cody looked up with a laugh. "Since when?"

"Fine. Just don't come looking for me to cook when Merlita up and takes a bus back to Chihuahua."

"Damn! Where the hell is that ticket?" Cody complained as he threw down an empty envelope. "Someday I'm going to get this desk organized. If I miss this flight, it will be tomorrow afternoon before I can get another one out.''

''That might not be such a bad thing. Give you a chance to talk to Sarah.''

''Pa—''

Walt cut him off with a forestalling hand. ''None of my beeswax, I know.''

Cody sighed. Might as well give in. He wasn't going to get away from Luna D'Oro today without discussing Sarah. ''It's just a little harmless fun, Pa. You remember what I was like as a kid, don't you? Always trying to pull a fast one on you and Mom and the bunkhouse crew? Nothing Sarah's done is malicious. In fact, you have to admit that some of her pranks are pretty clever for a twelve-year-old.''

''That isn't what you said last week when you turned on the air conditioner in the Rover and five pounds of rice flew out the vents and nearly scared you off the road.''

''*Surprised,* not scared.''

''Same thing.''

Cody rolled his eyes. He didn't want to argue. Especially when Walt was probably right. Sarah—his sweet, precious baby girl—had turned into a royal pain in the butt in the past couple of months. Mouthy. Disobedient. With enough practical jokes in her bag of tricks to torment the family every day for the next ten years. And he didn't want to even think about what her final school report was going to look like this year.

He stopped looking for the plane ticket long enough to glance at the picture he kept on his desk.

Sarah, of course. The candid shot taken last year at the ranch's annual cookout.

Pa's camera had caught her pressed up against Cody, all smiles and girlish delight, hugging him with every bit of the strength and love she had in her. Nothing in that pert little nose and dimpled grin looked even remotely defiant. Her pale sunlit hair was made for angels, not devils. If there was any hint of the stubborn, willful behavior they'd seen lately, it was in the slight clef in his daughter's chin. She'd inherited it from her mother. It was pure Daphne.

"Here's your ticket," his father said, rescuing it from beneath a pile of handbills advertising everything from horse auctions in San Antonio to Stampede Days in Laredo. He handed Cody the folder, and then another right beneath it. "And take this with you on the plane, too. Try *reading* it this time."

Cody slipped the plane ticket into the inside pocket of his buckskin jacket. He barely glanced at the flyer his father had shoved into his hand. He knew what the old man was up to.

The flyer contained information about a parenting conference that had taken place two weeks ago in Austin. Struggling to understand what was causing the change in Sarah's behavior, the two Matthews men had planned to attend, but at the last minute the deal Cody had made for Williston property had looked as if it might fall through. Walt had been forced to go alone.

He'd come back full of excitement and ideas and the flyer—with one name circled on the workshop list. A Virginia teacher and educational therapist named Joan Paxton had conducted a seminar on how to deal with kids suffering from attention deficit disorder. The blurb about her in the brochure was full of the kinds of things Cody hated most—sweeping praise from pompous-sounding academics and vague promises about what her lecture could accomplish. But Pa kept pressing Cody to contact the woman, see if she could give him some one-on-one advice.

Only one thing wrong with that idea, Cody had said. Sarah did *not* have attention deficit disorder. The flyer had been relegated to the read-when-I-get-around-to-it pile on his desk.

"I'm telling you, son," Walt interrupted Cody's thoughts. "The woman had every person in the audience taking notes. She knows her stuff. And if you'd talk to her, she might help us figure out what's eatin' Sarah."

Anxious to be gone, Cody was hardly listening now. Absently he asked, "Why would she be willing to talk to me in particular?"

"'Cause I asked her to."

That grabbed Cody's attention. "What? You didn't tell me that."

"I went up to her after the workshop and told her how much I enjoyed her speech. We got to talking, and before I left she said she'd be happy to discuss Sarah's problems with you."

"How could you do that?" Cody asked. He dragged a hand through his dark hair, striving for patience. "Look, Pa. Sarah is *my* problem. I don't want or need any stiff-necked, tight-assed schoolmarm telling me what's wrong with my kid. I haven't done such a bad job for twelve years that I need to call in reinforcements now.''

"I'm not saying you have. But what's wrong with asking for a little help? And come to think of it, have you done anything about hiring a nanny yet?''

"I haven't had time to call an agency.''

"You haven't *made* time.''

Unfortunately that was true. Cody had stalled on that suggestion. The idea of hiring full-time live-in help to raise Sarah rubbed him the wrong way. Sarah was twelve, for God's sake, not a baby who needed her diaper changed. Which was, by the way, the kind of thing *Cody* had done for her when she'd needed it. That and a lot of other things. Now, suddenly, he couldn't handle his own daughter?

"You didn't have help raising me after Mom died. I didn't turn out so bad.''

His father shook his head. "No, but I shoulda worked harder on that ornery streak of yours.''

Cody grinned. "I got it from you, didn't I?'' He headed for the door. "I've got to go, or I'll never make the plane. We'll talk when I get back.''

"Son?'' His father's serious tone brought him up short. "Here's something else you need to consider. How will you explain Sarah's behavior to her *other* Grandpa, if he decides he wants to become part of her life?''

Cody felt his heart drop. He couldn't admit it to his father, but that worry had been nibbling at him ever since Edward Ross had reentered their lives. So far, the Connecticut millionaire had kept a low profile, but if the old man ever decided to investigate the circumstances of his granddaughter's birth… Cody shuddered at the thought.

"He won't interfere in our lives, Pa," Cody said in a determined voice, more to convince himself than his father. "He's too busy hobnobbing with senators and movie stars. He doesn't have time for twelve-year-old girls who only want to talk about horses and how soon they'll get to wear makeup."

"Don't you believe it, son. What's Edward Ross been doing with his time since he's retired? His only child killed in a plane crash years ago. His wife dead, too. Then he finds out he has a grandchild—a girl who looks a heck of a lot like Daphne. You think he's not gonna want to be a part of her life? A *big* part?"

The older man slipped one arm out of his metal crutch support and rubbed his hip absently. "You're foolin' yourself, son. Believe me, at that age, a man looks back on his life and starts thinking maybe he should have done things differently."

Cody frowned, a little surprised by the remorseful tone in Walt's voice. His father had few regrets about the way he'd lived his life. The accident that had robbed him of the full use of his legs was about the only thing he might want to change. How different everything might have been if he'd never climbed up on that bull.

"Pa?"

His father seemed to snap out of his reverie. He straightened, fixing Cody with a hard stare. "So maybe you're right, and Edward Ross leaves us alone. That still takes me back to the point I've been trying to make. You know everything there is to know about raising cattle, Cody. Making land deals. Playing the stocks. But what do you really know about what goes on in a little girl's head?''

"I know she doesn't have attention deficit disorder, damn it."

"Let's be sure. I have the number for the private school where this gal teaches in Virginia. Alexandria's not that far from D.C., is it? You could stay over. I'll set it up for you."

Cody glanced at his watch. Only way he'd make the plane now was if he ran into no traffic at all and sprinted through the airport like a long-distance runner. Conceding defeat, he sighed heavily and nodded. "All right. Make the call to her. And set up all the appointments for nannies you want. Call me tonight at the hotel and tell me where and when to show up."

His father grinned. "You won't be sorry."

"I already am."

"This woman's sophisticated, intelligent. Did I mention her father was Alistair Paxton, the diplomat?"

"Ah, jeez, a blue blood. You know how I feel about that kind of woman."

"You're not fixing to make her your wife."

"You know what I mean. Just the thought of being around another Daphne-type, even briefly, makes my gut ache."

"All right," Walt said hurriedly, apparently eager to shore up any damage his words might have done. "You don't like her, you cut the conversation short and come on home. I'll have a dozen nannies waiting for you, ready to be interviewed. One of them is bound to please you."

"I can hardly wait," Cody said without enthusiasm and rushed to his car.

PROBABLY SHOULD HAVE mentioned her resemblance to Daphne, Walter thought, as he waved the Rover away from Luna D'Oro's front drive. But Cody was already riled up enough about being strong-armed into agreement, and he'd turn as prickly as a desert cactus if he thought he was being manipulated, as well.

Of course, everything else aside, meeting Joan Paxton would still be a good thing for Sarah. The woman was razor sharp when it came to kids. If Cody didn't let his ego get in the way, she might be able to help him cope with Sarah. God knows, reprimands, incentives and being sent to her room hadn't done any good with the girl lately.

Walt made his way slowly back to the rear of the house, where the hacienda's courtyard *portal* offered peace and quiet and a great view of the setting Texas sun.

He was worrying for nothing. When Cody met Joan, he'd see reason. He just had to listen to her for a few minutes, give her half a chance. And he would, because she was a looker, and Cody had always had an eye for pretty blondes. The fact that she bore a passing resemblance to Daphne, Sarah's mother, wasn't necessarily a bad thing, was it?

Walter frowned as he settled down on a chaise longue with a weary groan. *Oh, well. Too late now.*

Gently he lifted his legs onto the lounger. If he got

his right hip to stop giving him fits in a few minutes, he'd call her, set up a time when she and his son could get together. It was short notice, but Walt still had a little of the old Matthews charm in him. He could make it happen. Could be that by this time the day after tomorrow, Cody would either have hated her on sight and come home, or he'd be convinced she'd hung the moon.

Even with that damned resemblance to Daphne, Walter was betting on the latter.

AW, HELL, I SHOULD HAVE known.

Cody picked Joan Paxton out the moment she walked through the crowded lobby of the Alexandria Hotel, and he knew right off she wasn't going to have anything to say that he'd want to hear.

He'd been regretting the decision to meet the woman almost from the moment he'd agreed to it. When Walt had called him in his D.C. hotel room, the resentful, trapped feeling in his chest had gotten worse.

The Paxton woman would meet him at four in the afternoon in the hotel lobby, Walt had told him. Then—when he got home—there would be three interviews with prospective nannies waiting for him. From some ridiculous agency called Cultivated Kids, whose logo in the phone book, Pa had said, was a garden row of child-flowers, their faces beaming up toward the sun. As if Sarah was a crabgrass-clogged daisy who just needed a healthy dose of weed killer.

Damn Sam Houston's whiskers! He didn't need a

gardener for Sarah. He didn't need outside help with Sarah at all.

Truth be told, he liked her fine just the way she was. Bright. Imaginative. Sure, she was a handful. Had been from the moment she'd come wailing into his life without a single instruction manual. With Daphne horrified at the thought of being a mother, Cody had raised her almost single-handedly. He'd followed gut instinct and horse sense, and hell, she hadn't turned out so bad.

A little rough around the edges, maybe. A little wild and unpredictable at times. But he liked those traits in her. They made her an individual. They made her funny and interesting and someone he could be proud to call his daughter. Sarah was going to turn out to be one hell of a woman, not some watered-down, homogenized prima donna who only cared about the latest fashions from Paris and how hard she'd have to work to find a rich man to marry.

From behind a planter he watched the Paxton woman make her way to the hotel front desk. Oh, yes, he knew her type well enough. Tall. Blond. Prissy. Spoiled rotten, no doubt, by that diplomat father of hers.

He didn't know what it was about cool ice princesses that always got to him. But since Sarah's birth he'd had two serious relationships with women, and both of them had been carbon copies of Daphne.

The last one had ended six months ago. All right, so maybe he was willing to consider dating again—it got lonely at the ranch, damn it—but he'd never give another tall, uppity blonde a second look. They were just too much trouble, he'd told Pa, and he'd meant it. Which was probably why Walt had deliberately neglected to mention that Joan Paxton was a Daphne look-alike.

The severe, dark suit she wore said she was all business and it accentuated her height. She wouldn't have to lift her chin too high to meet his six-foot-three frame. She moved with stiff authority, like a general inspecting his troops, and her shoulders were thrown back as though she'd forgotten to take the coat hanger out of her jacket before she'd slipped it on. She looked like she'd forgotten how to smile, too, but he had to admit she had a nice, tight rear end that shifted prettily without being provocative.

Cody frowned as his insides twisted unpleasantly. Yep, she reminded him so much of Daphne that he had to resist the urge to check for his wallet.

Wearily he rubbed his hand over his face. It had been a long, tiring day. The boardroom fight with Williston's lawyers had reduced his brain to mush. If he really *was* going to be faced with a bunch of Mary Poppins wannabes tomorrow, he needed to relax. Not try to make nice with an aristocratic intellectual who'd take one look at him and decide he'd done everything wrong the past twelve years.

He watched Joan Paxton ask directions. She'd punished her hair by twisting it up into one of those silly French things that all but destroyed any pretense of femininity, but she couldn't hide the truth that her hair was one of her best features. The color of sunshine, tendrils that looked as fine and soft as a kitten's ear surrounded a pretty, heart-shaped face.

ANN EVANS   21

She turned her head to follow the concierge's pointing finger, and a few wisps of golden hair had the audacity to escape their French prison. Impatiently she lifted a manicured hand to smooth the disobedient curls back into place.

Glancing at her watch, she made a beeline for the hotel atrium where they were to meet in five minutes. He'd bet she'd never been late for an appointment in her life.

In another moment she had disappeared behind the jungle of plants and fake waterfalls that all fancy hotels insisted on cluttering up their lobbies with these days. But he could imagine her sitting there, glancing at her watch. Maybe tapping her foot.

Cody frowned again, then exhaled in disgust. What had Pa been thinking?

"No way in hell," he muttered under his breath.

There were other people he could consult about Sarah's behavior problems. Authorities of his own choosing. Not someone who would blame attention deficit disorder or him. Not someone who would probably suggest drugs that would turn his baby girl into a complacent little zombie with the personality of navel lint. *No!* No overbred blue blood was going to tell him how to raise his kid. And Cody was definitely not going to give said blue blood the opportunity to figure out that the Matthews household wasn't exactly what it seemed to be.

Instead, he'd send a bellman to her with a message. Apologize for the inconvenience, cancel the meeting. Perhaps sometime in the future, he'd suggest. A vague-enough promise he never intended to keep.

There was still Pa to deal with. He was a stubborn old cuss. Once he'd wrung that promise out of Cody, he wouldn't let up. There would be at least two more trips back here to D.C. to complete the Williston deal. Cody could hear Walt's argument now. Surely *one* of those trips would allow him time to reschedule a meeting with Joan Paxton?

Of course, if he and the schoolmarm didn't hit it off, he could say he'd given it his best shot.

He tipped his Stetson to the back of his head as an idea came to him. He was suddenly glad he hadn't had time to change out of his comfortable buckskin jacket and jeans. Boots and western garb would suit this interview just fine. If he'd learned one thing from his father, it was how to make a Texas drawl and good-old-boy attitude work for him. In the corporate world, he'd used his rough frontier persona more than a few times to set those bean counters on their ears.

Joan Paxton would be easy to chase off.

A little snake-oil charm. A lot of Texas arrogance. Maybe he'd even shamble into his best aw-shucks, dumb-cowpoke routine, the one that never failed to get a cackling laugh out of Merlita. Miss Joan Paxton would hightail it home but quick and count herself lucky to get away.

Leaving him with no chance of another meeting.

Leaving him to find his own solution to Sarah's wayward behavior.

He could spend the rest of the evening working out his frustrations in the hotel gym. Relax afterward in a hot whirlpool. Maybe he'd even stop by the hotel gift shop, see if he could find something to take back to Merlita. Just in case Sarah had been up to tricks again in his absence.

Striding toward the atrium, Cody's lips curved into a satisfied smile.

Ten minutes.

Tops.

CHAPTER TWO

THE ATRIUM was filled with tourists just back from a bus trip to Arlington Cemetery and businessmen anxious to unwind from meetings held in hotel conference rooms. Waitresses, ever cognizant of the big tippers, had come out of the piano bar and were circling the tables of men.

Joan Paxton sat with her head down, making notes in her appointment book. She wouldn't have minded a glass of water, but it was impossible to catch a server's attention, and she soon gave up.

She glanced at her watch again. The man was ten minutes late.

Not a good sign, Mr. Matthews.

She refused to think of him as anything but Mr. Matthews, regardless of the fact that Walt Matthews had told her that his son hated formality. What kind of name was Cody, anyway? It was like Howdy Doody. No real adult had a name like that. It made her think of cowboys and Indians and Wild West shows. Understandable, considering the man lived in Texas, but if William Cody Matthews was really the successful businessman his father said he was, you'd think he'd have used his more professional-sounding first name.

Stop, she told herself firmly. *You're just finding fault because you've been upset lately. Mr. Matthews isn't the reason your professional and personal life are in chaos right now. Don't take it out on him.*

Headmaster Mueller was the one who deserved her scorn. And quite a bit more than that if he didn't keep his roving hands to himself. Which he might not.

Last week, after he'd cornered her in the supply closet and she'd slapped him so hard her hand still stung the following day, he'd seemed so sure of himself, almost amused. After all, in spite of her solid credentials, she was still just a teacher at the school, while he was the man who had almost single-handedly built, financed and ran the Virginia Academy for Gifted Children.

If she ever touched him again, he'd told her, she'd be looking for another job. Her face felt warm even now to think that she had countered that threat with one of her own. That if *he* ever touched *her* again, he'd be looking for a doctor. Since that time he hadn't tried anything. But now she was always uncomfortable in his presence, feeling his eyes on her constantly, and the knowledge that she was under his scrutiny had begun to wear on her nerves.

How mortifying the whole episode had been. How unlike her. Struggling in a supply closet with a man old enough to be her grandfather. Threatening bodily harm to another human being. What would her father have said about such a tasteless display, such unlady-like behavior?

She stared down at the latest to-do list she'd begun in her book, not really seeing the words she'd written there. Distasteful as that incident had been, she supposed she could manage Mueller. It was her most recent argument with Todd that had left her reeling. A week ago, when the tension had finally come to a head at their favorite Italian restaurant, she had been stunned to watch their relationship reach an unexpected and bitter climax.

What happened? Joan asked herself for the hundredth time. Todd Ingles was the man she was supposed to marry someday, the man she'd known since high school, the man with whom she intended to share a lifetime of dreams. And yet, after she'd told him what had happened with Mueller, he'd been unsympathetic and uncommunicative. Unable to understand his attitude, she'd finally asked him what the problem was.

"Now, don't take this the wrong way," he'd said to her over a plate of spaghetti and meatballs. "But are you sure you haven't been sending Mueller the wrong signals?"

It was fortunate that the restaurant had been crowded and noisy, because Joan was so shocked she dropped her fork, and it clattered on the table. "What is that supposed to mean?" she asked when she could find her voice.

Todd shrugged as he twirled pasta on his fork. "Just that Mueller never struck me as a skirt chaser. You know his background, his education. He's been published in the *Journal,* for Pete's sake."

"Oh, I see," Joan had said, unable to keep the annoyance out of her voice. "A degree from Harvard prohibits you from being a lech?"

"I'm not saying that. He just seems too refined to play those kinds of high-school games. He's well respected. Monied. His ancestors are founding fathers."

"So are mine. And I'll bet my father never tried to put his hand up an employee's skirt. Are you saying I might have led him on?"

"Of course not. I'm just saying you might have misinterpreted the situation—"

"Todd, it's hard to misinterpret someone shoving their hand down the front of your blouse. He tried to kiss me."

Recognizing that he had chosen the wrong side in this argument, Todd reached over to cup her hand. "Well, why wouldn't he? You *are* a beautiful woman."

Joan withdrew her hand and stared at him. "Don't. You're only making it worse."

"All right, I'm sorry. But so he got a little frisky. He's probably feeling his age and trying to prove to someone that he still has what it takes to get a woman to look at him. You don't want to piss him off, do you? This job pays well. It's prestigious..."

Her mouth had gone dry. Carefully she took a sip of water and just as carefully replaced the glass on the table. She gave him a level, knowing look. "The only one at this table who cares whether Mueller gets...pissed off, is you. Isn't that right?" When Todd didn't respond right away, Joan folded her napkin and quietly laid it on the table. Her appetite had completely disappeared. "What are you afraid of?" she asked softly. "That when he retires next year and the board chooses a new president of the school, he won't give his endorsement to you because your girl-friend wouldn't...put out?''

"Don't be like this. You're not thinking straight. Tomorrow—"

"No, don't say anything more." It had occurred to her suddenly that she really did not know this man. They'd been together for so many years. When had they stopped communicating? "I know how badly you want your own academy, Todd, and how frus-trated you are that it's taking longer than you'd planned. I just never realized that you'd want it so badly you'd be willing to see me humiliated in order to make it happen.''

"Joan, I'd never let Mueller hurt you. I love you.''

"Do you? I wonder sometimes.''

And she couldn't stop wondering, even now, after she'd left him sitting in the restaurant alone, after she'd dumped the flowers he sent to her classroom, and after she'd boxed up her belongings and moved into a small apartment on the other side of town. She'd given up her own apartment two years ago to move in with Todd. She didn't know where she'd end up now, but she knew she couldn't stay at Todd's place one day longer.

Maybe when she went up to the Cape with her mother this weekend... Her mother had never been a fan of Todd's, but she could be quite objective when she chose to be. All those years as the wife of a career diplomat had rubbed off on her. Somewhere between the Burbanks' barbeque and the Olsons' regatta Joan would confess everything, ask for advice...

God, thirty-one years old and asking for advice on

her love life from her widowed mother. What was she thinking? She rubbed absently at her temple, realizing that she was getting a headache.

She turned her attention to the well-worn appointment book on her lap. With the tip of her pen, she ticked off the items on her list:

Buy new swimsuit for weekend
Birthday card for Mother
Haircut with Denise
Clothes to cleaners
Black pumps to shoe repair
Talk to apartment manager about light in the stairwell

She frowned at what she'd written. A compulsive list maker, Joan prided herself on her organizational skills and the ability to prioritize. There was nothing on this list that couldn't be handled in one afternoon. All of it was so mundane-sounding. So normal. And yet, it was reassuring in a way to know that in spite of her current difficulties at work and with Todd, the requirements of life still marched on, needing attention.

"A new bathing suit, huh? Ever try one of those French thong things?"

Joan wasn't the skittish type. The husky, male voice coming from behind her and laced with amusement didn't make her jump or suddenly swivel in her chair. It only annoyed her to realize that a total stranger was reading her notes over her shoulder. She turned her head slowly, prepared to make sure that a man with such odious manners would know just what she thought of him.

The first thing she saw was the belt buckle. Large, silver. It was a spectacle of male adornment that had been hammered and engraved by a craftsman's loving hands. Unfortunately not by a craftsman with any sense of style or taste.

It depicted the head of a long-horned cow, or at least that's what Joan thought it was. Behind the head was a wandering outline of the state of Texas. Or New York. Hard to tell.

Her eyes traveled upward, away from the snug jeans that delineated strong male thighs, past an elaborately stitched and fringed buckskin jacket. Her gaze stopped momentarily at the open neckline of a faded blue shirt. Fascinating. Not the shirt, but the glimpse of swirling midnight hair that covered a muscular chest. Thick and crisp and extremely touchable.

That interest unsettled her. Todd's body was nicely muscled, but practically hairless. His torso had the pale, smooth perfection of a Greek statue. Until recently, she'd thought it the most magnificent body in the world. Until recently, she'd thought Todd the most perfect man.

She lifted her eyes to the stranger's face. Sun-bronzed, with the hard features of a renegade, this man would never be called handsome. Rugged, maybe, but even that seemed too tame, too polite a term to describe him.

Suddenly Joan realized that her scrutiny hadn't gone unnoticed. One inquiring brow rose with devilish interest, and he winked. She would have been em-

barrassed to be caught staring if she hadn't felt that
his breach of manners warranted an indignant look.

"So what do you think?" he asked with a grin.
"About the swimsuit, I mean. You look like a gal
who wouldn't mind attracting a little attention. I know
I'd give you a second glance."

She wanted to tell him that as pickup lines went,
he had the worst she'd ever heard, but it was probably
better not to indulge in conversation with this man,
no matter how attractive he was. "I'm really not interested in your opinion," she said in the haughtiest
tone she could manage, and then added with her most
withering look, "or your attention."

The stranger faked a wounded look at her rebuff.
Then unexpectedly, he was shaking her hand as
though her arm was a pump and he was bent on drawing water. "Howdy. You must be Joan Paxton. I'm
Cody Matthews. Mind if I call you Jo-Jo?"

She barely registered the fact that this mannerless
cretin was the man she'd planned to meet. She was
stunned, but he had already flung himself into the
chair opposite her before she found her voice. "Actually I'd prefer being called—"

"Sorry about the delay, Jo-Jo, but I didn't think
you'd mind waiting." His dark brows rose again.
"How 'bout a drink? I'm parched." He threw back
his head, spotted a waitress nearby and bellowed,
"Hey, honey! We need some service over here."

Oh, God. Was this Walter Matthews's idea of a
joke? How could this Neanderthal be that sweet old
man's son? The man she'd met at the seminar had
been soft-spoken, asking her advice with an old-

fashioned courtesy you seldom saw anymore. But *this* man…after a few minutes in his company, she'd be certifiable.

The waitress came to take their order. Cody Matthews tilted his hat to the back of his head with one finger and turned his appraisal of Joan into a leer. "What's your pleasure, Jo-Jo?"

My pleasure would be for you to end this meeting and go away, she thought. And then the rest of that line of thinking faded as she got her first good look at his eyes. Remarkable. Startling robin's-egg blue in that darkly tanned face. Beneath the hat, his hair was solidly black, silky and crisp-looking, if just a shade too long to please a fashion editor. She felt a moment's regret that these two features should be wasted on a loud obnoxious moron like William Cody Matthews.

"Don't keep this little gal waitin', Jo-Jo." He turned a hundred-watt grin on the waitress and patted her arm. "Time's money, ain't it, honey?"

The waitress had obviously been well-trained. She didn't move a muscle. Joan was the one who bridled at such familiarity. It reminded her unpleasantly of the way Headmaster Mueller had begun his little games with her, finding those opportunities to touch and hug. "A glass of white wine, please," she said quickly, ordering the first thing she could think of to give the poor woman a chance to escape.

Cody's gut tightened. He should have guessed. Every woman in his life had loved wine. It was a drink to be sipped and fawned over, and personally, he had no patience for it. "Shoot," he said with a dismissive shake of his head. "Wine's no better than cow piss. Give me a double scotch. No rocks."

The waitress hurried away and deliberately he leered after her. Out of the corner of his eye he saw the Paxton woman stiffen. Her complexion had gone the color of new milk, and he knew he'd made one hell of a first impression.

Kind of a shame to blow her out of the water like this, 'cause up close she didn't look that much like Daphne, after all. Her nose was shorter and her eyes were nicer than Daph's had been. A warm brown. But she had the attitude down pat. That regal distain that had been Daphne's specialty and had eventually helped to kill their relationship.

"Mr. Matthews—"

"Call me Cody, gal. Mr. Matthews is my pa. 'Course he doesn't like that kind of formality any more than me. Reminds us too much of standing before the judge waiting to hear him pass sentence." He made a loud snorting sound. "And we've both been that route often enough. How 'bout you? You ever been on the wrong side of the law?"

She looked honestly stymied by that question. It was a good five seconds before she formed an answer. "No, I can't say that I have."

"No, of course you haven't. You're a diplomat's daughter, aren't you? You probably went to some snotty private school and got taken everywhere in your father's limousine and never once complained about having to put up with piano lessons."

"Actually it was violin lessons."

She was watching him closely now, as if he'd

turned into a bug stuck on a pin. He lifted a specu-
lative brow. "I'll bet you never even jaywalk."

Joan ducked her head to allow herself time to think.
There was something about the look in his eyes, the
way those words hissed out between his teeth, as
though he begrudged them. She realized that for some
reason he found her objectionable. It was odd, really,
when he was the one who was clearly being outrageous. But she'd never been the type of woman to
run away from a challenge. Surely, if she tried hard
enough, she'd find something worth salvaging from
this conversation.

She lifted her head to look at him sharply. "Mr.
Matthews, perhaps we could discuss your daughter?
Your father was very insistent that I make time to
speak to you."

He seemed to find her words extremely funny. His
laughter was loud and hard, bouncing off the nearby
waterfall and drawing the attention of several tables.
"Of course he was. Pa knows what I like, and he
really came through for me this time."

"Perhaps we should limit ourselves to—"

"I figure I owe him big time for picking out such
a looker."

She blinked in surprise, not sure she'd heard correctly. "I beg your pardon?"

"If you come to my place in Texas to evaluate my
kid, it doesn't hurt that you won't scare off the
crows."

"I see."

He slid forward in his chair until their knees nearly
touched. In a voice trimmed to conspiratorial tones,

he said, "'Course, it gets kinda lonely at the ranch. You get finished sizing up Sarah, the two of us might work on a little...bunkhouse etiquette." His finger touched her knee suggestively. The look in his eyes was glazed with self-assured passion. "You catch my meaning?"

"Yes. I believe I do."

She stood, so abruptly that the chair wheeled back on its castors and bounced off the lip of the atrium reflecting pool.

Cody stared up at her, expecting her to haul off and slap him. Instead, he watched her indignation turn into exasperation. He had to give her credit. If she was alarmed by his aggression, she hid it well.

He rose slowly, not sure what to expect. Her eyes glittered; he could see anger in their dark, chocolate-colored depths, and a curious...disappointment. With him? That jarred Cody, yet at the same time, he was aware of his own faint, peculiar sense of relief.

She closed her appointment book with a firm snap. "Mr. Matthews, I don't believe we can continue this discussion. I'm afraid this meeting has been a waste of time for both of us."

He tried for bewilderment. "Did I say something wrong?"

"I don't believe you've said anything *right*. Frankly, I find that strange, because your father struck me as sincerely concerned about your daughter's welfare. And he thinks very highly of you. I understand that you graduated from Princeton at the top of your class. That you've been very successful in your business and running a ranch, as well."

Her chin angled upward. The movement caused a few golden curls to escape along the nape of her neck. Cody found he had to resist the urge to nudge them back into place. He looked away only to meet up with Joan Paxton's glare of smoldering dislike. She wasn't finished with him yet.

"What I can't understand," she continued, "is why that sort of man would deliberately sabotage this meeting by behaving in a manner that can only be described as repugnant." She fished a handful of dollars out of her purse, then slapped the bag back under one arm. "I believe your daughter could use my help. For her sake, I'd like to give you the benefit of the doubt and assume that you've come to this meeting drunk."

"Nope," Cody protested. For good measure, he winked again. "But a few drinks for you probably wouldn't be such a bad idea. You could stand to loosen up a little. You're pretty uptight."

She released a ragged strand of breath, and a moment later he saw color leap to her cheeks. For one frozen moment he felt guilty. There was a sour taste in his mouth, as if maybe he *had* been drinking. *Let up, Matthews. You've gone too far now.*

But Miss Joan Paxton had more starch in her spine than he expected. The subtle flex of her facial features, the flare of her nostrils—she was struggling for control and winning. Her guard was up now. Her determination transformed her eyes, making them seem lit by fire from within. All bristling anger and indignation, she was damned near beautiful, so attractive that it ignited a sharp thrill in Cody's senses and al-

most made him forget just how much he didn't want
to have anything to do with someone like her.

"No, I don't believe you *have* been drinking."
Those few syllables were no more than chipped sliv-
ers of ice. "I would say there's only one other possibility."

"And what's that, Jo-Jo?"

"That your unfortunate daughter has a jackass for
a father." She tossed the bills on the table. "That
should pay for my drink. I wish you luck, Mr. Matthews. I suspect you're going to need it."

She pushed past him. He watched her walk through
the artificial jungle of the lobby, cutting a precise,
angry swath that could have rivaled anything Sher-
man had planned for Georgia. She didn't look back.
He didn't expect her to. The role he'd played for her
benefit had been Oscar caliber.

He found himself staring in the direction she'd
gone long after he'd lost sight of her. Staring…and
wondering why success didn't have a better feel to it.
He'd accomplished what he'd set out to do. He'd
made her despise him. That final look from her had
been sharp enough to slice steel, and maybe that was
part of what was bothering him. The fact that Joan
Paxton thought he was a first-class son of a—

Ah, hell, where was all this silly regret coming
from? So what if some high-brow diplomat's brat
hated his guts? Hadn't he learned a long time ago
how to separate his ego from the core of every dispute? People didn't have to like him. They just had
to give in.

He rubbed a hand across his jaw, his mind fleecy.

After today, he'd be glad to head back to Luna D'Oro.
If there was any place on earth he understood the how
and why of himself, it was at the ranch, surrounded
by the people who meant the most to him.

After adding enough cash to the table to cover the
drinks—including a generous tip for the uncomplain-
ing waitress—Cody stopped by the front desk. The
clerk handed him a pink message slip. It was from
Pa, urging him to call the ranch. Cody's gut belly
flopped at the word *emergency* underlined twice in
red pen. By the time he put a call through on the
lobby courtesy phone, chaos was already sliding
through his system, spreading tentacles of ice-cold,
sweaty fear up his spine.

Merlita picked up the phone, letting loose a string
of rapid Spanish when she realized it was him. Cody
cut in, and in weeping fits and starts, the housekeeper
explained the situation at home as his heart leaped to
his throat.

Sarah had been taken to the hospital.

THE STEAM OF HER ANGER carried Joan right through
the front door of the efficiency apartment she'd recently rented. She banged the door shut, then wished
she was the temper-tantrum type so she could take
pleasure in banging it shut again.

She was furious and frustrated and…disappointed.

William Cody Matthews had been a disaster. An
ill-mannered, backwoods baboon who hadn't deserved the courtesy of a meeting. She was tempted to
call his father and chastise the man for playing such
a cruel joke; it would have felt wonderful to channel

some of the outrage she felt right now. But she knew a better way to manage that.

Peeling off her jacket and shoes, she plopped down at the tiny kitchen table. Shoving aside a snowdrift of mail, she ripped a piece of paper from her notebook and carefully smoothed it out in front of her.

She felt calmer already.

All her life she'd used the same method to handle anger, disappointment and confusion. List making was her personal mantra, the worry beads she fingered to deal with any problem. As an only child growing up in a household where her father was seldom home and her mother was more interested in her social calendar than raising a daughter, Joan had found lists to be the perfect sounding board. Goals. Fears. Fantasies. Once written down, they became tangible. And once tangible, they became manageable.

A smile curved her lips as she remembered a few of the more important ones: *Reasons Why Father Really Can't Come Home for Christmas,* full of a ten-year-old's unreasonable self-pity. *The Pros and Cons of Attending College in Europe,* revealing an appalling desire to escape her parents. *Why I Will Make an Excellent Teacher,* a list that had given her the courage to admit she could never follow in her father's footsteps.

Oh, there had been plenty of harsh words exchanged in the Paxton household that day. But despite the stale rhetoric and hollow bribes and clever arguments from her father, despite the emotional extravagance that quickly became cruelty and bitterness from her mother, Joan had been adamant—thanks to the list curled in her hand in the pocket of her jeans.

Maybe there were better ways to deal with stress and emotion than making lists, but she'd yet to find one that worked as efficiently for her.

Her recent problem with Headmaster Mueller had never made it to paper. The idea of seeing any of *that* in bold print had been too humiliating. And her breakup with Todd—that had happened too fast. She was firmly convinced that both those horrid situations had turned ugly simply because she hadn't taken the time to deal with them in black and white, to weigh her options and make sensible decisions. The result was the emotional turmoil she was still trying to sort through.

Well, she wouldn't let William Cody Matthews occupy any more of her valuable time. Relegated to a list, he would become insignificant. Forgotten. And she knew just the list she wanted, too.

Across the top of the paper she wrote in big, block letters, *What Makes Cody Matthews So Obnoxious.* She smiled at the harsh directness of the words and wondered if she'd need a second sheet.

Ten minutes later she had a sizable compilation of sins. Feeling in control once more, Joan scanned the words she'd written, her frustrations released on paper.

Overbearing arrogance
Ego the size of the planet
Poor taste in clothes—especially belt buckles!
Beautiful bedroom eyes
Lascivious nat—

Her eyes bumped back up. Wait a minute. *Beautiful bedroom eyes?* Where had that come from? Those eyes didn't belong on her list.

Annoyed, she rose and filled the teakettle with water. Waiting for the whistle, she leaned against the doorjamb and stared at the list on the table. What unconscious imp had caused her to make mention of that man Matthews's eyes? She wasn't even sure what bedroom eyes looked like, for heaven's sake! She regarded the sheet of paper from afar, as though it was a confessional priest who had suddenly betrayed her confidence.

All right, so he had great eyes. She'd give him that. She was probably just missing Todd. And though she had no more than a street artist's impression of Cody Matthews—all surface and no insight—she was convinced his looks couldn't make up for that unbearable personality. Number four on the list was a slip of the pen—a harmless notation caused by inattention.

The teakettle whistled, and she jumped. With a cup of hot Earl Grey in hand, she shoved the list into the stack of personal papers she'd brought from Todd's apartment. She was not willing to give Matthews any more thought. Better to lump him into that worthless brotherhood of men like Todd who didn't know the first thing about how a woman's mind worked.

She spent the rest of the evening going through a box of mementos she and Todd had collected in their years together, throwing out most of them. By the time she crawled into bed, she felt physically and mentally drained, sure that her sleep would be deep and soundless.

But in the end, her subconscious mind turned traitorous.

Later that night, when sleep slowed Joan's brain to a crawl, her usual dreams of Todd faded into the recesses of her mind like phantoms. Instead, into a space where dreams hung like midnight stars, there paraded a herd of silver longhorns. They thundered across vistas of tall prairie grass that rippled slowly in golden waves.

Full of raw, earthy power.

Dangerous.

And chased by a black-haired cowboy whose eyes reflected the brilliant blue of a cloudless sky.

CHAPTER THREE

A WEEK LATER, Joan created a new and unexpected list—*The Pros and Cons of Finding a New Teaching Position and/or Relocating.*

She wasn't certain what had prompted her to make it. Maybe it was frustration over Headmaster Mueller's continued sly and silent observation of her. Maybe it was the impasse she'd reached with a sulky, unreasonable Todd, who'd withdrawn every cent from their joint savings account and refused to consider that some of the money belonged to her. Or maybe it was just the fact that the school term was nearly over. Around this time of year she was always overtaken by a slightly sad feeling of finality, the realization that her children were moving on, away from her protective influence.

Regardless of the reason, in the span of one evening she made the decision not to return to the academy in the fall. The next day she tendered her resignation before she could change her mind. Mueller seemed surprised and annoyed by it, and even Todd made an appearance at her classroom door, demanding an explanation that she refused to give.

Anxious not to lose the momentum of such life-altering actions, she took a fellow teacher's advice and sent an application and letters of recommendation to a small private school in Oregon. It seemed a daring change, so much so that Joan couldn't sleep for two nights after she'd mailed the letter.

By the weekend she was feeling disheartened. Every summer she had worked a temporary job. It helped financially and kept her busy during the months until school started again. Since moving out of Todd's place had been expensive, extra money in the bank would be especially helpful if she had to relocate. But the classifieds in Friday's paper indicated pitifully few summer jobs available, and by Saturday afternoon, a dozen job applications had yielded nothing promising.

Her job search over for the day, Joan went up the stairs of her apartment building slowly, her feet aching, her hair beginning to tumble down her neck. She retrieved her mail from the box, sighing over a couple of bills. If she couldn't find temporary employment, how long before her mailbox was stuffed with demands printed in increasingly irate colors? How long before even her tiny efficiency became unaffordable? Her head filled with gloomy thoughts, she fumbled to insert the key into her front door.

The lock was stubborn, as usual, the notches bent out of alignment by some previous tenant. She wiggled and shook the key, but the lock held tight. Shoving strands of hair out of her eyes, she tried to remove the key, but it refused to budge.

Today's failure coupled with this new irritation curdled Joan's frustration into anger. She glared at her key ring, dangling impotently from the lock. Nothing seemed to be going right lately. Not even a dime-store lock would cooperate.

Rattling the knob, she gave the door a hard kick that only succeeded in squashing the toe of her high-heeled shoe. "Open up, damn you. What do you think you're guarding? Fort Knox?"

The words bounced off the empty corridor walls. An open display of anger wasn't her style. She tilted her head back, concentrating on calming her breathing.

Stalactites of peeling paint hung from the ceiling, held in place by a network of cobwebs. Farther down the corridor one of the hall lights wasn't working. She hated this place. Moving so quickly out of the home she'd made with Todd had been a mistake, a sacrifice of common sense for the sake of foolish pride.

"If you break it off in there, I'm pretty sure you'll have to call a locksmith. And on the weekend, it's likely to cost a small fortune."

She jumped at the sound of the male voice behind her. The folded newspaper and handful of mail slid from her grasp to land in a haphazard mound at her feet.

She turned to see William Cody Matthews seated on the steps that rose to the next floor. With daylight sliding toward extinction, shadows lay heavy in the corridor. His features were cast in an odd half-light, and partially hidden by the newel post, he looked like a prisoner behind bars.

The first thing she noticed was that he was dressed very differently from the man she'd met nearly two weeks ago. The flamboyant Texas garb had been replaced by jeans and a sport shirt—the trappings of an average Joe. Well, not so average, she amended. He still wore that ridiculous belt buckle. Still had those great eyes, the blue gone almost to sapphire in the dismal light of the hallway.

Every nerve went electric at finding him here. She'd never expected to see him again, and she wasn't sure it was wise to be alone with him now. Her mind raced as she wondered what her next move should be.

She could see he'd caught her thoughts. He tilted a look of clear blue toward her, his eyes warm and engaging. "I was beginning to think you'd never come home."

If his affable attitude was meant to soothe her distress, it was a dismal failure. Her heartbeat quickened as he rose from the stairway, coming toward her with the easy confidence of a man completely in command of his surroundings. He nudged her aside so that he could reach the key still imprisoned in the lock.

"Let me try."

He worked the key slowly out of the lock, then began to reinsert it with all the finesse of a master locksmith. Twisting the metal this way and that, he slid back the bolt in no time. Instead of opening the door, Cody Matthews removed the key, then leaned against the jamb with his arms crossed over his chest.

"You know, old locks are like women. You have to go slow."

Her pulse stuttered. "Mr. Matthews—"

"It's like this," he continued, without acknowledging she had spoken. "You made the same mistake with this lock that I made with you. You tried force. Tried to make it behave the way you think it should, when what you really need to do is get a better feel for it. Find out what makes it work.''

"What are you doing here, Mr. Matthews?''

"I'd like to talk to you. May I come in?''

The thought was unthinkable. "Certainly not.'' She extended her palm. "My keys, please.''

She half expected him to refuse. Instead, he let them drop into her hand. She felt oddly relieved when his fingers found no excuse to touch hers. Before she could react, he bent to retrieve the paper and mail at her feet. The classifieds were on top. She noticed with resentment that he didn't bother to hide his interest in the ads she'd circled, leaving her with all her camouflage blown.

"Looks like you've had a busy day. Any success?''

"That's none of your business.''

He shrugged, seeming to take no offense. "No, it isn't, but I think I might be able to help you, anyway.''

"Oh, I'm sure you're full of lots of ideas that you think will help me. Unfortunately I'm not interested in any of them.'' A sudden thought made her look at him sharply. "How did you find me?''

"I was at the school yesterday afternoon, but I guess I missed you. A teacher friend of yours told me where you live.'' He glanced around the corridor, frowning a little. "She said you'd just moved here recently, but I have to admit, I don't see this place as quite your style.''

Her patience snapped. "I think you should leave.''

He smiled at her, seemingly unaffected by the sharpness of her voice. "But then you'd miss the opportunity."

"What opportunity?"

"The chance to see a jackass apologize."

She wasn't expecting that. Was it just her imagination, or was he not quite the same obnoxious man she'd met in the Alexandria Hotel? Still too bold. Still provoking. But the crudity had vanished. Of course, he could just be a very good actor... Through the intricacies of her own flaring sensations, she realized the mistake of engaging in any further conversation.

"I don't think—"

"Miss Paxton, I don't apologize well or very often—"

"Really? I would expect you spend most of your life apologizing for your behavior."

She read the accuracy of that dart on his face. He scowled, and then unexpectedly he laughed. For a moment his features seemed incapable of forged feelings, then he shook his head. "I knew you wouldn't make this easy for me."

"I can't think of any reason why I should. Can you?"

"Not a one. I was an ornery SOB the day we met, and you have every reason not to believe a word I say, but I'm honestly sorry we got off on the wrong foot." He expelled a heavy breath, ran a distracted hand across the back of his neck and pinned her with an earnest glance. "How about we start over? If you're too nervous to invite me in, we can go someplace neutral, have a cup of coffee. Crow's a lot easier to swallow if you have something to wash it down with.''

"You don't make me nervous," she said quickly, then chided herself for feeling the need to protest.

"I didn't think so. You're not the nervous type, are you?"

"No."

"Good. I need someone who's not afraid."

"I don't understand. And after the way you behaved, I can't believe you'd come here…"

She let the words trail away, aware of a sudden change. He was still watching her closely, and something flickered in his eyes. Desperation, uncertainty…the light was too dim to be sure.

"Listen," he began. "I *wouldn't* have come here—I'd have written off our meeting as a stupid mistake—but right now I can't afford to make any more. You were right about what you said. My daughter does need your help. So that's why I'm here. To apologize for my previous behavior and ask you to hear me out. Frankly, circumstances have made me pretty desperate."

His words had grown soft by the end of that statement, and his tone of voice carried a fatigue and fear so profound it stunned her. After a long silence she asked quietly, "What circumstances?"

"After you walked out of the hotel, I got a call from home. My daughter, Sarah, had been taken to the hospital with a concussion. It wasn't serious, but it could have been." Cody Matthews turned his gaze down the hallway, concealing his emotions as though he waged some private debate. Her eyes were drawn by the sight of muscles bunching along his jawline, and when he turned his head toward her again, his look was tame and collected. "Please. All I'm asking for is ten minutes of your time. This is hard for me, but my daughter needs something that I don't know how to give. Help me figure out what it is. And how to keep an emergency trip to the hospital from ever happening again."

Joan drew a deep breath, then let it out slowly. She felt a sense of panic, as though she were poised on the precipice of a very long drop, but his words had the power to catch her heart. A child in need? When had she ever been able to refuse an appeal like that? She slid past him to turn the doorknob, looking up at him at the last minute. "Ten minutes and a cup of tea," she said sternly. "I won't promise you anything more than that."

Within the confines of her tiny efficiency Cody Matthews seemed an overpowering presence, an invasion that left her self-conscious and uneasy. She should have known he wouldn't settle on the couch to wait. Instead, he wandered the room restlessly, as though he could find clues to her personality through the few items she'd bothered to set out. He said nothing, and it made her uncomfortable to watch him touching the fragments of her life in such a dismal setting.

He studied a small photograph of her parents and herself, an informal shot taken aboard the family sailboat. It was a silly tangle of arms and legs and wind-tossed hair—her father had scrambled into the picture at the last minute—but they were laughing and cuddling close. Many stately, stuffy pictures had been commissioned of Alistair Paxton over the years, but none of them meant as much to Joan as this one.

"Pa mentioned your father was *the* Alistair Paxton," Cody remarked. His finger skimmed across the picture, as though he could make contact through the glass. "He doesn't look much like the 'Dean of Diplomacy' here." He tossed her a sideways glance that was startlingly direct. "But then, that's probably why you like it, isn't it?"

She replied with a vague nod, a little thrown by his astuteness. Not even Todd had ever guessed the truth of her relationship with her parents. Before the conversation could become any more personal, Joan escaped to the kitchen.

She ran water into the kettle, then pulled china down from the cupboard. One of the cups clattered as she set it on the counter, tattling a tale of nervousness she'd claimed not to feel. The sound annoyed her. She'd once attended a State Department dinner, met the president, for heaven's sake. Who was this man Matthews to make her so jittery?

The water was ready in an irritatingly short time. Taking slow, steadying breaths, she came out of the kitchen bearing two cups and a new resolve to find out what Cody Matthews wanted as quickly as possible.

He'd made himself comfortable at the dining-room table that doubled as a desk. Like a good friend who'd stopped by for a bit of neighborly gossip. One ankle was crossed over the other knee, and he smiled at her as she joined him.

Determined to keep the conversation businesslike, she rescued a yellow legal pad and pen from beneath the uncharacteristic litter of paperwork that had been piled up for days on the corner of the table. "Do you mind if I take notes?"

"Suit yourself."

"You said your daughter suffered a concussion?"

"She's fine now and back at the ranch."

"How did it happen?"

He took a sip of the tea, not bothering to hide a small grimace of distaste. "She took a nosedive off one of the barn roofs."

"Intentionally?" Joan asked quietly, hoping that Sarah Matthews wasn't the self-destructive type.

Cody Matthews bit back an agitated response. "Hell, no. Sarah's not suicidal. She was trying to jump onto the back of her horse, like they do in the movies. She missed." After a pause, his fierce expression mellowed. "I suppose I ought to start at the beginning. How much did my father tell you about my situation?"

"He said you have a twelve-year-old daughter who's been behaving wildly—"

"Sarah is free-spirited," he interrupted. "Not wild."

"You asked what your father told me."

That calm response won a sheepish look from him. "Sorry. Go on."

"Your father attended my lecture on attention deficit disorder. He felt it might be the root of Sarah's problem."

"I don't believe my daughter has attention deficit disorder," Cody stated.

The brevity of that answer should have warned her off the subject. Instead, with slow deliberation, Joan set aside her pen, dunked her teabag one last time, then slipped it onto the saucer. She didn't look at him, but she was determined to persevere. Denial was a common reaction from parents of troubled children, and taking exception to his attitude would serve neither of them well.

After a moment she said, "I'm not a physician, Mr. Matthews. Nor have I met or even spoken to your daughter. So I wouldn't presume to offer a diagnosis."

"Damn," he said with a look full of regret. "I'm going to end up apologizing to you more in one day than I have in my entire lifetime. I'm sorry if I sounded defensive. Sarah's my only child, and I get a little crazy when this subject comes up. She's a bright, strong-willed kid. There's nothing wrong with that." He looked at Joan, as though daring her to disagree. "In fact, I happen to like her that way."

"How long has her behavior been what your family considers unacceptable?"

"Off and on for about two months. Worse lately."

That was a good sign. A recent change in behavior might indicate the problem was situational. "Have you spoken to your daughter about it?"

"I've taken away her allowance. Cut her riding privileges. I haven't spared the discipline, if that's what you mean."

"No, that's not what I mean. I mean, have you

talked to her about the way she's been acting? Tried to discover if there's a reason behind it.''

He made an odd face, one full of contradictions. There was regret there, but frustration and annoyance, as well. "Lately Sarah and I have had problems communicating."

"What about Sarah's mother? Has she spoken to her?"

He shook his head sharply. "Daphne was killed in a plane crash shortly after Sarah was born."

"I'm sorry—"

"Sarah doesn't ask about her mother. She doesn't even remember her."

Joan didn't like the way his face had become a chilling mask of banality when there was such bitterness in his voice. Had he loved Sarah's mother so much—still missing her even now, after all this time—that he could not discuss her? His abrupt statement was patently false, of course. What young girl didn't want to know everything about a mother who had never been part of her life?

Joan wanted to ask more, but the hot message glowing in Cody Matthews's eyes told her that lingering over this line of questioning would gain her nothing. It was absurd and frustrating to feel so much and know so little.

"Who else makes up your household?"

"My father. Merlita, our live-in housekeeper. Ranch hands."

"No one else?"

"No."

His mouth flattened, as though he was angry with

himself for allowing emotion to seize him, even temporarily. His fingers played along the rim of his cup a long moment. Long enough for her to notice that his hands were beautifully shaped and not at all what she'd expect from a high-powered businessman. Tanned and unmanicured, they were a workingman's hands.

She made a few more notes on her pad. When she looked up, she discovered that he was watching her intently. His thumbs were hooked under his belt; the slight movement of his fingers made the dining-room light shoot sparks from that preposterous buckle. Her hand stilled, but her chin inched upward. "Something wrong?"

"You take a lot of notes."

"They'll give me a better picture of your daughter's situation."

"May I read them?"

"Of course," she said, trying not to register anything but the mildest agreement. "If you feel that they threaten you in some way."

The look he gave her sent shivers down her spine. "You have a sharp tongue for a woman who's fresh out of work and just moved out on the love of her life."

The knowledge that he knew such intimate details about her personal life left her stunned, but she refused to show it. She met his eyes. Trying to modulate her voice, she said, "And you have quite a belligerent attitude for a man whose ten minutes are up and who still seems to need my help."

Not a flicker of a response crossed his face. Had

she overestimated her ability to carry her own weight in a contest of words with this man? A hush took over the room, unbroken except for the growl of afternoon traffic in the street. And then, just before his silence could unnerve her completely, he made a low sound in his throat that could have been laughter.

"All right," he said, and his face had lightened a little. "What else would you like to know?"

Relieved, she dived into safer water. "Has Sarah had a physical recently?"

"Yes, I had the doc check her out thoroughly when she was in the hospital last year to have her tonsils out. Nothing to worry about there."

"What about her education? What's that like?"

"Public school in Goliath—that's the nearest town of any size. I'd prefer better, but there's nothing private near the ranch, and I'm not going to pack her off to some fancy boarding school thousands of miles away, see her head stuffed with a bunch of nonsense and have her sent home only on holidays."

Joan showed no trace of opinion on this information, but secretly she was pleased by Matthews's determination to keep his daughter close to home. She herself had been sent to all the best schools abroad, and with a tinge of the old regret, she wondered if her parents had ever been as impassioned about her as this man seemed to be about Sarah. She shook off the thought immediately. Now was not the time to mourn for things that had never been. "Has the school done any special testing? What do her teachers think?"

"She's ahead of most of her class, but her grades

have been up and down this last semester. Her teachers say she's quick and eager sometimes, but often disruptive and disobedient. One of them—Miss Beasley—is the same crab-apple old witch I had when I was Sarah's age, so I don't know what to believe from her.''

"Do these behavior problems occur only during school hours?"

"No."

"During certain hours of the day or night?"

"No."

"Before or after meals?"

"No."

"Does she get enough sleep?"

"The kid sleeps like a rock."

"No insomnia? No nightmares?"

"Nightmares? No. Where are you going with this?"

"Sometimes the symptoms of ADD can mimic other problems. You have to eliminate other possibilities that could be causing this behavior. Dyslexia, for instance. Or anxiety. Even depression."

Cody made a face at that. "Sarah isn't dyslexic, and she has nothing to feel anxious or depressed about."

"Mr. Matthews, do you or any other family members suffer from ADD?"

"Absolutely not," he said firmly.

Another sore subject, she thought. But she had to be honest with the man. For Sarah's sake. "It tends to run in families. What about on her mother's side?"

"We don't have much contact with her mother's side of the family. But from Daphne...no."

Hesitation in that short answer caused her to snap a direct look his way, but judging by the look on Cody Matthews's face, this, too, was forbidden territory. She sighed, setting her pencil down. When she spoke, her tone was soft, carefully neutral. "I'm afraid this isn't going to help much. No single question or test can determine if a child has ADD. Have you considered taking Sarah to someone who can give her a complete neurological examination? Someone who can also work up a detailed history of Sarah's past?"

The soft illumination from the dining-room light revealed an evasiveness on his face. His eyes and mouth had become almost too indifferent, too implacable, yet there was an odd vulnerability in the mask of his features. As annoyed as she was with this deception, she felt moved by his desperation, because a man like Cody Matthews couldn't begin to fathom a once-loving child who now indulged in an insolent indifference to reason.

He looked down at his hands to see that he had made fists of them, and his brow furrowed as though he found the sight surprising. He played with the handle of his teacup, and she watched him wrestle with his reluctance. "I don't want someone poking and prying into family business, upsetting Sarah with a bunch of questions. I just want my daughter back."

The admission seemed torn from him, and he fell silent, into the pit of what he probably considered parental failure. Observing him, Joan felt sure there

was a weight of sorrow here she didn't fully compre-
hend, some dark, unknown current too strong to
chance exploring.

She could see now why his father had said Cody
Matthews was likely to balk at outside help, why he
had deliberately sabotaged their first meeting. He was
a proud man, a proud parent. He'd obviously been
determined to immerse himself in practicalities,
weathering Sarah's stormy behavior with a pragmatic
unsentimentality until the worst was over. Unfortunately the worst had stayed and stayed, until the man
was left with no more choices.

Matthews had turned his head, pretending an interest in the scratch of a magnolia branch outside the
window. Without thinking, Joan laid her hand on his
forearm to recapture his attention.

"Mr. Matthews, there's no shame in a father ad-
mitting he doesn't understand his daughter. The fact
that you're trying to help her now, that you're willing
to consider other alternatives, is a very positive
sign...."

The words trailed away as his head swung back,
his glance falling to his arm where her hand still lay.
He looked at her, and she thought the blue of his
short-sleeved shirt turned his eyes almost turquoise,
so brilliant against the sooty blackness of his lashes.
There was something new in the look he gave her,
something besides frustration and fatigue. It brought
a quick, suffocating tightness to her chest, alarming
in its intensity, yet carrying with it the gentleness of
a caress.

His head tilted toward her as though in puzzlement,

and when he spoke, his voice was low. "My father thinks you're some kind of miracle worker. Are you?"

"No," she murmured, suddenly barely able to draw breath.

He smiled, no more than a lazy curl of his lips. She wasn't sure whether it was one of acceptance or subtle mockery, but it was absurdly charming nonetheless, a smile made to make a woman melt. More disturbing, Joan realized how easily she could fall victim to it.

"I'm a man in need of miracles, Joan Paxton. Work just this one," he said in a silken tone, "and whatever you want most in life, I'll see to it that it's yours."

It was all silly imagination, wasn't it? The way his words seemed to work in some secret place within her. She felt as though her center of balance had radically altered, and that all the forbidden fantasies of last night's dream were on the verge of materializing into life.

His eyes were still on her. She lost the courage to hold his gaze and lowered her head—to discover that her hand was still poised on his arm. The hard muscled flesh felt warm. The feathering of crisp, dark hair tickled her palm. She disengaged her hand so quickly that an outsider might have thought she'd burned herself.

She rose abruptly. The stack of paperwork on the corner of the table slid to the carpet. Willing away her awareness of him, she picked up their cups in a rush that surely must have been embarrassingly noticeable. "What I'd like is a little more tea. How about you?"

By the time she finished speaking she was in the kitchen, so she didn't catch his response. She knew it was ridiculous, but the thought of rejoining him in the dining room, where the energy in the air moved like an invisible tide, seemed more than she could manage at the moment. Instead, she asked from the safe distance of the kitchen doorway, "Did you say you wanted another cup?"

He was bending to retrieve the paperwork from the floor, but he lifted his head long enough to give her a wry glance. "No, thank you. I'm not really a tea drinker."

She turned back to the kitchen counter, concentrating on pouring water from the kettle. The odd intensity that had crackled between them only moments ago had passed, but the silence was becoming uncomfortable. She should say something, shouldn't she? But just when she found an innocuous topic, he stunned her with his next words.

"So, you'll come to my ranch?"

Sure she'd heard incorrectly, she returned to the kitchen doorway, kettle in hand. "What?"

He was sorting through the jumble of paper, stacking it neatly into piles. "I want to hire you to come to Luna D'Oro. You can evaluate Sarah in person."

"I couldn't possibly."

He looked up at her. "Why not?"

"I have obligations here."

"No, you don't. I told you, I know all about your quitting your job, moving out on your boyfriend. One of your fellow teachers—Marilyn, I think her name was—seemed fascinated by the whole thing. She didn't have all the reasons why, but she liked to talk, and I know when to listen.''

''I'll definitely have to speak to her about that.''

''Money's not an issue,'' he continued. His blue eyes sparkled.

The still-hot kettle was almost unnoticed in her hand, and she repositioned her fingers around the handle. ''It doesn't have anything to do with money. I don't have the qualifications you're looking for.''

''I disagree. Do you think that when it comes to Sarah, I'd take suggestions from just anyone? I checked your credentials. In addition to teaching, you act as an educational therapist for your school. You were invited to take part in that seminar in Austin because of a paper you had published in *Higher Education*. You know your stuff. And while I may not agree with your findings, I think you'd be impartial. Objective.''

''It takes time to do a complete evaluation.''

''You can take as long as you like. You don't have a new job to start until the fall, do you? And only if you get that position in Oregon.''

''I'm definitely crossing Marilyn's name out of my address book,'' she muttered.

''But you'll come?''

''It isn't just Sarah who would have to be evaluated. It's important to know how she interacts with others in the family. It would mean a huge emotional investment from every member of the household.''

''I'll make sure everyone cooperates.''

She gave him a tight challenging look. "Including you?"

"If I have to."

She withdrew to the kitchen with the excuse that the kettle needed fresh water. While she ran tap water into it, she stared at the wall, thinking.

It was so odd, really, to be mouthing so many objections to Cody Matthews's idea, yet at the same time, to be overcome by a moment of complete exhilaration and conviction. She *could* help Sarah Matthews. She could help father and daughter develop coping skills if it turned out the child did have ADD. She'd experienced such conviction before, but never without gathering more information, and certainly never without at least meeting the child in question. But somehow, she just…*knew*.

Placing the kettle back on the stove, she drew a deep breath, thinking of the motherless and alienated child waiting back in Texas. Joan emptied her lungs, then returned to the doorway.

Matthews looked up from the papers he'd stacked on the table, giving her a questioning glance. "Well?"

"I'll do it." Annoyingly, he looked as if he hadn't expected any other answer. It made her tone sharper than she intended when she continued, "But for no longer than two weeks."

"All right. I think I should warn you that life on a ranch can require some getting used to. We're out in the boondocks, but we're completely self-contained. The land is unforgiving of mistakes, so it's my world down there. I'm blunt and demanding, and I run Luna

D'Oro on my terms. My people call me *el jefe grande*—the big boss. If that offends any of your female sensibilities, you'd better tell me now.''

She allowed a skeptical expression to flit across her features, refusing to be cowed by the note of challenge in his voice. ''Actually, you've managed to offend me so frequently in the short time I've known you, a few more transgressions will hardly make a difference.''

He laughed out loud at that. ''Why, Miss Paxton, you can be pretty blunt yourself.''

''Does that bother you?''

''Not at all. Just means it ought to be interesting. Let's call this a done deal, shall we?'' He extended his hand and she took it, meeting his gaze squarely as he smiled broadly at her.

He wrote out a check that seemed generous, but not foolishly so. Then he rose from the table. By the time they reached the front door, Cody Matthews had promised to send a messenger around with an airline ticket before the week was out. The idea of leaving Alexandria on such short notice was disconcerting, but better to make the break from her past a clean quick one, she thought.

''Someone will pick you up at the San Antonio airport,'' he told her. ''Although my foreman will probably pitch a fit at having to pick up another 'expert' to handle Sarah.''

Her brows rose. This was something she hadn't considered—that others had come before her and failed. ''You've brought others to your home?''

''Not like you. Nannies. Two in one week.''

"What happened?"

"Sarah gave the first one a series of interesting bedmates. I believe the one that sent her packing was a king snake." He cocked his head, and the movement allowed the lamplight to limn his mouth as it curled with amusement. "Harmless. But enough to scare a skittish woman, I suppose."

She sensed he wanted a reaction, and she refused to give it to him. "And the second?"

"My attorney advises me not to discuss the details of the case."

She frowned, unable to hide her surprise. "Mr. Matthews—"

"I'm kidding," he said with a laugh. "You need to lighten up, Miss Paxton. Are you always so serious?"

The teasing glint disappeared from his blue eyes, and for a moment she was stunned by the curious intimacy of his gaze. It reminded her of those moments at the table when her hand had been on his arm. She felt the power of physical awareness arc between them, a temptation to reckless things. It was gone in an instant.

Unsettled, she found her voice, wishing him a safe trip back to Texas.

"Pack for hot weather," he instructed.

She nodded blindly, but just as she was closing the door behind him, he snagged the edge of it with his hand. "One more thing," he added, and an unholy grin laced his features with subtle mischief. "This belt buckle is special. It was a gift from my daughter, so I wouldn't advise telling her what you really think of it.''

He was gone before she could ask what he meant by that. Scowling, she leaned against the door. While she didn't like that silly buckle, she'd never said a word to him about it, had she? She'd only—

The blood drained from Joan's cheeks. The list. All his flaws itemized on paper. What had she done with it? She hurried to the dining-room table where the papers Cody Matthews had retrieved from the floor now lay neatly stacked.

Two envelopes down, right beneath the electric bill, lay the list she'd compiled—*What Makes Cody Matthews So Obnoxious.* The words practically leaped off the page. ''Poor taste in clothes—especially belt buckles!''

Scathing.

Satisfyingly petty.

And listed right below it, where he could not have failed to read it, ''Beautiful bedroom eyes.''

CHAPTER FOUR

HE SHOULD HAVE SENT one of the ranch hands to pick her up.

In twenty-four hours he had to be in Dallas, negotiating his way past a school of legal sharks determined to chew up his plans for the property he'd bought in San Antonio. He should be gearing himself up for the mental gymnastics of that confrontation. Not bumping along the dusty, knotted ribbon of road that led to Luna D'Oro with Miss Joan Paxton seated primly beside him on the sun-cracked seat of the ranch pickup.

The truck smelled like feed-store molasses and needed new shocks. It was rattling the fillings right out of his teeth, for Pete's sake. He should have thought to bring the Rover. But it had been an impulse decision to pluck the keys from Tomas's hand at the last minute to run this errand himself.

He slid a glance across the seat as the pickup lurched into and then out of a pothole. The woman looked tired and uncomfortable, trying to hang on to that ramrod posture of hers, in spite of every rut and curve that threatened to toss her around the cab like a pea in a hollow gourd.

She'd hardly said two words since they'd left San

Antonio. There was a pinched look around her lips, and he wondered if some grievance against him was fermenting in her. She was probably angry because he'd taken one look at her expensive luggage, snorted in disgust and then tossed the bags into the truck bed with little more respect than he'd give sacks of grain.

He hadn't been able to help himself. In spite of his suggestion that she dress in casual, comfortable clothing, she'd come off the plane looking like a Madison Avenue executive: tailored suit, designer attaché case and an air of indomitability. She looked primed for a nine-o'clock appointment with a company president, not a twelve-year-old child. Cody knew that the moment Sarah saw her she'd become as balky as a barn-sour nag.

He felt some of his old rebellion and resentment rise. How could this haughty blue blood succeed where he could not? What had he seen in Joan Paxton that day in her apartment to make him think she'd have some special talent for figuring out what the hell was wrong with Sarah? The woman had admitted she wasn't in the business of working miracles, so why had he pushed her to take the job?

'Cause you're flat-out desperate, that's why. And if he wanted to deny that, he had only to remember last night—the latest go-round with Sarah over the poor showing she'd made for the school year.

She was already barely hanging on by her teeth in two subjects. Last week Miss Beasley had sent home a note about Sarah's final exam.

Maybe he ought to float the latest problem past Joan Paxton and get her opinion. No sense stalling.

Hells bells, wasn't that the reason he'd brought her here? He chewed the inside of his cheek a moment, thinking that the woman had one heck of a challenge ahead of her.

"Sarah's in the doghouse with me right now." He broke the silence. "I'd like to think that means she'll be on her best behavior, but there's no telling how she'll react to you."

Out of the corner of his eye, he saw her head swing in his direction. "Given what you've told me, I'm not expecting to be welcomed with open arms," she said mildly. "What did you tell Sarah was the reason for my coming here?"

"I told her that I knew she was having a hard time in school lately. At home, too. And that I didn't seem to be helping the situation much. I said you were an educational expert for children her age, and that you might be able to give us some advice."

"How did she respond to that?"

"Suspicious looks. A surly attitude. We ended up in an argument."

"Over what?"

"Her school progress reports this year have been going steadily downhill. Math. Science. Now history. Just before Sarah's last test, her teacher, Miss Beasley, sent home a note saying that because she didn't finish some big semester project, if she got anything less than a B on her exam she'd 'jeopardize her chances for promotion.' Which, if I remember correctly, is diplomatic teacher talk for being held back a year."

"So how did Sarah do?"

"She thinks she passed the test. We won't know for sure until we pick up her grades at the end of this week. But she's all in a huff. She got a real attitude when Beasley claimed she hadn't turned in the written portion of her project."

"What kind of attitude?"

"She called Miss Beasley a liar."

He sensed her grimacing reaction. "And your response to that?"

Cody took his eyes off the road for a moment to meet her inquiring gaze. "Personally, I think Miss Beasley is still the same dried-up, embittered old biddy she was when I had her as a kid, but I couldn't let Sarah call her teacher a liar. I lectured her until I ran out of breath and then sent her to her room without supper. I told her if she got held back a year, she could kiss her horse goodbye." He snorted, remembering what a storm of protest that comment had brought. "She still wasn't speaking to me this morning. When I told her I would be back around noon and she'd better be there ready to meet you at lunch, she just looked at me."

Joan Paxton nodded absently, and he wished he could tell what she was thinking. He switched his attention back to the highway.

"Why do you think she called her teacher a liar?" she asked after a long silence. "Why not just call her mean or crazy or too hard? Why specifically that accusation?"

He thought about it a moment, but came up empty. "I don't know. Maybe she felt cornered. Maybe she'd got caught not completing an assignment," he said at last, "and that was the first thing she could think to say."

"Is it possible she *did* complete it? That Miss Beasley is wrong?"

That approach surprised him. He'd expected her to state Sarah's behavior was classic ADD. "I'd like to think that Beasley's wrong, but Sarah's record on follow-through has been crap lately. More likely this is just one more project she decided not to finish." He slid a glance toward her. "And isn't sticking with a project a problem for ADD kids?"

She lifted an amused brow. "You've been reading up."

He shrugged. "Just trying to get a better feel for it."

She gave him a smile that made the interior of the cab feel suddenly airless, then turned her attention back out the window, seemingly absorbed in the flat, boring landscape. A few wisps of hair trailed against the high collar of her blouse, like gold filaments unraveling from a tapestry. He wondered why she insisted on confining it in that roll, when it would have looked magnificent caught in a stray breeze, swirling around her head and shoulders like the gilded hooded cape of some ancient warrior queen.

He was annoyed with himself for noticing, and for turning so fanciful all of a sudden. Experience always left its mark, and long ago he'd had his fill of women with flawless, aristocratic features who had very little going for them underneath all the window dressing. Sure, she seemed bright, in addition to good-looking. She might even have a spark of interest in him—if

he could believe that list he'd read in her apartment.
But there was no sense in trying to ignite that spark,
because it always got out of control, and sooner or
later they'd both end up burned. No more Daphnes,
he'd sworn six months ago. And he'd meant it.

He squinted ahead, down the long highway. She
was here to help Sarah. Not him. Whatever magic this
woman might be able to work with his daughter, he'd
better plan on staying immune to it himself.

SPARSE.

That was the only word that came to mind as Joan
watched the dry monotony of southern Texas parade
past her window. Nothing moved out here. No brooks
giggling over slick rocks. No ancient hardwoods com-
peting for space along riverbeds and waterfalls. Not
even a puff of dust as a jackrabbit sprinted across the
road.

The land here looked hot and hostile. Even the rock
formations dotting the landscape resembled the jagged teeth of some fire-breathing dragon, and the battered pickup seemed to be rattling them down into the
bowels of the beast.

As though he'd heard some unspoken complaint,
the man beside her notched up the air-conditioning.
Cool air fanned her cheeks.

''Gonna be another hot summer,'' Cody Matthews
said suddenly. His eyes flicked over her suit. ''Too
hot to spend it wrapped up like a New York banker.
You bring anything cooler?''

She tossed a quick look his way. In jeans and a
well-worn Stetson, he was once more playing the tall,

laconic Texan. "I'm sure what I've brought will be fine."

"Uh-huh. First scorcher we get, I'll be scooping you up out of a dead faint."

"I doubt that. I'm very adaptable." She kept her voice as smooth as whipped cream, having already decided that William Cody Matthews was a man who delighted in keeping a person off balance.

"We'll see," came his skeptical reply. He gestured over the steering wheel, pointing toward a line of dark clouds on the horizon. "Might get some rain soon. That'll cool things down a bit."

"It's much more dry and barren than I expected."

"You get used to it."

She couldn't miss the affection in his voice. "You like living here."

"I was born and raised here. My grandfather bought the property Luna D'Oro sits on when there was nothing there but an abandoned line shack. Pa got busted up on the rodeo circuit and decided to try his hand at ranching. Ended up striking oil, instead. Not enough to put us on easy street, but enough to add considerably to the land. Since that time, I've expanded our holdings, bought the house we live in now. I can't imagine living anywhere else but on the ranch."

That surprised her. "Your father gave me the impression that your business keeps you away from the ranch quite often."

"I don't know that I'd say 'often,'" he replied with a scowl. "More than I like, perhaps. I have an office in San Antone where I handle a small investment group. I spent a few years on Wall Street after I graduated from college, developed quite a knack for guiding new investors through the market.''

''But you decided to give up Wall Street and come back here?''

''It took me a while to realize that I'm not meant to live in a big city. Some people just don't take to it.'' His eyes raked over her. ''Any more than a hothouse flower could survive in a place like this.''

The implication that she couldn't stand up to a harsh south-Texas climate irritated her. As a diplomat's daughter, she'd done her share of traveling to far-off exotic places that had been much more intimidating than this environment.

''Mr. Matthews—''

''You think you could start calling me Cody? Or at least what everyone else on the ranch calls me?''

''*Jefe.*''

''Yeah. *Jefe grande,* actually.''

Of course, she thought. *When hell freezes over.* In her most agreeable tone she replied, ''Perhaps Cody would be easier and less formal. For Sarah's sake.''

He threw her a knowing look. ''I told Merlita to hold lunch for us. You like Tex-Mex?''

''Most of it.''

''I've asked her to take it easy on the jalapeños since we'll have a tenderfoot in our midst.''

''That's really not necessary,'' Joan remarked evenly, remembering times when she'd sampled native dishes so spicy they'd nearly burned the taste buds off her tongue.

Cody's gaze strayed to the floor of the truck cab,

where a brown, oblong case sat at her feet. She'd refused to see it carelessly tossed in the back with the rest of her luggage. "What's in there? You bring your own rifle?"

"Perhaps I should have," she said lightly. "No, it's my violin. I play for my own enjoyment, and I couldn't leave it behind."

"Fiddle player, huh? Never cared for it much. Always thought it sounds like two cats squalling in a back alley."

She gave him a thin smile, determined not to let him get under her skin. "What a colorful analogy. I don't believe I've ever heard that comparison."

"You any good?"

"Well…I've never had anyone call Animal Control. In fact, at one point in my life, I thought I wanted to play professionally."

"So what changed your mind?"

"Working with children pleased me more."

"Sarah's pretty good on the piano," he remarked when the quiet again seemed to have stretched a little too long.

"Perhaps we could practice together." After another thoughtful silence, she added, "That might be a way to make a connection with her."

"I wish I could believe it would be that easy."

She looked at him sharply. For the past few minutes there had been something in the air, an edginess between them. He was watching the road, but she sensed that the tension in his posture had nothing to do with driving.

"Mr. Matthews—Cody—you're still not sure I can help Sarah, are you?"

He seemed unmoved by the friction in her question, his attention focused on maneuvering a twisting curve. "I hired you, didn't I? I want you to succeed. And I don't doubt your credentials."

"That wasn't my question." When he made no response to that, she decided to push a little harder. "Is there something *personally* you dislike about me?"

He frowned. "No."

"From the very first moment we met, I've sensed a hostility in you that doesn't seem professionally motivated."

The frown darkened into a full-blown scowl. "You've got an overactive imagination."

"I would appreciate it if you wouldn't treat me like a fool."

The truck slowed suddenly as Cody braked and pulled off the road, gravel spewing from beneath the wheels. He pushed the gearshift into park and turned in his seat to face her, one hand draped over the steering wheel. His look was as precise and sharp as a knife blade, but she didn't sense anger. Only that he'd come to a few decisions of his own.

With one finger he tipped back the brim of his hat. "Okay. You want the short and skinny of it? I'm not crazy about you, but it's nothing personal. I just don't happen to like your type."

"What type is that? Female?"

Something flickered in the depths of his eyes. "Let me ask you a question. How much did you pay for that luggage back there? Or for those pearls you're wearing?''

Whatever Joan had been expecting from him, this attack on her belongings wasn't it. ''I beg your pardon?''

''Have you ever bought anything that didn't have a designer label on it? Or jewelry that didn't come from Tiffany's? I know your background. I know what your kind of privileged childhood does to a woman. What you expect out of life. Yes, I want you to succeed with my daughter. But I'm a little worried. Because I'll be damned if I know how you're going to 'connect' with her when you obviously grew up with a silver spoon in your mouth, and Sarah is all denim and cowboy boots.''

His words left her nearly speechless. ''You're serious, aren't you?'' When he remained silent, she continued, ''I don't know why I should bother trying to explain, but for your information, that luggage was a college-graduation present from my aunt. The reason it looks fairly new is because on a teacher's salary I don't get much chance to use it.'' She plucked her necklace away from her blouse with two fingers. ''As for these pearls, they're fakes. Good ones, but fakes all the same. If anything I own looks expensive, it's because I try to buy the best so that it will last a long time. Is being a smart shopper against the law in Texas?''

''Joan—''

''I won't make excuses for who my parents are or where I went to school or how many European vacations I took as a child. That's your problem, not mine. But your implication that it would somehow diminish my ability to deal with your daughter is ridiculous. It's like saying a writer has to have committed a murder before he can write a murder mystery.''

''Joan—Miss Paxton…''

She subsided with a sigh of displeasure. To her surprise, the sky had darkened in the past few minutes, threatening a summer squall meant to match her mood. How dare he form an opinion of her based on such paltry evidence? He didn't know anything about her. ''If you're really so concerned, it's not too late to take me back to the San Antonio airport.''

''Joan—'' he said patiently.

''I suppose now you're going to offer up another one of those 'Aw shucks, ma'am,' apologies of yours.''

''Not exactly.''

She snapped her head around to discover that he looked far from apologetic.

With no trace of irritation in his voice, he said, ''It's been my experience that women of your breeding and background follow certain patterns in life. Ones that I find personally annoying. If I've lumped you unfairly in that category, then I'm sorry, but I've seldom been wrong about this. I may not have wanted to hire you, but I've accepted that I need outside help. For Sarah's sake, I'd like us to get along, as I would want any business arrangement to progress. But we don't have to be…''

''Friends?''

''Exactly. I don't necessarily like or agree with

everyone I do business with, but that doesn't mean we can't make a go of it, does it? We're adults.''

"Well, at least *one* of us is," she muttered.

"You asked for the truth. I'm giving it to you."

She swallowed a variety of possible retorts and said calmly, "You're right. There's no reason why we can't make this work."

He released a long breath. "Good. I'm glad you're going to be sensible about this."

"You're the boss," she said, watching a tumble-weed dance across the road. *"Jefe grande."*

If he caught the sarcasm in her tone, he chose to ignore it. Instead, with a short nod of agreement and his jaw clamped as tight as an old turtle's, he restarted the truck and pulled back onto the road.

Twenty minutes later they bumped off the highway and onto a narrow dirt road bracketed by rough-hewn oak columns. Wrought iron formed a connecting arch overhead bearing the words Luna D'Oro, framed on either side by artfully depicted half-moons with an inset of the letter G.

"That's the ranch brand," Cody said, pointing to the ironwork as they drove under it. She could hear the pride in his voice. "You know any Spanish?"

"A little. Golden Moon," she translated. "Sounds very romantic."

"Yeah, for a while we took some kidding over the name from the other ranches. But in recent years we've offered some of the best crossbred cattle in the state, so they give us respect now." He inclined his head toward a small herd of healthy-looking cattle munching scrubby grass on a nearby rise. "That's

Luna D'Oro stock. From here to the house, everything you see is mine.''

The weight of the words and the way he said them made Joan glance at him. People, too? she wondered. It would be interesting to see just how much power this man thought he wielded in the lives of his family.

The dry pasture landscape gave way to an approach drive to the house. As they pulled to a stop in front of the place, Joan realized that *house* wasn't quite the right word. ''Oh, my,'' she said on a soft exclamation of surprise.

Cody grinned. ''I know. Looks a little like the Alamo, doesn't it?''

''All that's missing is Santa Ana's army surrounding the place.''

The long low profile of the house was part mission-style, part Southwestern. The thick beige adobe walls, deep windowsills and heavy mesquite doors looked like they could withstand an assault from the most determined desperado. Shoulder-high walls fanned out from either side of the house to form a square, like a protective barrier meant to keep a hostile world at bay, but through one open gate Joan glimpsed an inviting courtyard crowded with huge terra-cotta pots filled with flowering shrubbery.

Cody was retrieving her bags from the back of the truck, obviously enjoying her look of amazement. When he stood beside her, he said, ''Right after Sarah was born I bought the place from the bankrupt estate of a silent-film star. He played Davy Crockett in one of the first westerns they filmed in the area. It's sort of a rambling hodgepodge. But we like it.''

"It's wonderful."

He looked pleased by her praise. Lifting her bags, he said, "Bring your fiddle and come on in. I'll give you the nickel tour of the place after lunch. Something tells me you're going to love the *portal* that runs the whole back of the house. That's Spanish for covered porch, and it's the place we do most of our living."

She followed in his wake, enchanted by the fantasy feel to the house, as though she'd suddenly been dropped into an early Clint Eastwood movie.

"You should have seen it when I first looked at it. There was a tree growing in the living room that had taken hold in the mud and clay of the adobe. Pa and I did everything ourselves. Re-stuccoed, laid Mexican tile." He motioned toward the chimneys that indicated at least four fireplaces. "Even rebuilt the original kivas."

As they stepped inside, she was surprised to find that, in spite of the exposed beam ceiling, dark woods and thick walls, the rooms seemed light and cool, with none of the overpowering severity that Western architecture sometimes created. Anyone would feel safe and secure in a home like this, Joan thought, and yet, the structure was quirky and unique enough to invite exploration.

A stocky Mexican woman in a peasant-style blouse and colorful skirt hurried to meet them. She smiled broadly at Joan, and her black eyes twinkled. Cody introduced her as Merlita Soledad, the "best housekeeper and cook north of the Rio Grande."

"*Jefe* always makes free with the pretty words

when I'm about to put food on the table,'' Merlita claimed with a hearty laugh. Cody objected, but Joan could see that it was all in fun; there was a great deal of affection between them.

An older man she recognized as Walt Matthews joined them, shaking Joan's hand and telling her how nice it was to see her again. She noticed that he still leaned heavily on the metal crutch she'd seen him use at the Austin seminar.

Cody set Joan's bags down. "If you don't mind, we'll get you settled in after lunch. I'm starved. Where's Sarah?"

The housekeeper's smile died, and she looked fretfully at Walt Matthews. Even before the old man grimaced and shook his head at Cody, Joan knew what he was about to say.

"I'm afraid she's not here, son," he said. "We don't know where she's run off to."

CHAPTER FIVE

THE OPEN AIRY DINING ROOM sparkled in the noon light slanting in from the sunlit *portal.* A vase of zinnias added a splash of color and delicacy to the heavy rough-hewn table and chairs.

Pa was on his best behavior for Joan Paxton, had even put on a fresh denim shirt for her arrival. Cody listened to their soft laughter as his father shared a funny story with the woman about the "good ol' days" on the rodeo circuit.

As for the food, Merlita had outdone herself. Her best chilies *rellenos* could melt in your mouth today. The salsa was fresh, and her quesadillas offered just the right mix of spices, a little bite to them, but not intimidating. Yep, the food was great.

And it all tasted to Cody like dry sawdust.

He was trying hard not to seem fazed by Sarah's disobedience, but he could feel his heart pounding. Neither Joan nor his father had said anything about the tightness in his jaw or his lack of interest in the conversation. The Paxton woman slid a few glances his way every now and then, and he could sense a certain tension at the table. But he had ignored the question in her eyes, hoping that he looked calm, hoping that his face didn't show just how mad he was at Sarah.

In spite of his direct order to be present at lunch to meet Joan Paxton, Sarah had yet to make an appearance. He took a swallow from his water glass, trying to dislodge the lump of tortilla that seemed wedged in his gullet. *She'd better have a hell of a good excuse.*

He supposed he should have known Sarah would disobey him. She'd been at her most recalcitrant the past couple of days, and the news that still one more adult was coming to Luna D'Oro to interfere in her life had ended in another storm of tears and slamming doors. But he'd thought he'd made it pretty clear what he expected of her today.

The Paxton woman had doubtlessly picked up on how surprised and annoyed he'd been. He hadn't been able to hide that. Now she probably thought he was the most hopeless excuse for a father she'd ever encountered. A parent who couldn't even make his own child show up for lunch. No wonder he'd had to call in reinforcements.

As angry as he was with Sarah—and she'd find out just how angry soon enough—he was disappointed in her, as well. He didn't want this to be Joan Paxton's initial introduction to his daughter, a poor first impression that would have to be overcome. This wasn't who Sarah was. This surly, rebellious child they'd been seeing so much of lately wasn't the bright, sweet-natured little girl he loved more than life itself.

He found himself suddenly wanting to correct any bad opinion Joan was formulating. Pa's story was winding down. In the lull of conversation, Cody cleared his throat, and both Joan and his father glanced his way.

"She's not usually this disobedient," he suddenly said to Joan. "She knew I expected her to be here to meet you. I was pretty adamant about it, and I suppose she couldn't resist the temptation to misbehave."

The woman didn't pretend not to know what he was talking about. Nor did she look at him the way he had imagined she would, with mockery or superiority. Except for a little line of worry between her brows, she seemed contemplative.

"Cody's right," his father jumped in as though he'd received some nonverbal plea for support. "This isn't like her. She knows when he means business."

Joan tilted an eyebrow at Cody. When she spoke at last, her voice was softly modulated. "Is it possible that's exactly why she isn't here? That she *does* know when you mean business? And that this wasn't one of those times?"

His chest tightened suddenly. "I'm afraid I don't follow."

She took a drink from her glass of iced tea and after a long moment seemed to come to a decision. "Cody, please don't take what I'm about to say the wrong way, but is it possible that, by not being here to meet me, Sarah was doing exactly what you gave her unspoken permission to do?"

"Why would I do that? I invited you here."

"Yes, but not without expressing a great deal of skepticism about the work I do. You've made it very clear to me. Is it possible that when you told Sarah about the purpose for my visit, something in your body language or tone of voice or facial expression gave away how you truly feel? In effect, giving Sarah silent permission to negate it as well, the result being that she doesn't show up.''

"If I did so," he replied in a careful tone, "what purpose would that serve?''

"Avoidance. You know my visit here could expose unpleasant issues with Sarah. Perhaps this is an unconscious effort on your part to delay what you will clearly find objectionable.''

He bridled at the suggestion, but he'd be damned before he'd show just how much her words bothered him. His father had found sudden interest in his food, but he hadn't missed the old man's mouth twisting in amusement. Cody shook his head, like a doctor in the presence of some incurable disease. "I don't ask my twelve-year-old daughter to do my dirty work for me, Joan. If I really didn't want you here, you wouldn't be sitting at this table right now.''

"Please don't be defensive about this. I only pose it as a possibility.''

His father gave him a sidelong glance. "Sarah can read you like a book, Cody.''

The thought that his own father believed he was capable of sending Sarah unconscious instructions to disobey him stung more than Joan Paxton's accusation. He tossed his napkin on the table. "That doesn't mean—''

"Daddy!''

From the dining-room door a whirlwind of blue

denim and red stripes suddenly barreled into him.
Blond hair as mussed as a haystack, smelling of
horses and heat, Sarah threw her arms around Cody's
neck and hugged him.

Uh-uh. It wasn't going to be that easy. He turned
in his seat, keeping his voice under rigid control and
his face set like a statue's. After the claim Joan had
just made, it wasn't that hard to remain stony.
"Where have you been, Sarah?"

"Out on Ladybug. I forgot. Don't be mad."

The look in her eyes was sweetly pleading. He
shook off understanding and forgiveness like un-
wanted rain. "You were supposed to be here when
we got back. I made myself very clear on that."

"Well, I'm here now."

He cleared a tightness in his throat, aware that both
Pa and Joan Paxton were watching him. "Go wash
up," he ordered. "Then come back here."

She started to move away, but then she turned toward Joan, tilting her head in the woman's direction
as though she hadn't known all along that their visitor
had arrived. After a long moment of simply staring,
she said flatly, "You're Joan Paxton."

Joan held out her hand and smiled. "That's right.
It's a pleasure to meet you, Sarah."

The girl shook hands, but muscles worked along
her jaw, making her chin look uncommonly fragile.
"Grandpa Walt says you're a real smart lady," Sarah
commented. "You don't look real smart to me."

Cody's fist hit the table, and silverware jumped.
"Sarah!"

"Well, she doesn't," Sarah said, whipping back

toward her father. A barely suppressed panic had crept into her voice. "She looks like the last *expert* we had around here, and we all know that she couldn't find her butt with both hands."

He reached out to capture her thin forearm, giving it a shake. "What in the name of Sam Hill's gotten into you? Apologize. And then go to your room."

"Why should I?" she yelled back. "I'm the one she's come here to see, aren't I? How's she going to find out anything about me if I'm locked in my room?"

"I have never locked you in your room, and you know it. But right now, it's awfully tempting. I'm ashamed of your behavior."

She inhaled a sobbing gasp, glaring at him. Then suddenly, wresting her arm from his grasp, she shouted, "I don't care!"

In the next moment she ran out of the room.

No one at the table said a thing. Cody drew a deep breath, his heart lying like a heavy bucket in his chest. What should he do now?

He had no opportunity to consider options.

Then from the vicinity of the living room came the sound of a heavy crash.

"What the hell…!" Cody was out of his chair, shoving it back so hard that Joan suspected it had left skid marks on the beautiful Mexican-tile floor.

She rose and followed more slowly, joined by Walt Matthews, who looked worried by this latest outburst from his beloved granddaughter. The sound of Cody's raised voice and Sarah's shrill responses led them to the living room.

Joan and Walt stopped in the doorway. She had seen this room briefly after her arrival, when Cody Matthews had shown her into the dining room. Then, she'd been more interested in the tension emanating from Cody than the appointments of the living room. But she'd noticed the massive, comfortable-looking furniture, the creamy, uneven plaster so typical of adobe architecture and the occasional Western sculpture that clearly spoke of the Matthews family's love for their home state.

Now, in a matter of moments, Joan realized that one of those lovely art objects had been knocked off its pedestal. The thick, handwoven area rug had not been able to save the ceramic sculpture of a stallion and pony, muzzles touching affectionately. It lay in three pieces, and on either side of it stood Cody and Sarah. The anger in the room was thick enough to cut it with a knife. The child, wide-eyed, seemed ready to bolt, and her father looked both shocked and furious.

"I didn't do it on purpose!" Sarah wailed. "It was—"

"Stop!" Cody cut her off with the sharp slice of a raised hand. "Don't make matters worse by lying about it."

The girl took a startled breath and went white. She seemed very young and vulnerable. Joan wanted badly to intercede, but she dared not. Her position in the Matthews household was still too new, too tenuous to interfere in this fiery father/daughter battle for control. Besides, she wanted to see how the situation played out, and as long as it got no worse, the release of anger might be good for both of them.

The silence stretched on, long and uncomfortable. Joan could see the two of them struggling for some way to resolve the crisis. She continued to watch them silently, and beside her, she felt Walt stir in discomfort. He seemed about to step into the fray, and Joan quickly lifted her hand to his arm. The old man subsided immediately.

And suddenly Sarah whirled and fled the scene before anyone could say a word.

For a long agony of one or two seconds, Joan feared Cody might try to go after her. But after a step in Sarah's wake, he turned his attention to the broken sculpture, crouching to collect the pieces with quiet care.

The pony's ear had snapped off, as well as a large section from the stallion's mane. The breaks were clean, but in such obvious places that the sculpture would never be the same. After a moment Cody stopped trying to see if the damage could be repaired. Merlita had come up behind him, and he stood to place the pieces into her hands.

"Trash it," he told her.

Merlita muttered something in Spanish, then wandered toward the kitchen. Cody bent to tip the overturned pedestal upright. He glanced up at Joan, and she thought she'd never seen a man look so trapped and resentful.

He shook his head. "You must think we're—" He broke off, and when he began again, his voice had a resigned, desolate quality to it. "I don't know what to say. Sarah's never been deliberately destructive before...."

Walt spoke up. "It could have been an accident, son."

"Like hell, Pa," Cody said with a sharp shake of his head. "She's mad at me, and she wanted to show me just how much by destroying something she knows I value."

Joan was listening with only half an ear. Her thoughts were elsewhere, her eyes traveling around the living room speculatively. The statue of the stallion and pony had been pretty and sculpted by a talented hand, but there were obviously other, more expensive pieces placed randomly around the room. Why had Sarah chosen that particular statue on which to vent her anger? Almost absently, she remarked, "It looked like a lovely piece."

"It's one of a kind. I commissioned it from an artist in Laredo." Cody jerked away to slap his hand against a nearby trestle table. "Damn! I can't believe Sarah's behavior today."

"May I ask, was it your favorite?"

He turned his head to frown at her, clearly struggling to bring residual anger under control. "No. But it had sort of a special meaning for Sarah and me. I bought it on her tenth birthday. Ironically, it's called *Stable Buddies*. That's always been our private nickname for our relationship." He snorted in disgust. "At least, what our relationship *was*.. I'd hardly call us buddies now. And today the kid seems to hate me."

"Perhaps it's not as bad as it seems."

"I'd better go talk to her."

Joan caught his arm as he turned. "I'd like to suggest that you leave her alone for a while. Give both of your...emotions a chance to stabilize."

Cody looked uncertain. "I don't know. I don't want her to think she can get away with this kind of stuff."

"I'm sure she doesn't think that."

Joan gave him a small smile of reassurance, hoping to convey that the horrible scene they had all just witnessed had been painful and unpleasant, but not fatal. In fact, if what she suspected was true, she was actually quite hopeful for this father/daughter relationship.

SHE KNEW SHE WAS in trouble.

Big trouble.

She'd never yelled at her father before. And she'd never, *ever,* broken anything just because she was mad. Oh sure, they'd had fights sometimes, but she knew where to draw the line, just how far she could push. Not like today. Not when it got all crazy so fast that she hardly knew what she was saying.

Sarah threw herself on her back across her bed, folding her arms behind her head and staring up at the ceiling. Her nose felt stuffy, like she was gonna cry. She shook her head fiercely. She wouldn't. She couldn't. No one, not even Merlita, could think that it mattered to her one way or the other if she was sent to her room in disgrace.

With a minute turn of her head, she looked around, at the walls and shelves that held their accumulation of things she had saved her whole life. Familiar things. Treasured things. It brought her stomach up to her throat to think of never seeing any of them again.

Her room. But for how much longer? A week? A month? When they sent her away, would she be allowed to take any of her stuff with her? Probably not. From the conversation she'd overheard, it didn't sound like Grandfather Ross would want any reminders of Texas in his big house in Connecticut.

Three months ago she'd been called to her father's study to meet the old man for the first time. Her whole life had changed that day, and nothing was ever going to be the same again.

It still amazed her that Grandfather Ross could be related to her mother. In the pictures Sarah had seen of her, she could tell she was sweet and kind, like a fairy princess. Sarah thought it was easy to see why people had loved her, and certainly why her father had. He still couldn't talk much about her even after all these years.

But Grandpa Ross didn't seem sweet *or* kind.

"I'm your grandfather," he'd said in a quiet, very serious voice, and then he'd shaken her hand. He'd looked at her as if she was some alien creature, and when he smiled, there was no sparkle in his eyes like Grandpa Walt always got when he talked to her.

This new relative in her life scared her with all his talk about visits to Connecticut and questions about school and what she liked to do for fun. But what scared her most of all was the way her father had stood nearby, not saying a word, careful not to look in her direction. She knew him—that stiff posture, the way his head dipped low. He was upset, and whether it was with her or Grandfather Ross, she didn't know, but from that moment on she knew something wasn't right.

Later that night, of course, she'd found out the truth. Barely awake, she'd stumbled out of bed to get a drink of water and overheard Grandpa Walt and her father talking about it. That was the night she'd discovered that her father was going to send her off to live with Grandfather Ross.

That he didn't love her anymore.

For a long time that had been the hardest part. To realize that her father didn't want her around. That he was willing to let a complete stranger—related or not—finish raising her. She'd cried really hard that night, sobbing so long into her pillow that it had still been wet in the morning. Her red, swollen eyes had been a dead giveaway, but luckily Dad had taken Grandpa Walt to San Antonio that day to see the doctor about his hip, and Merlita was easy enough to escape. Sarah had ridden off on her horse, and only Ladybug knew how she'd spent the night.

But a person couldn't cry and stay sad forever. Grandpa Walt had always told her you had to get back in the saddle when life "tossed you on your keester." So on that day—three months ago—that was what she'd decided to do.

I'll show him, she'd repeated over and over again on the ride home. *I'll show him I don't love him, either.*

So what if her father didn't want her? Maybe she was tired of hot, dusty Texas summers. Maybe the

teachers were better in Connecticut, and she'd never
have to get the third degree from someone like old
Miss Beasley again. When it came right down to it,
why should she love her father? Work was all he
cared about lately, anyway, wasn't it? Maybe he'd
decided he liked making money more than he liked
raising a kid.

Still, it was hard to stay quiet and pretend nothing
was wrong. That she didn't care. Sometimes what her
father was planning made her so mad she couldn't
help but find ways to upset him. Like today, with this
new visitor who'd probably been brought here to fix
things between them.

Well, she'd see, Sarah thought. She'd find out.
There was no fixing some things, and this was one of
them.

Sarah's gaze wandered around her room, while she
mentally said goodbye to all the pieces of her old life
she'd have to leave behind when she went to live in
Connecticut. No Ladybug to help her win more barrel-racing ribbons at the county fair. No Grandpa Walt
to help her make hay-bale castles in the barn. Not
even any glow-in-the-dark plastic stars overhead.

She remembered last Christmas, the day her father
had helped her glue those stars to the ceiling. He'd
laughed and insisted that it didn't matter where they
went, stars ought to be random. But in the end he'd
been very careful to follow her instructions perfectly
as she read from a book the exact pattern of Pegasus,
her favorite constellation.

That had been a good day. The best. From all the

laughing and joking, she'd never have guessed that her father was getting tired of having her around.

Against all her efforts, a tear slipped out of the corner of her eye and rolled down into her hair. She swiped it away angrily. Sometimes it was so hard, she thought. Sometimes it was so hard not to care anymore.

AFTER SUCH AN EVENTFUL LUNCH, Luna D'Oro seemed ominously quiet. Walt had headed off to the stable. Cody had agreed, in short, terse sentences, that he would try to cool down by working in his study for a while. Sarah, presumably, was sulking in her room.

Joan took the opportunity to unpack, sorting her things into bureau drawers and the closet with her usual precise care as she pondered her introduction to Sarah and the child's relationship with her father. Clearly they were both hurting, struggling to cope with a change that neither of them understood or knew how to resolve.

Yet nothing Joan had witnessed today felt hopeless. While the exchanges between Cody and Sarah had been heated and passionate, there had been no nasty signs of irreparable harm done between them. In her years of counseling at the school, Joan had seen her share of arguments develop between parent and sibling. True to form, Cody had insisted on being the "adult" in the conflict, while Sarah had refused to back down. And when the child had realized she could not win the battle in the dining room, her only defense had been flight.

It was doubtful that the destruction of the statue had been an accident. More likely, it was Sarah's attempt to reassert her position in the argument. But even that might have an interesting subtext.

Joan wanted to explore the possibilities of that, and she found her chance a few hours later when she went into the kitchen for something cool to drink. While she sipped iced tea, she and Merlita talked. The cook was friendly and seemed to like having another woman around. She was also dispirited by the recent trouble Sarah had been causing. It was clear she loved the girl like a daughter.

Joan listened carefully, knowing that peripheral members of a family often had good insight into its problems. But she sat up straighter when Merlita told her that Sarah had emerged from her room no more than an hour ago.

Without a word to the housekeeper. Without a stop at the refrigerator for a soda. Just long enough to rescue the broken statue from the trash.

"She didn't break that statue on purpose," the older woman claimed. "She is crazy about *les caballos*. And she love that thing too much for that."

Joan gave the housekeeper a noncommittal smile. "Merlita, I need a favor," she said as she set her glass in the sink. It was time to put her theory to the test.

"*Sí, señorita.* Anything I can do to help."

"Actually, I was wondering if you have any glue."

A few minutes later Joan stood at Sarah's bedroom door. It was open, and inside Joan could see Sarah, hunched over her desk, deeply involved in some project. Joan could guess what it was.

While she watched, the girl huffed in despair and tossed an object onto the desk. As Joan had suspected, it was one of the broken pieces from the statue. The pony's ear.

Before she could be caught staring, Joan knocked on the doorjamb. The girl whirled in her chair, nothing close to a welcome in her face.

"Can I do anything to help?" Joan asked from the threshold.

"No," was the short, bitter response.

"May I come in, anyway?"

Sarah shrugged her thin shoulders. "I don't guess I can stop you."

"Of course you can. It's your room."

"You'd just tell my dad."

"Why would I do that?" Joan asked, as though such a thought was inconceivable. "I want to get to know you better. Wouldn't it be silly of me to make you mad right off the bat?"

The girl seemed to think there was some truth in that statement. She sighed and swiveled back to her desk. Over her shoulder she said sullenly, "Well, come in if you're going to. Look around all you want. You're not going to find anything weird."

"I don't expect to. Is there some reason you think that's what I'm looking for?"

"I heard Grandpa Walt and my dad talking. You're supposed to find out what's wrong with me."

"Gosh, I'd better get cracking then." She moved to the desk where Sarah sat ignoring her and leaned against it. Crossing her arms, she looked down at the girl and said in a serious tone, "Okay. So what's wrong with you?"

The girl didn't look at her right away. She sat for a few moments fingering the jagged edge of the broken sculpture. Then her eyes flickered upward, catching Joan's gaze quickly before skittering away again. "Nothing," she said quietly.

"Well, that certainly makes my job easier."

She knew where Sarah got some of her stubborn attitude. Her jaw was set in the same hard lines that her father's had been only a few hours earlier. On the desk lay a tube of common school glue, but the statue still lay in pieces.

"That glue's not strong enough," Joan said. Out of her skirt pocket she pulled the tube of household cement Merlita had given her. "Try this."

Joan wasn't surprised when Sarah made no move to take the tube. She slid the glue across the desk and then moved away, intent on learning more about Sarah from the girl's surroundings.

There were few surprises here. The bedroom was full of the kinds of mementos a girl caught between childhood and adolescence might collect. Knowing that Sarah was following her every movement, in spite of pretending otherwise, Joan finally stopped in front of a bulletin board covered with red, blue and purple ribbons. Second place in a spelling bee. First place in a barrel-racing championship. Dancing-school awards. School competitions. The girl wasn't without talent.

"You play the piano," Joan said, lifting one of the

first-place ribbons with the tip of her finger. "And very well, it seems."

Sarah was still pretending to inspect the broken pieces of the statue. "It wasn't that big a deal. They gave ribbons to everyone in the recital. So the losers wouldn't feel bad about themselves."

Joan had to suppress a smile. It seemed Sarah was aware of the latest efforts of educators to build self-esteem in children.

Beside the bookcase was a table holding a very elaborate handmade castle, complete with a well for drawing water in the courtyard and a toothpick jail for holding disobedient peasants. "Nice castle," Joan said. "Did you make it yourself?"

"Yeah. For all the good it did," Sarah muttered.

Joan frowned at the structure. It was intricately detailed down to the last cobblestone. She made a mental note to ask Cody if he had helped Sarah complete the work or experienced any problem in getting her to finish it.

Behind the castle, leaning against the wall, were six dolls in simply made medieval costumes. Bright red lines had been painted across the second and fifth doll's necks, and Joan took a wild guess. "Henry VIII's wives?"

Sarah's interest was caught at last. Her head swung in Joan's direction. "How did you know?"

Joan pointed to the neck of the second doll. "The beheading marks. Definitely poor Ann Boleyn and Catherine Howard. And the clothes are very true to the period. Did you make them?"

"Merlita helped me. It was part of my final semester project."

"You must have aced it."

The girl made a disgusted sound. "We haven't gotten our final grades yet, but Miss Beasley's probably gonna flunk me because she says I didn't turn in the written report part."

Joan caught a momentary tone in the girl's sullen voice—something angry and hurt—that made her want to go a step further. "*Did* you turn it in?"

Sarah swung back to the desk, obviously determined to seem as if she didn't care one way or the other. "It doesn't matter what I say," she said. "No one believes me. Not even Dad. He's probably told you that I'm a big fat liar and I should be locked away somewhere. Like Ann Boleyn in the Tower of London."

Joan laughed. "Well, he hasn't told me you're a big fat liar and I'll bet there aren't any towers in this part of Texas. He'll probably have to settle for locking you in your room. Oh, dear," she added, as though suddenly realizing that Sarah was in her room now because she'd been sent here. "It looks like you're halfway there to being Ann Boleyn already. Your father just hasn't locked the door yet."

The girl took a strange little breath. It might have been a laugh. She picked up the statue again, scrutinizing it. But the moment Joan approached the desk again, Sarah set it aside, pulled a book from the overhead shelf and began flipping through the pages absently.

Joan picked up the statue and one of the pieces.

She turned it over in her hands a few times as though giving it careful consideration. "You know, this really can be fixed."

Sarah shrugged. "I don't care about it anymore. It's just a stupid statue."

Hardly, Joan thought, but aloud she said, "Well, it seems a shame to send it to the trash bin. Let me see what I can do to help."

"I don't want it," Sarah objected quickly.

Joan ignored the protest and uncapped the household cement. The cleanest break was in the pony's ear. She ran a thin line of glue across the jagged piece. Sarah was furiously concentrating on her book now.

"I loved cats as a little girl," Joan said. "My father used to buy me the most beautiful figurines."

Sarah still refused to look at her, but the pages of the book stopped turning.

Joan sighed as she pressed the ear back on the pony's head. "Unfortunately I had a real cat who was fascinated with the top of my dresser. Ming would knock them over, and the legs always broke off. I ended up with the best collection of glued-together cat statues in the world."

She applied pressure to the reattached ear, having a sudden, vivid recollection of those years when her father had been an ambassador in the Far East. That little stray cat had been a household fixture for so long. It had broken her heart to leave Ming behind when the family had moved back to the United States.

The silence evidently got to Sarah. She tossed her head back to stare at Joan. She had beautiful blond hair, and it fell prettily over her shoulder as she fingered it back. But it was the cold look in the girl's eyes that made Joan's breath catch. "I don't like cats," Sarah said, and there was thunder in her scowl. "And I'd get rid of a cat that messed up my things that way."

Temper. Yes. But not apathy. That was a good sign.

Joan smiled mildly, wanting to keep her responses noncontroversial. "I suppose that would have been one way of dealing with the problem."

"That's what you do with things you can't fix. You get rid of them."

The bitter note in Sarah's tone made Joan look at the girl more closely. There was something else at work here, something that went beyond studied defiance and bad behavior. Aware of Joan's scrutiny, the girl looked away, but her sleight-of-hand wasn't quite successful. Her skin was flushed, her posture stiff, and in that quick glimpse of her eyes, Joan had seen the glisten of tears.

She wanted to delve deeper, but now was not the time. Later, when Sarah felt easier with her, when she'd figured out for herself that Joan meant her no harm. Then she'd return to that comment.

Forcing lightness into her voice, Joan said, "Well, I liked Ming a lot more than a bunch of ceramic statues, so I was willing to take my chances." She lifted her hand from the pony's ear, and it stayed in place. Setting the statue on the desk, she said, "See? Almost like new. You can try replacing the other piece, if you like. Holler if you want help."

Before Sarah could say another word, Joan left the room.

CHAPTER SIX

FROM SARAH'S BEDROOM Joan made her way to Cody Matthews's study, hoping to find him still there. She was in luck. The door was open, and inside the cluttered office furnished to suit a man's taste, she saw him standing in front of one of the bookcases.

He seemed lost in thought, and as she approached, Joan could see that his attention was focused on a picture on one of the shelves. It was a photograph of Sarah taken at a young age, seated on the back of a pinto pony.

An almost imperceptible movement of his head told her Cody was aware of her presence. She stood beside him, knowing that he must be wondering where that darling little girl in the picture had gone.

"She was just two in this shot," he said softly without looking her way. "Her legs weren't even long enough to reach the stirrups. Pa told me I was nuts for buying her a pony so soon, but I couldn't wait to teach her to ride."

He sounded tired and grim, like a man anticipating an endless series of challenges. She didn't know whether she had intended to come up close to him, but she did now, without much thought. Close enough to touch him, close enough to see the lines around his eyes and note that his hair, in addition to being soot-dark, was as thick as any boy's.

"You mustn't let what happened today dishearten you," she offered gently. "It's merely a symptom of some greater stress going on in her life right now, but it's one that can be resolved, I'm sure of it."

He turned his head to look at her. His eyes were unreadable, but for the briefest of moments she thought she could see past that confident Texas drawl, past the obstinate determination to be the father of a perfect child. It made her feel strangely close to him, made her want to offer comforting sympathy that went beyond mere words. She could feel her blood run faster in her veins.

This wasn't like her. She moved toward the chair that sat in front of a massive desk littered with paper. How annoying to discover that she had to concentrate very hard to remember why she'd come here.

Cody moved away from the bookcase, too. He sat poised on the edge of the desk, quietly, evidently waiting for her to continue. She pulled her notebook, which she almost always carried with her, out of her pocket.

"I thought we could talk about what I hope to accomplish in the next few days," Joan said at last. "But if this is a bad time…"

"No, no. In fact, I wanted to talk to you, too. Mostly to apologize for Sarah's behavior earlier."

"There's no need."

"You're very calm about the…reception she gave you."

"I assure you, I've had worse encounters with children who resent my entry into what they consider their private domain.''

"And your first impressions of Sarah?" Cody asked with a raised eyebrow.

"From what you've told me and from what I've seen for myself so far, your family structure here is very small and tight. I'm guessing Sarah doesn't want anyone to change the order of things, the rules and rituals she's comfortable with. She's frightened by my presence and the sudden attention that's been focused on her behavior. It's only natural that she expresses it in the most blatantly hostile way she knows. Even if it costs her dearly, as it did with the statue.''

He cocked his head at her, frown lines appearing between his eyes. "Costs *her?* What do you mean?"

"You said you bought that statue to commemorate Sarah's birthday. That you both saw it as a tangible symbol of your relationship. I'm willing to bet that statue meant even more to your daughter than it did to you.''

"And yet that didn't keep her from destroying it.''

Joan slid forward in her chair to stress her point. "But don't you think it's odd that of all the items in the room, she chose that sculpture?"

Cody shrugged. "It was a random choice made in the heat of anger.''

"I don't think so.''

"Pa thinks it was an accident.''

"I don't believe that, either,'' Joan said with a quick shake of her head. "I believe that even as furious as she was, Sarah couldn't bear to hurt you that badly. So unconsciously, she chose to destroy something that *she* loves.''

Cody looked doubtful. ''That's a little cerebral for a twelve-year-old, don't you think? Even for one as sharp as Sarah.''

''I'll give her credit for even more than that. The destruction of that particular statue is also an indication of the way she views your relationship lately. Damaged. On the verge of being destroyed completely.''

''Whoa,'' Cody said, clearly disbelieving now. ''She's just a kid.''

She had the sudden disconcerting thought that maybe she *was* reading too much into the incident. Why was she trying so hard to find emotional justification for Sarah's behavior? Because Cody Matthews would accept that more easily than a diagnosis of attention deficit disorder?

She shook her head. That was crazy. She'd never alter the reality of a situation just to please a parent. Especially one who'd been as skeptical and contentious as Cody Matthews.

Brushing aside those doubts, she said more firmly, ''I've just spent the past twenty minutes with Sarah in her room. Do you know what she was doing? She'd rescued that statue from the trash and was trying to piece it back together. You should have seen her face. She's not a good enough actress to hide how upset she was.''

His gaze sharpened. ''Did she talk to you?''

''She talked *at* me. But it was a start.''

''So where do you want to go from here?''

Joan sighed and settled back in the chair. "If you have no objection, I'd like to talk to her teachers as soon as possible. If school's just let out for the year, they'll be clearing out the classrooms, grading final exams. I'd like to get to them while Sarah is still fresh in their minds, but they'll need your permission to discuss her performance with me."

"I'll call the school tomorrow and see what needs to be done—although I'm not sure how helpful they'll be. Considering her behavior lately, her teachers will probably be glad to see the last of her." He ran his hand through his hair. "If she passes."

"Is there really a chance she won't?"

"I don't know. Sarah says I used to have faith in her and that I ought to trust her now. But I told you what Beasley said."

"I definitely want to speak to this Miss Beasley about Sarah's semester project."

Joan repeated the discussion she'd had with Sarah about all her hard work on the castle and doll costumes, and her indignation over the fact that no one seemed to believe she'd finished the written portion of the assignment.

Cody told Joan that Sarah had had no trouble completing the first two parts of the project, but that he couldn't speak for the final part. "I was in Dallas most of the week she was supposed to do it," he admitted a little reluctantly. "Helping one of my clients finance a big investment. You might ask Merlita or Pa if they saw any sign of it being worked on."

Joan nodded as she made a note in her book. She inclined her head toward the computer terminal on the corner of Cody's desk. "Could I have access to a computer? I've brought my own disks, and after I've had a chance to talk to her teachers, I'd like to run a couple of continuous-performance tests on Sarah. They'll help provide additional clues."

"I'll set you up with a password tonight. What kind of tests are you talking about?"

"They're very simple," Joan replied. "We can go over the contents of them if you like. Perhaps tomorrow afternoon?"

"I have to be in Houston tomorrow on business. In fact, I won't be home until the end of the week." He must have caught her small frown because his brow lifted. "Is that a problem?"

"For Sarah's sake, it would be better if you were here until she gets used to my presence. She may feel as if she's being deserted. Left to fend for herself."

He stood and walked behind his desk. With impatient movements he sifted through a stack of paper, suddenly all business. "It can't be helped," he said.

Joan had to swallow a stinging retort. He had no way of knowing it, but those very words had often been her father's response when he'd been called away from family outings, from birthday parties and school plays. The needs of his country had always taken precedence over the needs of his family, and though Joan understood now just how vital a part Alistair Paxton had played in countless international strategies, his absence had been almost unbearable to his young daughter.

She ducked her head to keep her annoyance from

showing, then chastised herself for drawing comparisons. Her personal experiences had no business here.

"Something wrong?" Cody asked when the silence stretched on.

"No," Joan denied quickly. "I'm sure we'll manage without you."

Only later, when she was returning to her room, did she remember that her words were exactly the same as her mother's had been all those years ago.

COMPARED TO LUNCH, Cody thought, dinner that night was a cakewalk. Sarah was on her best behavior, though making no bones about the fact that it was strictly against her will that she was present at all. Pa was still playing the good host at the table, and Joan Paxton, looking prim and schoolmarmish in another one of those high-necked blouses of hers, had remained polite, pleasant, but somehow distant.

Earlier Cody had made his announcement that he'd be away from home for a few days. He'd expected an explosion from Sarah, but she held it in, as if sensing that another show of anger would not be tolerated. After one blurted, tormented "But," she'd subsided. Pa frowned at the news. Joan Paxton merely took a sip from her wineglass, patted her lips dry, and then developed an excessive interest in the pot roast on her plate.

It was *her* attitude that bothered Cody most of all. Disapproval. It was practically oozing out of every pore.

What right did she have to disapprove? In spite of his skepticism, he was doing his best to accommodate her needs, wasn't he? Sure, there were some things about Sarah that he could *never* share with her, but he'd been cooperative, given her more access to his life than he'd ever given any woman. What more did she want from him?

He knew what was eating her. She didn't like the idea of going it alone the next few days. Not because she couldn't manage just fine at Luna D'Oro without him. Not because Sarah might be a handful without his presence. No. She wanted *his* participation. His wholehearted involvement. She'd already made it clear that the entire family had to be willing to explore their relationship with Sarah. And he was ready to do that. Up to a point. For his daughter's sake.

But not just now. Not when everything he'd worked so long and hard for had reached a critical point. There was too much riding on this deal in Houston for him to chance having a subordinate handle it.

If things went well, Cody would nearly double his holdings. The deal would ensure that extensive medical treatment would be possible for his father if his hip got any worse. It would keep Luna D'Oro solvent for the next generation of Matthewses. But more than anything else, it would allow him financial support if he ever had to fight to keep Sarah.

Maybe that wouldn't happen. Maybe all the noise Edward Ross was making about wanting to know his granddaughter better would cease once something else caught his interest. He'd been pretty quiet lately. But the possibility of all that Ross capital being used to uncover the truth—the ugly truth—made Cody break out in a cold sweat.

If there was trouble ahead, he needed to be ready. By God, he wasn't about to lose Sarah just because he couldn't afford to hire the best attorneys in the country.

He couldn't share those fears with Joan, of course. They were too personal and would lead to too many dangerous questions. Besides, they had nothing to do with what Sarah had been up to lately. If Joan was as smart as everyone seemed to think she was, she wouldn't need that kind of information, anyway. Why confuse the issue?

Light laughter brought Cody out of his reverie.

His father had been sharing the story about the two of them cleaning out the fireplace kivas shortly after Cody had bought the house and discovering a colony of harmless fruit bats in one of the chimneys. Pa was doing a comic impersonation of two grown men trying to escape a house full of terrified bats.

Joan's eyes were sparkling. Her cheeks were flushed from the wine, and when she smiled at his father, the smallest trace of dimples snuck in.

She was a confusing woman. Fascinating, he admitted, but confusing. Aloof, analytical one moment. Soft and full of wry good humor the next. And caring, too. When she'd stood next to him in the study, he'd felt her ability to understand and empathize with what was running through his head at that moment. It had aroused his interest, and then her proximity—the scent of her hair, the warmth of her breath—aroused him even more. In a basic primitive way that he hadn't experienced in a long time. A damn long time.

He'd have to watch himself around her. Keep a clear head. He didn't need woman trouble on top of everything else he was trying to deal with right now.

"Isn't that right, Cody?" his father asked.

"I beg your pardon?"

"I said, Joan ought to see all of Luna D'Oro, and she can borrow one of our horses to ride out with me one day this week." To Joan he said, "We'll have to take it slow because of my darn hip, but you'll get to see the place."

Luna D'Oro land was an impressive sight, and Cody thought how much he'd like to be the one to show it to Joan. But she was better off with Pa, who'd be delighted to share the history of the place with an interested newcomer and probably wouldn't think twice about what she looked like in a pair of snug jeans.

"I've told Joan she's to make herself at home here," Cody said, giving the woman a thin smile. "Can you ride?"

"It's been a few years," she acknowledged. "But I used to ride all the time when my family moved back to Virginia from Europe."

He could picture that. Some snotty country-club stable, where everyone posted politely on well-groomed bridle trails and hardly got a speck of dust on their jodhpurs.

Managing to keep disdain from coloring his voice, Cody told her, "We ride western, and our remuda isn't a bunch of sedate Sunday hacks. If you think you can handle one of them, you're welcome to pick out a mount.'' He turned toward Sarah, who'd been demonstrating her displeasure with this conversation by repeatedly sighing noisily. ''You know the stock, Sarah. Why don't you help Joan choose one?''

The girl stared openmouthed at her father. ''I'm not a stablehand.''

He felt his annoyance rise, but instead, he said calmly, ''No, you're not. While I'm away, you're the lady of the house and the closest thing I have to an official hostess for our guest. How about helping your old man out here?''

Obviously the implication that Cody would be relying on Sarah for the next few days, that she could be trusted to behave in a responsible manner, brought her objections to a standstill. Looking shocked, she muttered, ''I guess I can. If it's that important to you.''

''It is. Thank you, Sarah.''

He had to resist the temptation to smile. These were the first civil words that had passed between them all day. Cody felt good. Maybe the situation wasn't hopeless, after all. Maybe as a father he wasn't completely inept.

His glance met Joan's. She smiled in his direction ever so slightly. Silent approval.

His gut kicked—hard—as though his stomach was tied up in knots. It was stupid, Cody told himself, to take so much pleasure in that one tiny look. He took a deep swallow from his wineglass, deciding that, in spite of everything, it was a very good thing he was going to be away from Luna D'Oro for a while.

THE NEXT MORNING, promising to treat her to the best chili lunch in Texas, Walt Matthews dropped Joan off in front of Goliath's one-and-only school.

Making her way to the administrative office, Joan thought it didn't make much difference where you taught kids—in a small drafty old building that had been designated a historic landmark or in a rambling bunch of portables on scrubland. By the end of the term, all schools looked pretty much alike. Abandoned lockers hanging open. Cases filled with dusty trophies. Tattered banners hanging across hallways, urging support for one team or another.

The children were gone now, but she expected to find most of Sarah's teachers still in their classrooms, tying up loose ends. She succeeded in talking to three of them in two hours. The trio—two women and one man—were harried, but willing to share their opinion of Sarah. All of them described the girl as a bright and imaginative student, but they also recalled, without exception, times when she had been moody, disorganized and disruptive in the classroom. Although she had passed all their classes, two of the teachers were disappointed. They'd expected better results from her. One of them even voiced the suspicion that Sarah had attempted to sabotage her final grade by deliberately answering test questions incorrectly.

Joan wasn't sure what to think. Some of Sarah's behavior was classic ADD—her inability to sit quietly for very long, her tendency to blurt out answers instead of waiting to be called upon. But none of the teachers Joan interviewed had found the girl unable to sustain attention and focus, and no projects had been incomplete. It was a curious mix of symptoms, and by the time Joan reached Miss Beasley's classroom, she was hoping this older, more experienced teacher would offer more definitive clues.

She was about to grasp the knob on the door of Miss Beasley's room when the door flew open, and she nearly collided with a thin, thirtyish woman coming out. Joan offered an apology, but the woman ignored her and barreled down the hallway, her heels voicing sharp staccato sounds of disapproval all the way.

Inside, Miss Beasley sat hunched over her desk, furiously making checkmarks on the paper in front of her. Joan assumed she was still grading exams—not the best time to discuss Sarah. In fact, the teacher didn't seem to realize she had another visitor, and Joan took the opportunity to look around the classroom. If Cody was correct, this was the place where Sarah did her poorest work, the place where she was most in danger of failing.

Joan could see why. If Sarah did suffer from ADD, even the mildest form, this classroom was hardly an environment she could thrive in. The room was small, a hodgepodge of shuffled paperwork, overflowing bookcases and poor lighting. Even the desks were a problem—they were much too close together to allow for any kind of quiet study or concentration. She felt a trace of sympathy for the poor woman who had to teach in this environment and wondered what Miss Beasley had done to deserve it.

Her sympathy died a little as the teacher looked up, giving her a sour, suspicious glare that must have

withered many a student's courage. "Now what?"
the older woman demanded. Her worn, tired features
were lined with tension, and the quality of agitation
in her voice left no doubt about how much she re-
sented this interruption. "If I get one more parent
trying to coerce me into raising an F to a D, I'm going
to call Security."

That explained the last visitor, Joan thought. With
her hand outstretched and a friendly smile on her face,
she crossed to the teacher's desk. "Actually, I'm on
your side. I'm not a parent, I'm a teacher." She introduced herself, mentioning where she had taught in
Alexandria, information that caused Miss Beasley to
lift one gray brow.

"Are you my replacement?" she said with a touch
of frost in her tone.

"I beg your pardon?"

"I'm retiring this year, thank the Lord. And if
you've come here looking for some free advice, I
haven't got any. You'll have to find out what to do
just like I did. The hard way."

"No, I'm not your replacement, though I'm sure a
new teacher would love to hear what you have to say.
You must be the resident expert, after nearly forty
years of teaching."

Miss Beasley's posture lost some of its stiffness.
She tipped her head sharply. "Closer to fifty. And not
a one of them easy, I'll tell you."

Joan nodded in sympathy. Miss Beasley was
strictly an old-school educator, loads of experience,
but a little confused and a lot jaded by the changes
that had taken place in education over the years. The

rules were different now. Mountains of administrative paperwork. Classes too large. Parents who took no interest in their children's work. Disrespectful students. Obviously she was a woman who expected to be treated deferentially, but Joan would have bet her last paycheck that Miss Beasley hadn't had a class she really enjoyed teaching since Nixon had resigned.

And what, Joan wondered, had she thought of Sarah?

"I'm sure you're quite busy…"

"I am."

"But I was hoping we could talk for a few minutes. I've been asked to come here by one of your student's fathers, William Matthews. Sarah's dad."

"Sarah!" Miss Beasley yelped. "What's that wretched child done now?"

In spite of her determination to be diplomatic, Joan felt her blood start to heat. No wonder neither Cody nor Sarah had any use for this abrasive woman. Taking a deep, calming breath, Joan said, "Nothing, I hope. I've been asked to evaluate some of Sarah's recent behavior. I've done quite a bit of work with children suffering from attention deficit disorder, and Mr. Matthews asked me to—"

"That young lady does not have attention deficit disorder," Miss Beasley interrupted, crossing her arms over her stomach. Her mouth was pinched and unpleasant. "The only thing wrong with Sarah Matthews is the same thing that was wrong with her father when I had him in my class twenty-five years ago. Not enough hand-to-backside contact. Spoiled. Spoiled rotten."

Joan ducked her head, trying to hide her irritation. She wouldn't get answers if she antagonized the woman. "I'm sorry to hear she's been such a problem for you. It's rather odd, since she seems very enthusiastic about history, and I've seen the project she worked on—the castle and Henry VIII's wives."

"Oh, she's very enthusiastic about what she *likes*. But give her something she doesn't like, and you get nothing but excuses and rebellion. Her father was just the same. And no less disrespectful, either."

"I wonder, could I see her grades?" Joan asked, pointing to the dog-eared grading book that was open on the desk. "I have a permission slip from the office to look at them."

The woman indicated she had no problem with that by tossing her hands in the air. She slid the book across the desk. It collided with a mountainous stack of what appeared to be test papers, some of which fluttered to the floor. "Look all you want. The sad truth is there for anyone to see." With what could only be taken as a self-satisfied attitude, she added, "Oh, I imagine there will be lots of tears in the Matthews household come Friday."

"Then you're going to fail her?"

"I certainly am."

Joan found Sarah's name in the book and ran a finger down the column of test scores over the school year. It wasn't easy to decipher. Miss Beasley's handwriting was messy and difficult to read, with numerous erasures and crossed-out numbers. Sarah might not be organized, but neither, it seemed, was her teacher.

The scores weren't great, but not a complete disaster. She'd passed the final exam, but the incomplete project in the last semester had killed her average.

With a sigh of disappointment, Joan replaced the book on the desk. Miss Beasley has gone back to grading papers. She clearly had no interest in discussing one of her least-favorite pupils any further.

Pressing her fingers against her pursed lips, Joan took a turn around the crowded room, thinking hard. Something was not right here. While there were definite problems in some of Sarah's other classes, none of the teachers Joan had talked to had actively disliked the child. What had gone wrong with this student/teacher relationship?

She looked around the room again, noting the lack of any organization in the myriad stacks of student term papers. The woman was obviously overwhelmed with work and struggling to make sense of her students' projects. If Sarah had been telling the truth, if she *had* completed the written portion of the assignment, was it possible it was buried in this room somewhere? And if so, how likely was it that this teacher would be willing to give Sarah the benefit of the doubt?

"Miss Beasley," Joan called out from the opposite side of the room. The woman looked up in displeasure. Joan took another deep breath, knowing that she had to go very slowly, very carefully. "The final-semester project is the one score that stands out from all the rest. She's not an A student, but she's not failing, either. Is it possible, just for argument's sake, that she *did* turn in the written portion of the assignment?''

''No.'' Flat and uncompromising.

''Please. Could we consider it for a moment? I know how crazy the end of the school year can get. I can also see how overworked you are.'' The older teacher straightened in her chair, becoming defensive and guarded. Quickly Joan tried to take some of the sting out of her words by reallocating some of the blame. ''Sarah does seem rather scattered. It's possible she brought it in, but didn't follow your instructions to put it in the right place.''

''She never follows instructions.''

Joan ignored that complaint and rifled through the closest stack of paper. ''I'd be happy to help you look for it.''

''Miss Paxton,'' the woman said, standing abruptly, ''I'm not sure I like your insinuation. I'm not in the habit of losing a student's work. I'd like you to leave now.''

''Passing this class is important to Sarah's future. If there's the slightest chance that—''

''There isn't.''

''Mr. Matthews thinks—''

''I'm sick and tired of hearing what parents 'think,''' the woman snapped, slapping her hand down on the desk. ''They choose to shut their eyes to the fact that their little darlings simply don't tell the truth. Sarah did not complete the assignment, and that's that.''

Annoyance with this obstinate old woman had Joan clenching her fist in the pocket of her skirt. She wanted to shake her, tell her that this rigid, cynical attitude had no business in a classroom full of young, eager minds. Poor Sarah and the other pupils who had been forced to put up with her this past year. How had they all managed?

A sudden thought occurred to her. How *had* the others managed? Taking a chance she asked, "Miss Beasley, is Sarah the only child who did not turn in her assignment?"

"I don't see what that has to do with anything. Or what business it is of yours."

"When I came into this classroom, another woman was coming out. She was upset. Was she a parent of one of your students, here to complain about an unfair grade? You just said you were tired of hearing what *parents* think. Plural. Have there been others recently disagreeing with your final grades?"

The woman flushed beet-red with anger as the accusation found its home. "You have no right," she said in a trembling voice. "No right at all to question my credentials as a teacher."

Out of patience now, Joan strode across the room to stand directly in front of her. "And you have no right to take some sort of petty revenge on William Matthews by failing his daughter unjustly. Fail her if she really didn't do the work. But if there's a chance that she did, that somehow it's misplaced or been overlooked, then you have an obligation to get at the truth."

The woman blinked rapidly, but Joan thought she could see uncertainty in her eyes.

"You're retiring," Joan said more gently. "Don't

leave teaching without being certain that you did the absolute best you could by your students.''

Miss Beasley, age, fatigue and bitterness in her face, stared at Joan. Then a glacially slow accumulation of coldness swept across her features. ''I suppose I could look again.''

Offering a small smile, Joan reached out to squeeze the woman's arm supportively. ''Thank you. I won't ask for anything more than that.''

TRUE TO HIS WORD, Walt Matthews treated Joan to lunch, taking her to a hole-in-the-wall diner called the Western Way Café. Joan ordered the house specialty, chili in a hollowed-out corn bread bowl.

''I should warn you,'' the waitress said, ''it's got a kick to it.''

''I hope so,'' Joan replied. ''What's the point in eating chili if it's bland?''

The waitress agreed, scooped up the menus and disappeared into the kitchen. With a sigh, Joan settled back in her chair, then noticed that Walt was smiling broadly at her.

''What?'' she asked.

The old man shook his head. ''Nothing. Just thinking that Cody doesn't know half as much about women as he thinks he does.''

''What does *that* mean?''

''He told Merlita to bring the spice level of everything she cooks down a notch to keep you from starving while you're here. But I'll bet you'd do fine.''

''You can't live in some of the places I grew up in

and stay a delicate flower. I'm sure some of the native dishes I ate would curl your son's hair.''

"I might like to see that,'' Walt said with a grin. "Tell me about your childhood.''

They talked for a while about the cities her father's work had taken them, the things that had shocked or amused her as the child of a diplomat, the countries that had taken her breath away with their grandeur or frightened her with their sheer crush of people living on top of one another. She glossed over the personal relationship she'd had with her parents, and Walt was polite enough not to press.

When the conversation dwindled and her chili had been consumed, Walt pushed back his own empty plate and laughed. "Yep, Cody's got a lot to learn about jumping to conclusions about people. And if I know my son, he hasn't hesitated to express his opinions.''

"No, he hasn't. Without actually saying it, he practically accused me of being a snotty rich bitch who thinks she's better than he is.''

Walt tipped forward in his chair, thumping his iced-tea glass down on the table. "That damn fool! You should have conked him over the head. I didn't raise him to have such poor manners, and I don't mind putting a knot in his tail even now.''

Smiling at the image of this much older, much physically weaker man taking on someone as imposing as Cody, Joan shook her head. "That's not necessary. I believe we've come to an…understanding.''

Walt gave her a smile that made his tired eyes look full of mischief. "I don't doubt you can hold your own with him. Otherwise I wouldn't have suggested you in the first place." He reached across his plate to empty another packet of sugar into his tea. "I hope you won't judge him too harshly. Living here, Cody's gotten out of practice being diplomatic. Or a gentleman. He sure hasn't had much luck lately with women."

"I find that difficult to believe."

Walt flicked a quick, oddly pointed look at her. "Do you?"

She found herself stammering, "I mean…he's obviously good-looking. A man of some means. I think some women would find him very attractive."

"Oh, they do, they do," Walt said with a dismissive wave of his hand. "But his last serious relationship of any consequence he had with a woman was over six months ago. And that turned out to be a disaster."

Joan couldn't resist. "What kind of disaster?"

"Cody met her at a livestock auction. He thought she was the sort of woman who might understand and appreciate living on a ranch in Texas. Turned out she worked for some big advertising firm in Chicago and was only visiting her father. But Cody's stubborn. He tried to make a go of it for a while. But her first real stay at Luna D'Oro was enough to settle things once and for all."

"She didn't like it here?"

"Evidently not. Cody and me, we came in from branding cattle one afternoon, and she had Sarah dolled up and wearing enough makeup that she looked like a hooker."

Joan winced. "Oh, dear. I can imagine Cody's reaction to that. Not his little tomboy Sarah."

Walt nodded sharply. "You got that right, but he didn't say anything. Leastwise, not to Sarah. Then the next night at dinner, Sarah asks if we were always going to live in the 'sticks' or were we ever going to move to the big city. You could see the influence that was being worked there. Next thing I know, I heard doors slamming and saw two sports car taillights heading down the front drive. That was the end of Miss Chicago."

They laughed together. Then, after the waitress had come to take away the dishes and leave the bill, Joan said quietly, "You know, Sarah's not always going to be Cody's little girl."

Walt looked suddenly serious. "I don't want to be around the day he realizes that. As far as he's concerned, the sun rises and sets on that child."

"It's always difficult for a single parent. Does Sarah ever talk about her mother? She seems to know very little about her."

A wariness came into the old man's eyes. "I think that's the way Cody prefers it."

"Any particular reason why? I'm asking because it would definitely help me to get a better picture of Sarah's mind-set."

Unexpectedly Walt scraped back his chair and rose. "You know, Cody's the one you'll have to ask. I've already spilled more about family business than he'd ever cotton to."

He scooped up the check and headed toward the cashier. Joan was left to follow in his wake, the questions in her mind still unanswered and leaving her more curious than ever.

Outside on the sidewalk, the sun was beating down unpleasantly. Joan made a move toward the ranch truck, which was parked nearby on the curb. Walt touched her arm to grab her attention.

"Would you mind waiting in the truck a few minutes while I head across the street to the pharmacy?" he asked. "I need to pick up a refill of pills for this bum hip of mine."

"Not at all."

He gave her the keys to the truck, and Joan watched him make his way across the road. She liked Walt Matthews a lot and wondered how a man so easy to talk to could turn so uncommunicative when it came to the subject of Sarah's late mother. Had there been bad blood between them? Had he disapproved of Cody's choice? Whatever the reason, he was right, of course. Cody was the one to give her answers.

Mindful of the heat, Joan hurried to the truck. She was unlocking the door when a hand descended unexpectedly over hers. Hot and sweaty and dirty.

"Hold up there, pretty lady," a raspy voice said, and Joan turned her head to find herself face-to-face with a wild man.

It wasn't really a wild man, though anyone might have mistaken him for one. Dressed in cheap grubby clothes, his hair unkempt and a week-old growth of beard on his face, the man who had clamped his hand around Joan's wrist gave her quite a scare at first.

But then she saw his eyes—bleary, bloodshot,

empty. The man smelled of gin, and Joan had run into his kind often enough on the streets of Washington, D.C., to know what she faced now. A panhandler.

"Let go," she said in a firm voice. "If you're looking for money, this isn't the best way to get it."

"You think I want your spare change?" the man asked with a little huff of incredulous laughter. When she jerked her wrist away, he released it. "I want more than that, and I know how to get it."

She frowned at him, seeing for the first time that beneath such an unpleasant exterior had once been a young, handsome man in fairly good shape. Lean and still strong—she'd felt that strength in his grasp. Her gaze scanned the street, but no one seemed to be around at the moment, and all she heard was the sound of a stray dog barking in the dusty little plaza that made up Goliath's town square.

The man seemed to sense her sudden uneasiness. "You got nothing to be afraid of from me," he said. "And nothing I want, either."

She had been cordial long enough, Joan thought. "Good luck, then," she told him, and turned away, eager to put a solid, locked steel truck panel between herself and this disturbing man.

"Got a message to deliver, that's all," the stranger said. "You give Cody Matthews a message for me."

Joan swung around. This man knew Cody? Suddenly this was not the chance encounter she'd thought it was. "You know Mr. Matthews?"

He grinned, displaying a full set of neglected teeth. "Mr. Matthews? I'm on a first-name basis, sweetheart. You tell Cody that Roger's in town. You tell him that I want to see him. And soon."

"I don't understand—"

"You don't have to. He will. You just tell him that he's got something that's mine, and he hasn't finished paying for it yet."

As Joan continued to stare, the man stepped back. He turned and loped into the alley that ran beside the café, merging into the shadows like a wraith. Feeling cold in spite of the heat, Joan unlocked the truck, slipped into the passenger seat and relocked the door immediately.

CHAPTER SEVEN

IT FELT LIKE GOING to the electric chair. Slowly Sarah went down the Goliath-school corridor, heading for the administrative offices. It was finally here. Judgment day. The day report cards would be handed out.

She'd hoped to delay the inevitable by having to wait until her grades showed up in the mail. But as he'd promised, her father had come home from Houston only two hours ago and now sat waiting in the Rover while she marched into the school to get the verdict. If she failed Beasley's class, had to repeat history in summer school, she'd never hear the end of it. But worse than that, she'd lose Ladybug. If that happened, she might as well go and live with her Grandfather Ross, because the only thing that she could still count on at all was her horse, and if *she* went... Sarah didn't want to think about that.

At the office, the line to pick up report cards was long. Like a condemned prisoner, Sarah fell in behind the last boy.

To keep her mind off of potential disaster, she thought about the past few days at Luna D'Oro. While her father had been gone, she'd expected the time to be awful, but to her surprise, it hadn't been.

Dad had told her Joan Paxton was a teacher, but

she didn't act like any teacher Sarah had ever known, and nothing like those nanny people her father had hired. Joan left Sarah alone most of the time. And when they were together, mostly she just listened. She never talked about bad behavior or being good or offered fake sympathy about how hard it was to be a kid nowadays. She hadn't scolded or lectured. The tests they did were easy and sometimes fun, although Joan never explained what she'd learned from them. And of course, Sarah refused to ask, even though she'd have given anything to see what Joan kept writing in that notebook of hers.

She knew that Joan had been to see her teachers, but gave no clues on how that had gone. Instead, she talked about movies she'd seen and favorite books she'd read and told funny stories about the places she'd lived as a kid. She'd traveled all over the world, but she never failed to say how pretty the sunsets were from the *portal* behind the house. She liked music a lot, and after listening to her practice her violin after dinner, Grandpa Walt had clapped and begged her to play for him every night. She did, asking Sarah if she wanted to join her on the piano. When she'd refused, Joan hadn't acted as if it was any big deal.

The mare Sarah had picked out for her seemed to please her, too. Grandpa Walt took her on a ride twice—a lot for him, since he always had such pain in his hip and leg. Sarah watched them disappear over the rise at the end of the long drive—and didn't know whether she was envious or relieved that she hadn't been asked to tag along.

All in all, Sarah thought, it had been a pretty quiet

three days while her dad had been gone. And even though she told herself she didn't care about him anymore, it was nice to know he wasn't going to have a stroke about what she'd been up to during his absence.

Her grades, of course, were a different matter entirely. Stroke levels there, for sure.

Her turn at the counter came at last. Sarah crossed her fingers as she ripped open the envelope and quickly scanned her grades. An A in reading—that had been a cinch. Science, math, English—not her best showing, but nothing that could get her killed. The real test was still ahead. Sarah's heart skipped a beat in her chest. World History—*D!*

Beasley had passed her!

Her eyes jumped to the bottom of the page. *This student has been promoted to the next grade level...*

As thrilled as she was to see that she hadn't failed her year, Sarah's eyes went back to the final grade for history. How was that possible? Beasley had practically told her she intended to flunk her. Had the old witch made a mistake? Finally gone round the bend? Sarah glanced around the room, almost expecting someone to shout and point a finger, accusing her of somehow manipulating her grades. But everything looked right. Everything looked...wonderful.

Sarah flew out of the admin office before anyone could change that. She couldn't wait to show her father, who'd probably be as shocked as she was, but pleased that she hadn't totally disgraced him. Wait until she told Grandpa Walt. And Merlita!

She pounded down the corridor, then slid to a halt

as she realized she'd just whizzed past her old history classroom. Through the glass pane that covered the top half of the door she was surprised to see Miss Beasley at her desk, filling a cardboard box with items from the drawers.

Entering quietly, she looked around her. It seemed so different without all the kids or any of the maps and posters stuck on the walls. Except for the presence of Miss Beasley and the blue stain on the wood floor where Eric Stonebridge had spilled paint one afternoon, it was almost unrecognizable as the room where she'd spent so many hours being tortured.

"What do you want?" Miss Beasley demanded, making Sarah jump. Then spotting the telltale envelope in her hand, she nodded, with that sharp little movement of her head that always made her look like a hawk ready to pounce on a mouse. "Oh. Got your grades, did you?"

"Yes, ma'am."

"No doubt you're pleased."

Pleased? She didn't know the half of it. Still, the woman looked old, really old. Sarah knew that she hadn't made it any easier for Miss Beasley this past year. Filled with sudden gratitude and a touch of shame, she said meekly, "Yes, ma'am, I'm glad. I just came in to say thank you."

"Don't thank me. A D's not that much better than an F in my book." She stopped shoving personal items into the box and scowled at Sarah. "Now what's that frown for? What's the matter with you?"

"I guess I'm not sure how I ended up passing. I thought you said—"

"I know what I said." The woman turned and pinned Sarah with a narrowed glare that made the girl take a step back. "Let me tell you something, Miss Matthews," she said in a nasty, soft tone. "You're a very lucky girl to have convinced someone to take your side about your schoolwork."

Sarah frowned even more, wondering if her father had spoken to her teacher, after all. During the last argument over her slipping progress report, he'd sworn she was on her own. "My dad—"

"It's a good thing for you I'm retiring. A very good thing."

Miss Beasley went back to plopping things into the box. It was the first time Sarah could ever remember seeing the top of her teacher's desk looking so clean. Only a small pile of colorful report covers—probably the last of the project assignments—lay on one corner.

"After the way your father sent that woman in here," Miss Beasley muttered, and Sarah wondered if she was even aware of her presence now. "Trying to browbeat me into giving you a better grade. I had half a mind to file a formal complaint with the school board."

That's exactly what you have, Sarah thought. *Half a mind...* Her ears pricked up. "What woman?"

"That arrogant young lady from Virginia that your father hired to be his...his henchman."

"You mean Miss Paxton?"

"In all my years of teaching I've never had any adult speak to me so disrespectfully. Not even my worst parent ever accused me of—" The elderly teacher seemed to suddenly realize that she wasn't alone. She gave Sarah a frosty, annoyed look. "I'm very busy right now. Did you have something specific you wanted to say to me?"

Confused, and a little unnerved, Sarah said the first thing that popped into her head. "I'm sorry I wasn't a very good student sometimes. I still learned a lot. Really."

Her teacher seemed momentarily surprised. Two spots of color appeared on her thin, wrinkled cheeks. "Well, I'm pleased to hear that, at least." She looked away, then spying the pile of reports on her desk, rescued one from near the top of the stack. "By the way, you can have this back."

Sarah recognized it immediately. "My report! You found it!"

"*I* never lost it," Miss Beasley snapped. She shook her head as if she was talking to an idiot. Actually, Sarah thought, it was pretty much the way she talked to all her students. "If students don't follow direction and put reports in the place I assign them, should it be my responsibility to unearth them? I think not."

"But I thought—"

"Sarah Matthews." The woman stopped her with a disgusted huff. "You complain when you get a failing grade. Don't tell me you're going to complain when you get a passing one, too."

"No, ma'am," Sarah said quickly, realizing that Miss Beasley didn't want to talk about this subject anymore. She was probably trying to hurry out of the school, get to doing whatever it was that cranky old biddies like her did when they retired. Thumbing past the cover page of her report, Sarah smiled at the grade she'd gotten. "Thank you again," she said, and this time she meant it. "I hope you enjoy your retirement, Miss Beasley."

"I certainly intend to," the old woman said, a little less sharpness in her voice. She didn't look at Sarah again.

Eager to escape, Sarah charged out of the room and down the corridor. She felt like shouting for joy. Promotion! A passing grade in history! And her written report on King Henry—found! Proof that she hadn't been forgetful or lazy...or lying. Wait until her father found out.

IT WAS NEARLY DUSK by the time Joan arrived back at Luna D'Oro after her afternoon trip to Goliath's one and only department store. A few days of struggling with the Texas heat had finally convinced her to concede defeat and purchase cooler clothes. She'd intended to buy cotton dresses, but the selection had been limited, so she'd settled on a couple of casual sport outfits. Then, as she was leaving the store, she spotted a rack of something else entirely.

Acting on a whim—something she rarely did—she decided to try on one of the loose peasant blouses and flowing Mexican skirts that the store carried an abundance of. Merlita had been pestering her for days to try her native style, claiming that women in her country knew how to beat the heat.

Joan hated to admit it, but they were right. The colorful skirt and shoulder-hugging white blouse made her feel delightfully unburdened. She bought one more of each and told the saleswoman not to bother boxing up the one she had on. She'd wear it back to the ranch. In the dressing room she even let her hair down from its usual twist, combing her fingers through it until loose curls covered her bare shoulders. She couldn't wait to show Merlita the transformation.

Walt had lent her the ranch truck, and she had felt only a moment's discomfort as she made her way to the store's small parking lot. She didn't want another confrontation with the mysterious, unsettling Roger, but he'd been nowhere in sight.

That short meeting had been the only dark spot in what had been a very pleasant, productive three days. The man's cryptic message to Cody was none of her business, though she certainly intended to tell him about it as soon as he returned. In the meantime, she'd casually asked Merlita and Walt if they knew anyone named Roger. They didn't, and her description of the man had brought only blank looks.

Determined not to read anything ominous into it, she'd been able to put the incident out of her mind for the most part.

Walking through the hacienda, shopping bags still in hand, Joan headed for the dining room. Merlita wasn't there. In fact, the table wasn't even set.

Hearing the faint clink of silverware and dishes, Joan followed the sound to the *portal* and discovered the housekeeper setting the large glass table with bright blue and yellow Mexican crockery, champagne flutes and fresh flowers. Although it wasn't quite dark yet, torch lamps burned along the low wall that divided the house from the walkway that led to the stables, giving the *portal* a mellow, golden glow.

"*Buenas noches,* Merlita," Joan called to capture the woman's attention. "We're dining al fresco tonight?"

"*Sí, señorita.* A little fiesta." The woman turned then, catching sight of Joan's new look. She gasped and clapped her hands together. "*Madre!* You did it!"

"I did! You were right, it's ten times cooler." Joan threw her arms wide, the shopping bags dangling from both hands. She wiggled her hips so that the full skirt swirled back and forth. Remembering the playful claim the housekeeper had made just yesterday, she said, "So what do you think? Do I still look like a *gringa* American afraid to show off the shape of her body?"

"No, ma'am, you sure don't," a male voice said from behind her.

Joan whirled to find Cody Matthews on a ladder beside the archway that led to the *portal.* He was in the process of securing a *Congratulations!* banner to one side of the arch. At least, he had been. Right now, he was staring down at her, a grin as wide as Texas stretching across his lips. Irritating, but she supposed any woman would notice the way the black of his shirt only intensified the darkness of his hair, and the practically indecent way his trim jeans rode his hips.

Walt had told her Cody should be back today. But if she'd known he was so close, she'd never have... But here he was, looking as devilishly handsome as ever and obviously amused to catch her acting silly.

She did not expect her reaction to seeing him. Not the flutter of her pulse. Not the airless constriction in her lungs. She stood straighter and wished with all her heart that one shoulder of her new blouse hadn't seen fit in that moment to slip even farther down her arm.

Merlita didn't help the situation. "You look beautiful, Señorita Joan. Doesn't she, *jefe?*"

"She does indeed."

Joan swallowed her embarrassment. Lowering the shopping bags, she forced herself to look up at him. "I didn't realize you were back."

"Could you try not to sound so disappointed? I've had warmer receptions from my horse." He cocked his head at her as he leaned into the ladder. "Looks like you decided I was right about the suits. I'm glad I'm not going to have to pick you up out of a dead faint, after all."

The conversation was getting much too personal. Uncomfortably so. She gestured toward the banner by lifting her chin. "Who are we congratulating?"

"Sarah."

"She passed!"

"Yep."

"Even Miss Beasley's class?"

"Yep."

"Oh, that's wonderful!"

He gave her a quick, disbelieving look. "A miracle is what it is."

Worried, Joan moved toward the ladder. "You didn't say that to her, did you?"

"Of course not," he said with a scowl. He descended a couple of rungs so that they were nearly face-to-face. "Give me some credit. I said I'd suspected all along I was underestimating her ability to pass her final exams."

"Good. She needs positive reinforcement."

"Dinner in twenty minutes," Merlita stated, then stepped back to observe her table.

"I've got to change," Joan told Cody, and started to move past him.

His fingers against her bare skin stopped her and sent tingles up and down her arm. "Don't," he said in a low voice, and when she frowned, he added with a smile, "It's a celebration, Jo-Jo. A fiesta. You'll fit right in." His eyes drifted over her speculatively, and then he caught a dangling curl between his fingers. She felt the momentary pull against her scalp, then it was quickly gone. "And leave your hair down. It softens your features."

She shook her head, not knowing whether she was more annoyed by the audacity of those statements or delighted by the little frisson of pleasure that went up her spine when he'd said them. Annoyed, she decided. That was definitely the safer of the two reactions. "I'm not trying to look soft," she told him.

"I thought you weren't going to be afraid to show off your body, *gringa?*"

"Stop twisting my words."

He laughed. "I'm only practicing my positive-reinforcement techniques."

"Practice them on someone else. I don't suffer from low self-esteem."

"No, I don't imagine you do." He squeezed her

arm lightly. "But come as you are, anyway, will you? For Sarah's sake."

SHE DEBATED about changing into something more professional, but the dresses in her closet looked uninviting, as did the jeans and denim shirt she'd ridden in yesterday. Besides, as Merlita had said, dinner tonight was supposed to be a festive occasion.

Taking a long hard look in the mirror, Joan tried to figure out what Cody had meant. *Softer.* What kind of backhanded compliment was that? Her features didn't appear to be one bit softer because of a different hairstyle. She leaned closer to the glass. At least, not much.

Annoyed with herself, Joan caught her hair in one hand and started to twist it on top of her head. She let the mass drop a moment later. She wouldn't put it up. Why should that man think it mattered to her one way or the other what he thought? Cody Matthews was so aggravatingly...male. But she didn't have to let him affect her, did she? Absolutely not. Snapping off the lamp, she left the bedroom and went to join the party.

Everyone else was already seated, and she was forced to take the chair directly across from Cody. There was a moment of awkward silence, which she tried to cover by repositioning her silverware and unfolding her napkin.

Walt made flattering comments about her appearance, and even Sarah agreed that she looked "different" with her hair down. Cody was complimentary, as well, saying nothing that could be considered out

of line this time, but Joan found herself avoiding eye
contact with him all the same. Irritation lanced
through her. Todd had always been free with compliments. Her reaction to Cody's should have been no
different. And yet, they left her with an intangible
feeling that eluded definition.

Dinner was a chaotic, lively affair. Merlita had
pulled out all the stops. She brought out so many
plates of her Mexican specialties that she must have
cooked all day. The table sparkled in the moonlight
and warmth of the nearby torches. The air was surprisingly cool and clear for early summer, the night
silent except for the occasional whinny of a horse in
the stable.

Joan sat and watched the interaction of the family
members. Sarah was more animated than she'd ever
seen her. She and her father were dealing splendidly
with one another, laughing, teasing, talking rapidly.
Walt chimed in when he could get a word in edge-
wise. Cody made a humorous but heartfelt toast to his
daughter. Sarah turn as red as a tomato, coughed on
the one sip of champagne her father had allowed her,
then pretended that was the reason for her flaming
cheeks. Tonight no one could have guessed that only
days ago there had been tears and harsh words between them.

It was a pity it couldn't always be this way, Joan
thought sadly. For probably this harmony wouldn't
last. Over the past few days Joan had begun to draw
her conclusions about Sarah's behavioral problems,
and while none of her findings indicated attention def-

icit, neither were they likely to make Cody Matthews happy.

Her eyes strayed to him and made the discovery that he was watching her while he listened to Sarah launch into a gossipy story about her piano teacher. The gleam in those blue depths and the small smile curving one side of his mouth told Joan how pleased he was with the way the evening was going. Tomorrow, she thought. Tomorrow would be soon enough to discuss her findings with him.

"Daddy, are you listening?" Sarah asked.

"Every word, buttercup. Miss Boyette is marrying a man ten years younger than she is."

"Yes. And they're moving to Dallas. So I guess that means no more piano lessons. Right?"

He leaned toward her and flicked a gentle finger across her nose. "That means a new piano teacher."

Sarah rolled her eyes dramatically. "Da-ad, I hate the piano. I'm no good at it. Even Miss Boyette says I stink."

"I doubt that. But if you do it's because you don't practice," Cody replied mildly as he speared a piece of mesquite-grilled steak. He tossed a look at his father. "Did she practice while I was gone?"

"Nope. Not a note."

"Grandpa!"

"Sorry, but you know it's true," Walt said. He brightened suddenly and snapped his fingers. "Say! How about playing a duet with Miss Paxton after dinner? This party could use some entertainment."

Sarah's glance flicked around the table, landing on Joan with her usual lack of enthusiasm. Clearly she didn't want to spoil the mood by being difficult, but she also didn't want to align herself with someone she'd been pretty successful in avoiding. She returned her attention to her grandfather. "I thought you and Dad were going down to the calving shed after dinner."

Walt shrugged as he passed a dish of *flauntas* around the table. "No hurry. One of the hands will come get us if we're needed." By way of explanation to Joan, he added, "Our best bull, Vindicator, is gonna be a proud papa sometime soon. But in the meantime, I'd rather listen to the two of you than twiddle my thumbs with Cody, waiting to catch a newborn calf."

Joan wasn't about to lose the opportunity to connect with Sarah. "I'd be delighted."

"I don't know," Sarah hedged. "I've heard her play, and I'm not sure I could keep up..."

"I know a few contemporary tunes. Even one or two western songs."

Sarah gave up with a resigned sigh. Taken with the idea, Walt grinned and nodded approval. "There you go. Should be fun." He turned his attention to his son. "Cody, did you know that Joan plays a mean violin? Music so sweet I swear the cattle we brought in two nights ago bed down pretty as you please. Even Vindicator, and you know how cantankerous that old boy can get on a full moon."

Cody laughed and shook his head in disbelief. "Pa, I thought it was the harmonica that was supposed to soothe restless cattle, not violins. And the corrals are awfully far away."

"Sound carries on a clear night. You ask the hands if they haven't noticed a difference."

Joan leaned closer to the older man. "I might be better off playing for the cattle, Walt. Your son's already told me that he doesn't care for fiddle music."

Walt made a tsking sound. "Well, Cody's got to learn to keep an open mind." He rolled a meaningful eye toward Sarah, who was busy turning her napkin into a robber's bandanna. "About more things than just music. Isn't that right, son?"

Cody only frowned and took a final sip of champagne.

After consuming thick slices of Merlita's Mexican cocoa cake, the party broke up. Sarah trudged off to find her music books, and Joan returned to her room for her violin and her own music. Walt claimed that it was still too pretty a night to go indoors, and Cody agreed, then pushed the upright piano—which was on casters—onto the first tier of the *portal*.

Merlita brought out better lighting for the performers. When Cody claimed that the dishes could wait and invited her to join them, the housekeeper settled on a nearby chair, her face full of eager delight. Walt, leaning heavily on his metal crutch now, settled onto a chaise longue with a relieved sigh. Cody seemed content to remain in the background, resting a shoulder against one of the adobe pillars. From where Joan stood near the piano, he seemed like a shadow man, his eyes indecipherable, his body partially obscured by a pot of fuchsia bougainvillaea that trailed out of a wrought-iron basket affixed to the wall.

The impromptu concert wasn't nearly as bad as

both Joan and Sarah had expected. Sarah fumbled her way through "Für Elise," then gained a little confidence and executed a second piece with a modest amount of skill. She wasn't the horrible pianist she'd said. So as not to take unfair advantage, Joan chose a simple version of a Bach partita when her turn came, then lost herself in her favorite, Paganini's "Caprice."

Together they struggled through a minuet. No one seemed to mind that it was played rather slowly for Sarah's benefit. Once, when the girl lost her place in the music and seemed about to give up entirely, Joan gave her a "Keep going, you can do it" look. And she did.

With their best selections behind them, their audience clapped and called "Encore" as if they really meant it. The musicians took bows, and when Joan lifted her eyes and her gaze collided with Sarah's, some of the wall the girl had built between them seemed to crumble as she gave Joan a small smile.

In honor of their surroundings, Joan accompanied Sarah on "Yellow Rose of Texas," then "Buffalo Gal," which brought Walt sitting up on his chair to sing along. Sarah's selections got simpler after that, and by the time she coerced her father to slide next to her on the piano bench and pound out one side of the duet "Heart and Soul," everyone was getting pretty silly.

Joan watched Cody as he interacted with his daughter—tickling, laughing, deliberately impairing her efforts on the keyboard. *This is what they need more of,* she thought. *One-on-one time.* Whatever problems

Sarah might have, she blossomed in her father's company. That much was obvious.

"Heart and Soul" went faster and faster, but they finished it more or less together, then fell against each other in relief. The connection between them was so strong in that moment that Joan felt a trickle of envy. For years she'd dreamed of having that kind of relationship with her father, but it had never happened.

The conversations she'd had with Sarah suggested that, particularly of late, Cody had been putting his work ahead of everything else. Evidently, business in the San Antonio office had taken him away from Luna D'Oro often, and when he was home, he was frequently distracted, closeted in his study for hours on end. She had confirmed this with both Merlita and Walt Matthews, and it worried her.

She knew firsthand how disastrous absentee parenting could be. Tomorrow, Joan made the mental note, she would have to discuss this with Cody. More time spent with Sarah and less time away from home was essential for his daughter.

"What's the matter, Joan?" Cody broke through her thoughts. "Okay, so I'm not conservatory-trained, but I'm not that bad, am I?"

Unable to resist teasing, she threw his own words back at him. "It sounded like two cats squalling in a back alley."

The remark must have caught him off guard, because he laughed hard. Full-throated. The twinkle in his eyes became a devilish glint, and suddenly Joan stopped thinking of him as Sarah's father and started to think of him as a man. A very sexy, attractive man.

Disgruntled to find her thoughts about him wandering yet again, she tried very hard to conjure up in her mind the list she'd made of all his sins.

Fortunately the party ended a few minutes later when Tomas appeared on the *portal,* looking uncomfortable about having to interrupt a family gathering. Both Walt and Cody excused themselves and followed the stablehand down the dark path to the barns.

Merlita began clearing dishes away, and Joan returned her violin and bow to the case. Sarah captured sheet music and stowed it in the piano bench. She was about to leave the *portal* without a word, but Joan felt compelled to stop her.

"Good night, Sarah," she called out. "And congratulations again on passing."

The girl turned, and even in the moonlight Joan could see the flush of embarrassment on her cheeks. Being rude didn't really come naturally to her. "Thank you. I guess I'll see you tomorrow."

"Yes. And by the way, thank you for playing with me tonight. I enjoyed it. Perhaps we could—"

"I think we did all right," Sarah quickly interrupted. "But we don't have to perform for them every night if we don't want to. We have television, you know?"

Before Joan could reply to that, Sarah raced for her bedroom.

Oh, well, Joan thought. Baby steps. Even the smallest connection was better than none at all.

CHAPTER EIGHT

A RAP ON HER DOOR brought Joan out of a sound sleep. The last thing she'd remembered last night was that she had not found an opportunity to give Cody the message from Roger. Glancing at the travel alarm on her bedside table, she saw that it was now nearly one in the morning. She hurried to the bedroom door, wondering who could possibly be wanting her at this time of night.

It was Tomas, from the stable.

He ducked his head by way of a greeting and said softly, "Miss Paxton, *Jefe* sent me up here to get you. He'd like you to come down to the calving shed right away."

"What?" Joan asked, trying to knuckle sleep out of her eyes. "What are you talking about?"

"He said please come. And to bring your violin."

"My violin?" Thoroughly confused, she yawned and swiped hair off her face. "Are you sure?"

"*Sí, señorita.* And he said you're not to get—" he frowned, trying to find the right words "—gussied up. You must come *andale,* in your skivvies if you have to." Tomas's ears were crimson as his gaze fell to the tiled floor. "*Perdone, señorita,* but those were his exact words."

Joan had no idea what this summons could be about. "All right," she told the embarrassed man. "I'll come." She pulled her robe over her pajamas quickly, slid into slippers and snatched up her violin case. "Lead on, Tomas. But your *jefe* better have a good reason for this."

The calving shed was a dilapidated little building on the backside of the stables. Walt had shown it to her during a tour of the ranch. There was nothing remarkable or high-tech about it.

When Joan entered the shed, she discovered Cody and Walt in one of the two dimly lit stalls, trying to coerce a rather large brown cow into holding still. The beast was having none of it, however. It tossed its head several times and sidled back and forth on the bed of straw, once almost pinning Cody against the wall.

"Welcome to the calving shed, Joanie," Cody said, sidestepping the cow. He smiled at her, then frowned as he took in her appearance. "Darn, I was afraid we'd wake you up."

"What's this all about?"

At the other end Walt was barely holding on to the animal's halter. His crutch leaned against the wall. As Tomas edged past Joan and entered the stall, Walt stepped back and allowed the younger man to take his place. He slipped his arm back into the crutch support and motioned with it toward the cow. "This ornery critter is having a baby. And we need your help."

"I don't know anything about delivering babies,"

she protested, wide awake now. "I could never even watch when my cat had kittens."

Cody laughed. "Relax, Prissy. We'll take care of the birthing." She noticed now that he was wearing rubber boots and a vinyl vest. While she watched from the other side of the stall, he slipped a plastic sleeve over one arm and unexpectedly shoved his entire arm into the back of the cow. The poor thing reacted by emitting a low sound of discomfort. "Damn it!" Cody grunted. "Ease up, sweetheart, we're trying to help you here."

Openmouthed, Joan grimaced. "Aren't you supposed to have a veterinarian for this sort of thing?"

"According to his service, Doc Swain is on the other side of the county tonight. By the time he'd get here, she'll have dropped this baby." Cody looked at his father, his face contorted with pain. "She's still so constricted she's about ready to separate my hand from my arm. I don't know, Pa. The calf could be breach."

"Breach?" Joan said in a soft voice. "That's bad, isn't it?"

"Could be. We can't find out until we get her to calm down a little. That's where you come in. We'd like you to play your violin."

"You're not serious!"

"That's what *I* said. But Pa thinks differently."

Walt spoke up. "I wasn't kidding earlier. The cattle seem to like the sound of the music. And we've run out of ways to convince this poor mama here to relax so we can get her baby out."

Cody had rescued his arm and was peeling the plastic sleeve away from his shirt. "I guess we're getting desperate enough to try anything. Better that than lose them both. So will you do it? Play something. Anything."

The cow was moving more restlessly now, throwing her head so forcefully that poor Tomas, short and rail thin, was having difficulty standing. Walt moved to help him maintain a hold, while Cody stroked the animal's hindquarters.

"All right," Joan conceded, knowing that she couldn't stand there any longer and do nothing. Almost to herself, she said, "I suppose I could play Tchaikovsky. I don't know how well I'll manage under these conditions…"

"She's not a music critic for *Variety,* Joanie. Just play it."

"Yes." She knelt and threw the catch on her violin case. Infuriatingly, her hands were shaking. Rescuing the bow and instrument, she stood upright just in time to get a very unpleasant view of the procedure Cody intended to try to ease the birth of the calf. She felt herself go white. "Cody, I think I should tell you…" She licked her lips, feeling her stomach starting to swoop and dive.

He took his eyes off the cow for only a moment. "What's the matter?" he asked quickly, seeing her distress. "Sam Houston's whiskers, you're not going to faint, are you?"

"No. I mean, I hope not. It's just that I'm not very good with blood. I know it's silly, but—"

He was suddenly there beside her, pushing her down on a three-legged stool he'd hooked with one leg. "Sit," he ordered. "You can play from outside the stall without having to see a thing. Don't stand up, and don't stop until I tell you to. All right?"

"Yes. I'm sorry."

"Just play. You'll do fine. And so will she."

It was almost surreal. Here she was, sitting in her pajamas in a poorly lit stable at midnight, trying to think what to play on her violin, while on the other side of the wooden wall a helpless cow struggled to give birth.

Maybe not so helpless. While Joan tried to gather her thoughts, she could hear the cow kicking and plunging against its restraints. There were tortured sounds from the animal and a few curses from the men. It seemed as though they had the devil himself trapped in the stall.

Joan frantically jumped into the first piece she could think of, Handel's "Bourée." It sounded horrible, but lively, at least.

The animal's fretful sounds grew louder.

"Play something else," Cody called, grunting with some unknown effort. "You're pissing her off. Watch her head, Tomas, watch her head. We have to keep her on her feet a little longer."

Trying to shut out the sounds of the struggles, Joan said, "Maybe Handel is too strident. Maybe Saint Saens would be better..."

"Joan!"

Good Lord, she was babbling. Grimly she moved into "The Swan" from Les Carnaval des Animaux. At first there was no discernable difference in the sounds coming over the wall. She closed her eyes and prayed as she played, hoping that the poor calf would be born all right, that the mother wouldn't inadvertently hurt any of the men trying to deliver it, but most of all, praying that this situation would be over before she ran out of music. *I'll practice,* she promised, looking heavenward. *I'll practice every day if you'll just make this be over soon.*

Eventually, and certainly beyond Joan's expectations, the suffering animal really did seem to calm down a little. The kicks against the boards became more sporadic, and while Joan could hear labored breathing, the cow no longer sounded tortured. Nor did the men. Joan could tell that *something* was going on, but she wouldn't have looked if her life had depended on it. Whatever problem that had delayed the calf's entry into the world, it seemed to be resolving itself.

"Come on, little one," she heard Cody coax. "I've got you. I've got you now."

Thank goodness, Joan thought. She was on her third go-round of "The Swan."

"It's almost over," Cody called. "Hang in there, honey."

"I'm trying."

"I was talking to the cow," he shot back, and all three men laughed.

"Oh."

She began to play more loudly. When it came to the violin, it seemed as if compliments from Cody Matthews just weren't going to materialize.

Half an hour later it was all over. Having done her part, the cow stood in one corner of the stall and looked balefully at Joan, who hung over the stall door and watched the still-wobbly calf stumble its way around the straw.

"He's so small," Joan said in a soft, awed voice. "Will he be all right?"

Cody came up behind her to look into the stall. He'd cleaned up a bit at the nearby sink. The smell of mild soap mingled with the scent of pure, sweaty male. "He'll be fine," he assured her, and she heard the tired relief in his voice.

The calf bumped its snubbed nose against its mother, discovering her milk supply. The cow nudged the newborn closer and blew heavily out through her nostrils.

"She looks pleased," Joan remarked. "You'd never know I tried to torture her with Handel."

Cody chuckled. "What were you thinking?" he asked in a low, amused tone that vibrated close to her ear. "Everybody knows cows like Saint Saens best."

She could feel his breath stirring strands of hair along her neck. It occurred to Joan that they were almost alone. In near darkness. Walt had turned in for the night, and Tomas, stuck on the night shift, was still busy in the stall, forking fresh straw onto the floor. He couldn't possibly see them from where he stood. She felt a little shiver of something chase up her spine and knew that, whatever it was, it had nothing to do with the night air.

Turning, she retrieved her violin case from the stool where she'd placed it. Trying to speak in a normal voice, she said, "Well, unless you have another midnight concert in mind, I think I'll turn in."

His eyes traveled over her. She realized that the
satiny thickness of her robe wasn't much of a barrier
between them, that the collar of her new turquoise
pajama top was cut much lower than she'd remembered it being when she'd seen it in the store. Self-
consciously, she lifted her violin case across her
breasts, only to discover that her hands were still
trembling a little. Cody noticed.

"Good grief," she exclaimed in embarrassment.
"I'm shaking. Isn't that silly?"

He took her fingers between his to halt their movement. "It's delayed reaction to the excitement. Take
some deep breaths." She did as he suggested. After
a moment or two he smiled, though he still didn't
release her hand. "There. Isn't that better?"

No. Oh, no, not at all. "Yes."

He began to massage her hand carefully. He
frowned as he ran his fingers up hers, then tilted her
hand toward the light. Touching the callus on her
forefinger, he asked, "What's this from?"

"Calluses build up from using the violin strings.
Anyone who regularly plays a string instrument gets
them." She tried to extricate her hand, and then was
immediately sorry because it only made him tighten
his grip. She told herself that it was only the late hour
and her own weariness that made it seem as though
fire licked her palm. "They're not very attractive,
but—"

"On the contrary. I think your fingers are very
sexy." Before she could stop him, he dipped his head
and pressed his lips to them. Joan's heart suddenly
seemed to be lost somewhere in the region of her

throat. "God, I'd never have guessed a woman as self-possessed as you couldn't stand the sight of blood. You were a good sport," he murmured softly. "Thank you for helping out."

"You're welcome."

Now there really was fire in her hand. It came from Cody's lips and tongue, which moved in slow intriguing patterns over her palm. She stared, enthralled, as his touch ignited a second fire low in her belly.

She had no idea how much farther he might have gone or how much she might have allowed him to, for Tomas chose that moment to speak up.

"You want me to get her ready for weighing, *jefe?*" His voice floated over the stall wall.

Cody stopped immediately. His head was still over her hand, and she could feel his lips stretch into a smile. "Yes, Tomas," he replied. "Let's get her measurements." He stood straighter. His fingers captured her wrist. His eyes were on her face, full of regret, but his words were for Tomas. "I'm going to walk Miss Paxton to her room. I'll come right back to help you."

She wanted to tell him she could find her way alone, that she wasn't at all sure she wanted his company. She was much too susceptible to this man tonight, had been from the moment she'd walked onto the *portal* and seen him on the ladder. But he was already urging her to follow in his wake, leading her to the rear of the house.

He didn't say a word, and by the time they reached the *portal,* she was almost herself again. That unexpected moment of intimacy in the shed might never have happened. And then suddenly, he stopped, as though remembering something he'd forgotten. They were near the pillar where he'd watched the concert earlier. He turned and gripped both her shoulders in his hands, his eyes intensely determined to find hers in the silver moonlight.

"Joan," he began in a very serious way, and then quietly, simply, said, "I want to thank you."

To cover her returning uneasiness at being so close to him again, she decided to go for a light tone. "You've already thanked me. To tell the truth, I wasn't that good. If I ever decide to change careers, tonight's performance is definitely not going on my résumé."

He took a step toward her, so that she had to take one back. The rough texture of the plastered adobe was suddenly against her spine, and a long finger of bougainvillea slipped across her shoulder.

"I don't mean about the calf," he said. "I meant, for coming here. For doing what you're doing with Sarah. Pa's told me how patient you were with her while I was gone. I've seen you watching her, watching *us*. No matter what I'd like to believe is the true reason for my daughter's problems, I know you're trying to help. Tonight she was so much like her old self. And we've jumped a big hurdle—Sarah passing her year. You had a lot to do with that."

The reminder of that day with Sarah's teacher jogged her memory of a different meeting entirely. "Oh, Cody, I'm sorry. I meant to tell you this earlier, but I haven't had a chance to speak to you in private. A rather unpleasant man stopped me on the street the other day and gave me a message for you. I thought he was a panhandler at first—''

Cody frowned. "What message? Who stopped you?''

"A man named Roger. He didn't give a last name, but he seemed to think you'd know him.''

The change in Cody was remarkable. It wasn't a trick of the light—he was suddenly very angry, and just as suddenly, determined not to show it. "What did he say to you?'' he asked in a quiet, firm voice.

She repeated every word exactly. It was easy enough since they'd been burned in her brain. What wasn't easy was accepting that Cody had no intention of revealing what any of it meant. There was a long pause while he digested the information, but as was his maddening habit, he clearly considered the subject off-limits. Since no part of Roger's comments had involved Sarah, any questioning by Joan would simply look like nosiness. Still, she couldn't resist a weak attempt for explanation.

"It was very weird. If you'd like to discuss it, I—''

He'd been staring off into the night, but now his head snapped around. "Did he hurt you in any way?''

"No, of course not. I just—''

He smiled and gave her arm a small, reassuring squeeze. "I'm sorry you got dragged into any unpleasantness. It shouldn't have happened, and it won't happen again. Roger and I have unfinished business, but that's all it is. Business. You won't see him again.''

"He looked very down on his luck.''

Cody's response came too quickly. "He is, and

that's something I think he blames me for. But I'll work it out with him. Please don't concern yourself about him any longer.''

"Is there anything I can do to help?"

Like a shutter going down over a window, she sensed his withdrawal from the subject. There were going to be no answers.

"You don't need to champion my cause," he said in a lighter tone. "Although you probably could, couldn't you? I understand you faced down that old lioness Beasley for Sarah's sake. How do I thank you for that?"

"Sarah deserved to pass. She wasn't lying, Cody. She really did do the assignment."

"I know that now. I should have believed her. She told me what happened this afternoon when we picked up her report card. Did you know she talked to Beasley?"

"No."

"I don't think the old bat told her the complete truth, or maybe Sarah didn't understand all of it, but I heard enough to be able to fill in some of the blanks. Beasley wouldn't have passed her if you hadn't gone in and twisted her arm."

"I did no such thing," Joan protested. "I only convinced her that, in all fairness, she should look again for Sarah's written report. She must have taken that suggestion."

"Some suggestion," Cody replied with a low laugh. "She called you my henchman."

Joan's jaw dropped. "Henchman! That's ridiculous. I wasn't rude. I was simply firm and persuasive in my arguments.''

Even in the poor light, Joan could see Cody's eyes sparkling with mirth. "I'll bet all your arguments are persuasive. But Beasley wouldn't back down easily. I ought to complain to the school board about incompetence like that. She calls herself a professional?''

"I'd let it go. She's old. She's retired now. She can't do any more harm. I felt rather sorry for her, actually. She was clearly overwhelmed and looked absolutely stunned when I said the things I did.''

He reached out to slide a wayward strand of hair back behind her ear. "Old witch probably didn't stand a chance. I've seen you with your dander up, remember? Hell, I've been a victim of that cool, calm indignation of yours myself. Leaving me standing there in the middle of the hotel lobby..."

"Oh, you poor thing," Joan returned in mock sympathy. "If I remember correctly, you deserved it." His hand still lingered along the side of her face. She pushed it away firmly. "And you hardly seem terrified of me now."

His teeth gleamed white as his grin widened. "No, ma'am. What I am is...attracted. In a very powerful way."

"What about that conversation we had in the truck? About my being the kind of woman you don't like?''

He scowled. "Pa's right. I need to learn to keep an open mind."

"I think I like you better with a closed one."

He leaned nearer, tilting a quizzical look at her. "Don't fight it, Jo-Jo." He ran a finger under the left side of her jaw, and the tickling feel of his touch made her breath shudder. "Do you know, earlier this evening, while you were playing with Sarah, all I could think about was how lucky that violin was. Tucked under this soft, sweet chin. You almost seemed to be caressing the wood. You can't imagine what that did to me." With one fingertip, he drew her chin up, so that their eyes met. "You're the lady with all the psychology degrees under your belt. What do you make of that?"

Her heart raced, but she couldn't allow him to take advantage again. She chose sarcasm to fend him off. "That you're probably the kind of man who always wants what he can't have."

"I can't?"

"No. You can't."

"Why? You're unattached. So am I."

"Unattached. But uninterested, too, I'm afraid."

He laughed. "That's a lie. I saw your list that day. Remember? You like my eyes. What else?"

So much for hoping he'd be gentlemanly enough not to ever mention the list she'd made. "Did you read the rest of that list?" she asked in a stern tone. "It's full of all sorts of things I *don't* like about you."

He moved closer still, and now his mouth was almost touching hers. She felt his lips playing at the corner of her own. "Hmm," he said absently. "Be sure to add kisses to the list." His mouth grazed her cheek, so delicately that it woke shivers in her. "Put them in my plus column."

"Cody—"

His lips stopped that protest. He was done with

tender touches, it seemed. His kiss was quick, hard and deep. Her mind pirouetted. She could hear her pulse pounding in her head.

He pulled away before she really wanted him to, no less out of breath than she. "What do you think? Tell me you didn't like that."

"I think..." It took her a moment to focus. "I think you are unforgivably presumptuous."

He caught her chin. "Add that to your list, then," he said in a playful tone.

Then he was gone, heading back down the path to the barns, leaving her to confused, light-headed feelings of delight.

CHAPTER NINE

"DAMN IT TO HELL and back, Dennis!" Cody snapped into the phone. Then he lowered his voice so as not to wake the whole family. "It's seven o'clock in the morning."

"I waited as long as I could, Sleeping Beauty."

"You know that's not what I'm talking about. I've been home less than twenty-four hours. There should be no reason why I have to head back up there now. I'll see McBride and Emerson on Monday." He blew out a disgusted breath, plotting his investment partner's dismemberment. "You can handle this, Dennis. You know that."

Dennis Wagner, whom Cody had known from the old days when they'd both worked for an investment firm in New York, wasn't easily intimidated. He laughed, and Cody could picture him in his Houston study, feet propped up on the corner of his desk, which was always annoyingly neat. "I know that. You know that. I think even Emerson knows that. It's McBride who's getting antsy. He's not much of a gambler, you know, and if he pulls out of this deal, he may take Emerson with him."

Seated at his own desk, Cody set the phone receiver down on the blotter, trying to get his irritation under control. He didn't want to get on another plane. He didn't want to go to Dennis's office in Houston. And right now he didn't want to spend any more time with their two top clients, McBride and Emerson, who were starting to behave like nervous old women over this deal. He wanted to stay here, at Luna D'Oro. For a variety of reasons. But it wouldn't help matters to take his frustration out on Dennis.

After a long moment he picked up the receiver again. In a curt, crisp tone he said, "There's nothing for McBride to be nervous about. He's going to make a heck of a lot of money on this. We all are."

"But not without a little sacrifice on our parts. I know you've been working hard for a month to put your end of it together. But we can't let it slip through fingers at the last minute just because we're not willing to do a little baby-sitting until Monday. Hell, my wife has tickets to the symphony this evening and thinks this is just my way of getting out of it." Dennis's voice went lower, as though confessing an irritating truth. "The fact is, while both Emerson and McBride like my track record in this sort of risky venture, they *trust* you completely. You can offset any objections they come up with. Stay here at my place this weekend. By Monday afternoon it will be a done deal and everyone will be happy."

"I don't want to be gone from here all weekend."

"It wouldn't be the first time."

"I know that," Cody snarled. "But Sarah's been a holy terror lately—" He stopped, not wanting to share personal problems with the man, no matter how close they'd become recently.

"You said it yourself, Cody. It's a heck of a lot of money."

They both remained silent for several long moments, letting those words settle. If he refused to go, Cody knew that Dennis could handle Emerson himself. But if something went wrong, if McBride started to waffle in his resolve…everything Cody had been working toward the past month would be for nothing.

Dennis was right, damn him. Cody had to go.

"I'll be on the next flight out," he said, and hung up before he could change his mind.

He sat back in his chair, rubbing his forehead distractedly. The traumatic events of last night's calving and the late hours had left him feeling fractured, grumpy. He had a hard time thinking of what he could say at breakfast to keep Sarah from indulging in a temper tantrum. He didn't think he had the patience right now to handle one. He wanted what he'd seen last night—the sweet little girl he'd fallen in love with the day he'd first held her in his arms.

Thinking of last night, he realized there was another reason he didn't want to leave the ranch this weekend.

Joan.

He was damned if he could see any sense in pursuing a personal relationship with her. Hell, he was even on record for saying as much. She was, after all, one of those blond Daphne-types with cool, keep-your-distance scorn, which never failed to get to him, but Joan Paxton added a new dimension to the mix.

She was sensitive. She liked underdogs. Her sympathy for Miss Beasley had shown him that. And she really liked Sarah. He could see it in her face when she thought no one was looking. He didn't know why. He'd willingly die for his daughter, but nothing in the girl's exchanges with Joan indicated the woman should feel the same way.

All right, so it was hard not to like someone who was willing to stick up for your kid. But he was discovering that it was easy to be intrigued by Joan for other reasons, as well. She was more than a pretty face; she had smarts. She had a good sense of humor and a sweet way of tilting her head to look at you that made his gut ache. A sweet mouth, too, that did a lot more to him.

He turned his head, hearing Merlita rustling through the kitchen cabinets as she got breakfast ready for the family. Time was short. He'd have to get moving if he was going to catch the only morning flight to Houston.

He had no choice. He had to go. Maybe some of Sarah's good mood from last night would spill over into the weekend. Maybe he'd ask Pa to take her into town, buy her some new shorts for the hot summer that was bound to be ahead of them. No, maybe Joan would be a better companion for something like that. Girl stuff. Sarah would surely miss him less if he sent her into town with a fistful of money and instructions to spend it any way she wanted.

There was still one last problem to see to, of course. The most unpleasant one of all.

Thinking of last night, the discovery that Roger Gleason had popped back into his life at a very bad time, Cody pulled the Goliath phone book out of his desk drawer. There was only one cheap motel in town, and he was sure that was where he'd find the man. From Joan's description, Gleason hadn't bettered his lifestyle any, and even the lowest, meanest bar in the county wasn't open this early.

Cody gritted his teeth, trying to prepare himself for another encounter with the man. Maybe the son of a bitch needed more money to get his life back on track. It must be so, Cody thought. Otherwise, why would Roger have shown up here, nosing around for another payoff?

A payoff Cody knew he'd have no alternative but to hand over. And pretty damn quickly, if he was going to get up to Houston anytime soon.

He called the Wigwam Motel, and sure enough, a Roger Gleason was registered. The voice that answered the room phone sounded sleepy and about a hundred years old.

There was no need for introductions. They'd never liked each other, and there was no use pretending otherwise. Cody lowered his voice and tucked the phone against his chest. "You ever come near anyone in my family or anyone staying in my home again, and you'll never see another cent. No matter what you threaten to do. Do you understand me, Roger?"

"Got your attention, didn't it?" the man said with a yawn. "She's pretty. She your new girlfriend?"

Cody ignored that and the impulse to hang up. "I'll be at your motel in about an hour. Try to be sober when I get there."

"Bring your checkbook."

"I know what you want."

"And I know what you *don't* want."

The truth of that taunt was like bitter acid in Cody's gut. But it was too late to stop now. For almost ten years Roger Gleason had been turning up in his life, and the pattern, right or wrong, had been set. All that remained was determining the amount of money Cody would have to shell out this time.

"Someday this is going to be over," Cody bit out. "That pickled liver of yours will kill you. You know that, don't you?"

Roger laughed, a thick, unpleasant sound. "I don't need a social worker, man. I need a fat check. Just bring it."

"One hour," Cody agreed, and hung up.

Resolved to make the best of a bad situation, Cody rescued his briefcase from underneath a stack of books and went to pack his garment bag.

Much as he worried about the deal with Emerson and McBride, he was much more concerned about getting rid of Roger. There would be little time for haggling, so this reappearance was probably going to cost him plenty. More than the fifty thousand he'd given the man three years ago. Considerably more than Cody could comfortably afford. But that was just too bad, he thought with a grimace.

There was just no way he could leave town knowing that Sarah's *birth* father was sleeping in a drunken stupor less than twenty miles away.

SARAH WALKED into the kitchen, still in her short pajamas. She was starving, but she knew how to keep hunger at bay. Merlita always made lemon-poppyseed muffins for breakfast on the weekend.

The housekeeper was on the kitchen phone, and wordlessly Sarah grabbed a still-warm muffin from the basket on the counter. The smells in Merlita's kitchen always made her happy. Maybe today she'd coerce her father and Grandpa Walt into riding up by the river. Or over to the water tower. It had been so long since they'd had a picnic there. Sarah was feeling so good this morning she wouldn't even put up a fuss if her father insisted on bringing Joan Paxton along.

Last night had been kind of nice. Someone different at the table who didn't talk about cattle or football or the deadliest dull subject of all, the stock market. Any woman her father had brought to Luna D'Oro previously had only been interested in herself, and definitely not interested in talking to a kid. But Joan acted like she didn't mind at all. And last night she'd looked like she'd know about the things that had begun to intrigue Sarah lately—like makeup and hairstyles and clothes that weren't just for riding horses. No. Joan Paxton wasn't completely horrible.

Her mouth full of muffin, Sarah perched on one of the stools, wondering if Merlita would be willing to pack a lunch for them today. Sometimes she had to be charmed into things like that. Sarah yawned and waited, listening to the housekeeper speak slowly into the phone to someone who was clearly not understanding every word of what her father called Merlita's "Spanglish."

"No, no!" the woman said impatiently. "Not this

afternoon's flight. *Boba!* Don't you understand plain English? This *morning's* flight to Houston. One ticket. Señor Cody Matthews. He can pick it up at the airport, *sí?''*

Sarah placed the remains of her muffin back on the counter. Her appetite had evaporated. She should have known this good feeling couldn't last. Her father was leaving again. Wanting to be away so quickly that he'd asked Merlita to make the flight arrangements while he was probably packing right now in the bedroom.

She wouldn't go see if it was true. Why let him think it mattered to her one way or the other if he left? Besides, he was probably busy rehearsing his speech for the breakfast table. Business to attend to...important meeting...blah, blah, blah. She knew she'd be expected to sit there and take it. No fights. No yelling. Just acceptance.

Back in her bedroom, she crawled under the covers. She blinked hard, just in case tears tried to come. No way she'd let them.

But what had she done wrong? Last night had been great, like the old days with her father. They'd been having so much silly fun. He hadn't acted like he didn't want her around anymore, and she'd completely forgotten how much she was supposed to be hating him.

Yet somehow it hadn't been enough. It didn't make him...want to stay.

She sat up in bed, refusing to give in to self-pity. She wanted to yell. Smash something. Across the room on her desk, the sculpture of the stallion and pony—now showing its repair only if you looked real hard—seemed to mock her. Fat lot of good that had done.

Maybe something else would get his attention. Make him stay. Maybe something worse would make him see she wasn't going to be pushed aside that easily. Forgotten.

Angrily she went through a mental list of possibilities. She could set fire to something, but that was dangerous, and someone might get hurt. She could jump off the roof again, but then *she* might get hurt. Another trip to the emergency room didn't hold much appeal. Besides, that probably only worked once. If she didn't break her neck, her father would blast her into next Sunday. Not because he cared about her, but because last time she'd scared Grandpa Walt white and made Merlita cry buckets. So that was definitely out. She supposed she could run away, but where would she run to? And wasn't that sort of what he wanted, anyway? To be rid of her?

She sat up straighter as sudden inspiration struck. She still had one or two tricks up her sleeve. She'd have to get back and forth to the bathroom without anyone seeing her, but it was possible. And who around here paid attention to anything she did, anyway?

HAVING TOSSED AND TURNED for what remained of the night, Joan wasn't surprised that she'd slept later than usual.

The smell of Merlita's strong coffee pulled her out of bed, and she was just heading down the wide hall to the kitchen when she became aware of a commotion near the vicinity of Sarah's bedroom. Now what? she wondered, and veered in that direction.

She found Cody standing on one side of Sarah's bed, Merlita on the other. Between them lay Sarah, the heavy comforter pulled up to her chin, a thermometer tucked in the corner of her mouth. She looked white as a bedsheet, and her eyes kept darting worriedly between her father and Merlita.

"Anything I can do to help?" Joan asked as she moved into the room.

Cody glanced at her, his brow creased with lines of concern. "Not unless you brought a medical bag to the ranch, along with your violin," he said. "Sarah's sick this morning."

He looked back at his daughter uncertainly, rubbing his chin. Joan noticed that he didn't look like a man who'd had a late night helping a cow give birth. In fact, he had obviously showered and shaved, and his clothes were all business, not at all what she'd expected on a Saturday morning. It made her wish she'd been a little more particular about her own dress.

She reached the end of the bed just as Merlita removed the thermometer from the girl's mouth. *"Madre dios,"* the housekeeper muttered as she squinted to read the numbers. "It's 102, *jefe*."

Cody pulled the desk chair up to the bed and sat. His hand brushed his daughter's cheek, then her forehead. "I can't feel a fever," he said softly. "What's the matter with you, buttercup? Does it hurt anywhere specific?"

"No, not really," Sarah replied on a shaky voice.

"Sort of all over. But don't worry, I'm sure it will go away. You catch your plane. I'll be all right." She turned her head away from his hand. With a grimace and groan, she added, "It's probably not my appendix or anything serious like that."

With her arms crossed over her waist, Joan watched this little byplay between father and daughter with interest. It surprised her to hear that Cody was leaving Luna D'Oro so soon. Leaving Sarah. Again. But unlike the last time, the girl didn't appear angry. She seemed resigned. That could be because she wasn't well. Couldn't summon the strength for a good argument. But wasn't it odd that her face wasn't flushed if her fever ran so high?

"No, I don't think it's your appendix," Cody said with a gentle smile. "You had that out when you were three. You just don't remember it."

"Oh, yeah. That's why I have that scar."

"Uh-huh."

"Then it's probably the flu," Sarah said on a gaspy little breath. Her hand popped up from beneath the covers so that she could cough delicately into it. "I'll stay in bed all day and not let it turn into pneumonia."

"Shall I call the doctor, *jefe?*" Merlita asked anxiously.

"Not yet," Cody said, his eyes fixed on his daughter's face. "Sarah, I can't stay home today. I have to go to Houston. I've got no choice."

"That's all right, Daddy. Really."

Sarah closed her eyes on a weary sigh. She looked

very small and pitiful under the enormous comforter. Cody swore under his breath and rose.

"Lita, let's try to get her temperature down with a couple of aspirin. I'm going to check to see if anyone has an afternoon flight." He touched his daughter's forehead. "Just rest, Sarah. I'll be back in a little while."

She nodded without opening her eyes. Both Merlita and Cody left the room. Joan continued to stand at the foot of the bed to watch Sarah. Her chest rose gently with every breath. Lying there so peacefully, she might have been a sleeping princess in a book. But interesting enough, beneath her pale eyelids, Joan could see the movement of the girl's eyes, flashing back and forth as though trying to determine which direction trouble might come from.

Joan went to the side of the bed and sat on the edge. The mattress dipped and Sarah opened her eyes. Wearily, as if it took great effort. "I'm sorry you're not feeling well," Joan said. "I had hoped we could take a ride today."

"Maybe some other time," Sarah said with a sigh. "When I feel better."

Joan lifted the back of her hand to the girl's throat. "Your father's right. You're not hot."

"The heat's all inside. My temperature..."

"Why don't we take it again?" Joan suggested. "Just in case Merlita didn't read it right."

"Sure," came the weak reply.

As Joan picked up the thermometer the house-keeper had left on the bedside table, her hand brushed the half-full drinking glass that sat beside it. She didn't want to take the chance of dumping water all over Sarah, so she picked up the cup, intending to put it on the other side of the lamp.

Her hand stilled in midair.

The plastic cup was hot to the touch. Extremely hot. And though one sniff of the contents told Joan that it was indeed nothing but water, there was no way Sarah would find it drinkable. In fact, it wouldn't be much good for anything that Joan could think of. Except perhaps…for heating something. Possibly the temperature of one devious young girl determined to keep her father at home?

Her gaze swung back to Sarah's face. The truth was there, and as though she knew it, Sarah turned her head away, pretending to find interest in a poster of horses galloping across a snowy field. Except for the sudden thrust of her stubborn chin, she was completely still, as though waiting for Joan to make the accusation.

"You know," Joan began softly, "you mustn't make your father frantic with worry. If your temperature goes too high, he'll have you in an ambulance heading for the hospital. That isn't what you want. Is it?"

The girl said nothing. But after a long moment her head moved minutely back and forth.

Joan smiled down at her. *She's like I was at that age,* she thought. Joan had never pulled a stunt like this—heating a thermometer in a glass of hot water. She wouldn't have dared. But there were similarities. *She's scared. Wanting her father's attention, yet refusing to let anyone think she needs it.*

Joan wanted to reassure her somehow, but she doubted Sarah would welcome anything she had to say. Her face was still turned away, and Joan resisted the temptation to get her attention by touching the soft pool of golden hair that spread across her pillow like melted honey.

"This will be our little secret," Joan said. "You work on...making a miraculous recovery. I'll talk to your father. See if I can convince him to stay home."

SHE FOUND Cody's bedroom door open and saw him inside, putting shirts on hangers in the garment bag that lay open on his bed. His movements were jerky, harassed, as though he was annoyed he'd waited so long to pack.

Regardless of the true nature of Sarah's "illness," it surprised Joan a little to see that he still intended to leave. What if the girl really had been sick?

"You couldn't get a later flight?" she asked from the doorway.

"I don't need one."

"What about Sarah?"

He opened his right hand and held it out toward her. The tips of his fingers were white. "I was talking to the airlines when I noticed this. Baby powder from her cheek when I felt for fever. Gave her a nice wan look, don't you think?" He shook his head. "Little brat. I ought to tan her hide for giving me a scare like that. And for trying to trick me into staying." He tossed a tie into the puddle of clothes he'd pulled out of his closet. "Pneumonia, my ass. I don't know how she managed the high temperature trick, but when I get back on Monday, I intend to find out.''

So he knew. Well, maybe that wasn't such a bad thing. It might help Joan make him understand. There was so much she wanted to tell him. Was now the right time? After watching him for a moment, she made her decision and said simply, ''Cody, please don't go.''

''I have to,'' he replied, hardly breaking the rhythm of his efforts to pack quickly. ''She's faking. She's not any sicker than I am, Joan.''

''There are more ways to be sick than running a fever.''

Still concentrating on his bag, he glanced at her, a stern look that indicated he didn't have much patience left. ''Make your point, Joan. I have a plane to catch.''

''Don't. Stay here and be with your daughter. For her sake—''

''It's exactly for her sake that I have to go.''

''I don't understand that, but how you run your business isn't my concern. Sarah is. And all I know is that this 'illness' was her way of calling out for help.''

He had moved into his bathroom. She heard the medicine cabinet open and close. ''That's why I brought you here, isn't it?'' he called out to her. ''To figure out what kind of help she needs.''

''I'm not talking about attention deficit disorder.''

He came to the doorway of the bathroom, shaving kit in hand. His face was very serious. ''Are you saying you don't think she has ADD?'' he asked quietly.

Joan moved into the bedroom. She closed the door behind her, then leaned against it, as though to ensure that no one came near enough to hear this discussion. "No. I don't think she does."

He looked taken aback, and Joan realized that he really hadn't expected that answer. He was silent for a long moment, staring down at the kit in his hands as though it was the most important thing in the world. "Well," he said on a huge sigh, "that's good to hear."

"Yes, but I think there are other problems I haven't been able to pinpoint yet."

His head jerked up. "What kind of problems?"

"Do you remember when you came to my apartment in Virginia? We talked about things that can mimic ADD. The possibility that Sarah might suffer from learning disabilities, anxiety, even mood disorders that could closely resemble ADD. You ruled out quite a few of them, but now I'd like you to reconsider."

He was silent, digesting her words, but she could tell he didn't like what he was hearing. His jaw was clenched so tightly she could see the muscle in his cheek flexing even from across the room. He looked defeated. She didn't doubt for a minute that this was not what he wanted to hear about his daughter.

"Fine," he said at last. He snugged the shaving kit into the bottom of the garment bag. "We'll get to the bottom of it when I come back."

She wanted to shout at him. He was a frustrating, pigheaded fool. She took a few steps forward, trying to think of ways to add weight to her argument.

"Can't you see how desperately she needs you right now?"

He'd pulled rolled-up socks from his dresser, and now he threw them into the garment bag. "Look," he began gruffly. He stopped, obviously trying to get his temper under control. At last he drove his hand through his hair and turned toward her. "What do you want from me? Do you know how hard it was to even *consider* the possibility that Sarah might have ADD? But I brought you here, because I couldn't take the chance any longer that she might need something more than I could give. Now you want me to believe that there's something else wrong with her? Well, I don't buy it," he said with a shake of his head. He pointed to Sarah's room. "Look at this stunt, Joan. It's nothing more than a spoiled little girl who just wants to have things her way. Maybe that's my fault, too, but that's all it is."

Joan shook her head. Her own anger was starting to rise in the face of his unwillingness to see the seriousness of the situation. "It's so much more than that. And she's not a *little* girl, Cody. She's a young girl on the verge of becoming a young woman. In a household, an environment, that caters to men. Merlita's the only female influence she's had, but your housekeeper can't take the place of a mother."

Cody swore. "She can't miss her mother. I told you, she never even knew Daphne."

"What she's missing is the nurturing influence a mother can give. Someone who can help guide her through the next few years, which are very difficult for girls. Everything from first monthly periods to first

dates to first kisses are ahead of Sarah, and she's
scared to death of facing those things alone."

"Did she tell you this?" he asked shortly.

"Of course not. She's much too stubborn and
proud to expose her fears that way. But if you'd spent
the last few days listening to her the way I have,
you'd see that situational stress is really a factor here.
But I've been picking up something else from her,
too. Something that's so frightening to Sarah that she
can't even articulate it. I think it has something to do
with fear of abandonment, as if she thinks—"

"Abandonment? By me?" he asked incredulously.
He made a sound of disgust and turned to zip up one
side of the bag. His clumsy movements told her that
his anger had just about reached its limits. "You almost had me, Jo-Jo. But you're way off base on that
one."

"Why is that such an impossibility?" she argued
back. "A lot of her bad behavior centers around you,
doesn't it? She doesn't want *you* to leave the ranch.
She desperately wants *your* attention."

"If she wants attention from me, then I'd think
she'd be on her best behavior, not acting like a little
demon."

"Don't you see? In Sarah's eyes, *bad* attention,
even in the form of punishment, is better than no attention at all. Conflict shows her that there are feelings involved. That you must care about her."

"Sarah knows that I love her."

He wouldn't look at her. She was furious now herself. She moved closer, so that his eyes were forced
to meet hers. "Why? Just because you say it? Or

because you buy her things? Is that all you think it takes?"

His irritated movements stilled. "You're overstepping, Joan."

"Do you love your daughter or not?"

He straightened, and she knew she'd made a tactical mistake. "Son of a..." His voice was a snarl. "If you were a man asking me that... Of course I love Sarah."

She gripped his forearm. "Then stay here and help me find out what's wrong."

"I can't."

"You mean you won't."

"All right, then that's what I mean. I won't."

Her fingers dropped from his arm. She stared at him, stunned that he couldn't or wouldn't see what needed to be done.

He lifted his garment bag off the bed, gave it a good shake and hooked it over his shoulder with one finger. Finally he looked at her. "I don't believe or accept everything you've said to me," he told her, and his voice had lost its nastiness. "But even if I did, neither one of us can fix what's wrong with Sarah in a weekend. Not *this* weekend. When I get home on Monday, I'll sit down with you. We'll go over this again and again if you want. But right now, I have to get to Houston, and Sarah just has to accept that." After a heartbeat, he added, "So do you."

That was the end of the discussion. She straightened, lifting her chin. *"Sí, jefe."*

His lips twisted in a small smile at the sarcasm. He started to move past her, and when he stood nearly shoulder to shoulder with her, he said, "After last night, this isn't the way I envisioned spending the weekend."

She refused to be moved by the potent warmth of his voice. She'd been an idiot to believe she could see past that rough, arrogant exterior, that she had glimpsed some inner part of him—a part he didn't like anyone to see. If he was willing to leave Sarah now, there was nothing in him that she could admire and respect.

She turned her head a fraction of an inch in his direction. "Last night should never have happened."

"Perhaps," he conceded. "But it did. And I don't regret it."

She looked at him without blinking. "I do," she returned coldly. "Have a safe trip."

CHAPTER TEN

JOAN SPENT SUNDAY MORNING in her room, writing an obligatory letter to her mother and jotting down thoughts in her notebook.

After Cody's departure, what remained of yesterday had been unbearable. She knew that he had spoken briefly to Sarah, but whatever he'd said hadn't helped much. The girl had eventually made an acceptable recovery from her "illness," then had moped around the house the rest of the day. She was monosyllabic in her responses to Joan. Not even Walt could get a smile out of her. Merlita, unaware of the girl's earlier subterfuge, fretted that Sarah had come down with something beyond the scope of her thermometer.

Luna D'Oro and everyone in it seemed to be holding its collective breath, waiting for something horrible to happen.

To count the day a complete loss, Joan had also received a letter forwarded by her mother. From Todd.

In his precise, elegant handwriting, he begged her to reconsider their breakup. He apologized for upsetting her, and even suggested they meet to discuss what could be done to salvage their relationship. He couldn't bear to think about running a private school without her, he said, and surely after all their years of planning together, she couldn't imagine anything else for herself, either.

The problem was…she could.

She read Todd's letter and realized that she didn't mourn the loss of their dream any more than she mourned the loss of him. She felt…nothing.

She hadn't expected that. Anger maybe, when she remembered his willingness to dismiss Headmaster Mueller's actions as a figment of her imagination. Suspicion even, that this letter spoke more of lost career opportunities than undying love. But not this total lack of interest in resurrecting a relationship that had once been the foundation of all her hopes and aspirations. Could it really be so easy?

Maybe she hadn't given herself time to think about it. Maybe this trip to Texas had come too soon. Whatever the reason, it frightened her how little she missed *any* part of her life in Alexandria.

She found herself fretting—almost panicking—about whether she'd get the job at the Oregon school. Not because it would be the answer to everything, but because she couldn't bear to think of a future where there was nothing worth holding on to. No lover. No husband. No lifetime career plan.

Even now, she told herself, she ought to be setting some goals for herself. Where was she going when her time here at Luna D'Oro was over?

The thought left her feeling surprisingly depressed.

Returning Todd's letter into the envelope, she stuffed it in the back of her notebook. She could call him later, tell him that it was really over between them. She tore off several blank sheets from her notebook, deciding that what she needed now was a return to the comforting and logical progression of her problem-solving lists. She had just placed her first header on a page—*Reasons a Move to Oregon Will Be Good for Me*—when there was a knock on her door.

It was Merlita, wringing her hands.

"Señorita Joan, can you come to the living room? There is a visitor."

"For me?"

"No, *señorita*. It is Sarah's grandfather." She stepped closer. "Her mother's father," she said in a low, almost reverential tone. "Señor Walt rode out this morning with some of the hands, and I do not know where Sarah has run off to. I told the gentleman no one is here right now, but he insists on waiting to see Sarah. Can you come, *por favor?* I do not know what else to do with him."

Joan backed away to slip into her shoes and check her hair in the vanity mirror. She was presentable, at least. "Was he expected?"

"I do not think so," Merlita said, relief apparent on her broad features. "Thank you, *señorita*. He's in the living room. I have coffee to bring. Right away."

Joan headed for the living room, curious about this new visitor, who seemed to so unsettle Merlita. She touched the housekeeper's arm as she started for the kitchen. "Merlita," Joan said. "Is there something not right about this man? Something I should know?"

"No, *señorita*. It's only that he never comes here. Only once that I know of. And I do not like that neither Señor Walt or Señor Cody are here to meet him.''

That didn't sound too ominous. So Sarah's maternal grandfather was practically a stranger to the Matthews household. That was a shame for Sarah, but not too surprising. Though Cody had told her very little about his relationship with his late wife and even less about his in-laws, she'd always sensed that the two families had not stayed close.

She entered the living room to find a well-dressed man standing by the large fireplace that took up one corner of the room. He turned at her approach: a silver-haired, reed-thin gentleman with sharp, cold eyes and an unexpectedly wide mobile mouth. He smiled at her.

Joan offered her hand. "Hello. I'm sorry none of the Matthews clan is around right now. I'm Joan Paxton."

"Edward Ross," he returned. His handshake was firm, in spite of the fact that she could feel every one of the joints in his fingers. "I should have called, but I've just finished some business in Corpus Christi, and a stop here didn't seem too far out of the way before my flight tonight. I was hoping to spend a little time with Sarah."

"I don't know where she is, I'm afraid. Probably on her horse. She's too quick for me to keep up with her."

One white brow rose at that information. "This is a rather large spread. She's allowed to roam the place completely on her own?"

"I'm sorry," Joan said. "Did I give you the im-

pression I'm her nanny? I'm not. I'm a..." She
stopped, thinking that there was no need to disturb
the man further by stating what her true purpose at
Luna D'Oro was. "I'm just a friend of the family."

Edward Ross's gaze sharpened. "Cody's friend?"

"Yes," she said quickly. Then realizing that
"friend" could imply a very different meaning, she
added, "Well, I haven't known him that long, really—"

They were interrupted at that moment by Merlita,
bearing an enormous silver tray with coffee service
and a plate of her homemade cinnamon buns. She set
it on the ornate Spanish sideboard, leaving them to
pour cups of the aromatic brew themselves.

After they both had coffee in their hands and had
settled on couches facing each other, Joan wondered
what she could possibly say to hold this man's interest for more than a few minutes at best. He seemed
ill at ease in her presence and disappointed that no
one was here to greet him. She wished she knew more
about this relationship, but no one, not even Walt, had
been forthcoming about the Ross side of the family.

After the clink of silver spoons and rattle of cups
became too much, Joan cleared her throat. "You said
you had business in Corpus Christi. Do you live in
Texas, Mr. Ross?"

"Connecticut," he replied with a tight smile. "I
find Texas rather...overblown, I'm afraid. It's like
this house. There's nothing real about it. It's like the
set of a western movie."

He sounded rather smug, and Joan repressed the
urge to pick up the nearest Remington statue and

throw it at him. "That's a shame," she said, instead. "I'm rather fond of Texas. It's brash and exciting and unpredictable."

"It sounds as if you're describing a person, not a state."

She didn't argue that. The claim was embarrassingly true, she realized. She stared into her coffee cup, wondering where such an effusive description of a state she hardly knew had come from. It had to be nervousness talking, she decided, but what did she have to be nervous about? She smiled at him. "Too many westerns as a child, I suppose. My mother was mad about John Wayne."

He nodded sagely. Uncomfortable silence again, broken only by the clock on the mantel ticking off the minutes. This time, it was Edward Ross who cleared his throat. "Is Cody expected back anytime soon?"

"No. He's in Houston. On business, too, it seems." He frowned at that, making her feel defensive for no reason she could put a name to. "Isn't it a shame that Sunday has become just as busy as the rest of the week now?"

"He has a business to run."

Her father would have said something like that, she thought. Perhaps Cody had a lot more in common with this man, after all. It reminded her how annoyed she still was with him, so that she said more harshly than she intended, "True, but he's also a father, and Sarah won't stay a child forever. He ought to stop and smell the roses."

"I'm afraid I didn't learn that until long after my

own child was grown. And by then, it was too late.''
He took a sip of coffee and then sat studying his cup.
''My wife always said I was too wrapped up in business, but I never listened to her. Now they're both
gone.'' He looked up. ''My wife—Margaret—passed
away not too long ago.''

She had misjudged him earlier. His eyes weren't
cold. They were a deep, warm blue. Like Sarah's.
''I'm sorry,'' she said, and meant it. ''I know you
lost your daughter. It must have been devastating for
you.''

''It was. More than you know.''

Suddenly she felt sorry for him. In spite of his ex-
pensively tailored suit, the precisely trimmed hair, the
air of affluence, he was just a lonely old man who
would probably go home to a dark, empty house
somewhere in Connecticut.

''How fortunate for Sarah to have you,'' Joan said,
trying to find a way to turn the topic of conversation
to something more upbeat. ''My grandparents on both
sides died before I was born. I missed the experience
of having them in my life.''

He nodded understandingly. ''I took retirement two
years ago, and I'd like to spend more time with the
girl. I'm hoping that will be possible.''

''I'm sure Sarah would love that.''

He looked at her oddly. ''Cody seems to be managing fine without my involvement. He may even prefer it.''

''Perhaps you've misunderstood,'' Joan said, offering encouragement. ''If anything, he'll probably welcome it. Sarah's quite a handful for him.''

He set his empty coffee cup on the table next to the couch. "Really? More than he can cope with?"

"I wouldn't say that."

"Do you think the girl misses her mother?" he asked unexpectedly.

"Every girl needs a mother to go to in times of need."

Ross seemed to take the remark quite seriously. He moved forward on the couch. "Does she have many 'times of need'?"

"Of course," Joan said. "What twelve-year-old girl doesn't? She's destined to drive her father to distraction by the time she's sixteen. Cody already has a heck of a time keeping up with her." It occurred to her that this might be the perfect opportunity to find out if ADD ran in the Ross family. But how to approach the subject? "Do you mind if I ask—was your daughter a challenge for you and your wife?"

"My wife, no. I was another matter. Daphne never listened to a word I said. She was defiantly determined to do as she pleased. I was busy building a business, and it was easier to let her go her own way."

"How did your daughter meet Cody? In Texas?"

He settled back on the couch again. "Cody wasn't living in Texas when he met Daphne. He was my financial adviser on Wall Street. My first, actually." He shook his head and smiled, obviously recalling those early years fondly. "He was quite a character back then. Full of sass and vinegar. He was always on the verge of getting fired, I remember. But he had an uncanny knack for the market, and no one could dispute that. He helped take my company public. In many ways he was the one who cemented my success.''

''Then you were pleased that your daughter wanted to marry him?''

He rose, and something in his face brought Joan to her feet, as well. He took a deep breath as his gaze found hers. ''Miss Paxton, I believe you have the wrong impression about my relationship with Cody. We aren't related by marriage. Sarah's my grandchild, but Cody never married Daphne.''

His words stunned her. ''I'm sorry. I didn't realize…''

He buttoned his suit jacket. Again he looked at her strangely, but this time it seemed as if the warmth of their conversation had dissipated. ''He got her pregnant, but he'd already decided he hated New York and wanted to come back here to work with his father. When Daphne refused to come with him, he abandoned her.''

''But he's raised Sarah. How—?''

There was suddenly a blur of movement as Sarah bounded into the room.

''Grandpa Ross! Look what I can do!''

Tousled hair flying, clothes mussed and covered with dirt, she came to a halt directly in front of Edward Ross. Then, unexpectedly, unbelievably, she bent forward and spit on the tile floor. A stream of brown juice—recognizable as chewing tobacco—splattered the tips of her grandfather's polished wing tips.

''*Sarah!*'' Joan gasped.

"For God's sake!" Edward Ross exploded in the same moment.

Sarah looked up at her victim. Her mouth dropped open in horror, and she went white. Her grandfather reached out to grasp her sleeve, but he wasn't quick enough. She twisted away and fled the room.

Calm, Joan thought. *Be calm.* There was a long, painful silence. Then, mustering her will, she hurried to the sideboard to snatch up several napkins from the silver tray. She knelt, wiping tobacco juice from the floor and Mr. Ross's shoes, while he just stood there staring down at her.

"I'm so sorry..." Joan said, her voice barely audible even to herself. "Please don't judge Sarah too harshly. She's a very rambunctious child. Full of pranks and—"

"Pranks!" the man snapped. He bent to finish the job Joan had begun, and when he straightened, she could see that he was so angry he was shaking. "I have never, ever, witnessed such unforgivable behavior in a child. What kind of life does she have here that she plays with chewing tobacco and dresses like a street urchin?"

"Please. Let me explain—"

"What possible explanation could there be for what just happened?"

"She's been having a difficult time lately—"

"Then where is her father? Why isn't he here to see her through it?" Ross's fury had abated a little. The anger she'd glimpsed in his eyes had been replaced by profound sadness. "I don't mean to shout at you, Miss Paxton. It's quite clear to me that you're just as shocked by Sarah's behavior as I am. I think I should leave now. Will you let her father know that I'll be in touch?"

"Of course. But won't you stay a little longer, let me find Sarah? I'm sure she'll want to apologize."

"That's not necessary," he said briskly, and began walking toward the front foyer.

When Joan closed the heavy pine door behind him, she exhaled in relief. What a dreadful incident. How would she explain it to Cody? He was going to be furious with Sarah.

Merlita came up to her, her dark eyes full of uncertainty. She'd probably heard the commotion all the way back in the kitchen. "The visit? It did not go well?" she asked.

Joan shook her head. "No, Merlita. It surely did not."

SARAH WAS SICK. Really sick this time.

After running out of the house, she'd tried to reach Ladybug's stall, but she hadn't made it. The side of the barn was as far as she could get before she lost everything—her breakfast, the apple she'd shared with Ladybug, the disgusting remnants of the tobacco she'd tucked in the corner of her mouth—everything. She retched and retched until there wasn't anything left, until hot tears flooded her eyes under the force of her rebelling stomach. Finally she sagged against the rough boards of the barn, her head pillowed in her arms.

She wanted to die. Right here. Right now.

She didn't ever want to go back into the house.

Never wanted to see Joan Paxton again, either. Or face her father. And if she ever saw her grandfather Ross again, she'd probably die of shame right on the spot.

Why had she done such a stupid, stupid thing? It had seemed like a great idea at the time. Still angry with her father, it felt like the best way to show him how bad she could be if he wasn't here to keep her in line. And if her grandfather Ross thought he had a perfect little granddaughter, if he thought she'd go to Connecticut and be some sort of angel, she'd show him. She'd show him good.

She'd found the tin of chewing tobacco on the ground outside the barn this morning and stuck it in the back pocket of her shorts. Grandpa Walt would know which one of the ranch hands to return it to. Then she'd walked into the kitchen and heard Grandpa Walt talking to Joan Paxton. Only, she realized soon enough that it wasn't Grandpa Walt's voice at all, but Grandpa Ross she heard talking in that soft, clipped way.

It scared her.

Was he here to take her back to Connecticut? Was that why her father had left yesterday? So that she couldn't cling and beg him not to send her away?

But listening at the kitchen door, she didn't hear him say anything about hauling her back to Connecticut. So there was still time, she thought. Time enough to convince him that the last thing he wanted was to have her for a live-in granddaughter. This was her chance. She couldn't ignore it.

Thinking hard what to do, she'd shoved her hands

into her shorts and encountered the tin of tobacco. She'd popped a small pinch of the stuff in her mouth before she could lose her nerve, then shot past Merlita and into the living room. It was only after she'd done the deed and looked up into her grandfather's face that she lost all her nerve. Sure, the old man had looked angry and shocked, but horrified as well, as though she'd grown a second head right there in front of him. The flush of excitement at carrying off such a trick had given way instantly to embarrassment. She'd wanted him to hate her, but the realization that he found her disgusting flooded her with shame.

What should she do now? she wondered. Her father would be furious, and she'd probably be grounded for a week. Or a month. But had she managed to save herself today? Was her fate still sealed? Surely Grandfather Ross wouldn't want her now. But if he did, what then? Did they have military schools for girls in Connecticut?

The questions went round and round in her head, and she could feel the panic and fear coming back, too. She didn't want to be such a baby, but she couldn't help it.

She was sobbing so hard into her shirtsleeve that she didn't hear Joan come up behind her. It wasn't until the woman placed her hand on Sarah's shoulder that she realized she was no longer alone. She whirled, on the defensive, knowing that Joan had been just as shocked, just as disgusted as her grandfather.

"Are you all right, Sarah?" Joan asked, bending a little to search Sarah's face.

Tears still blurred her vision, and she tried to wipe

them away quickly. "I'm fine. And I don't need any help from you. Go away."

"Sorry. I can't do that," Joan told her, and before Sarah realized her intention, she'd captured her wrist and was tugging her toward the calving shed. "Come with me."

The shed was empty, full of midday shadows. Joan led her to the huge stainless-steel sink, turned on the cold-water tap and placed a gentle but firm hand on the back of her neck, urging her to bend forward.

"Rinse your mouth out. Splash some on your face, too. You'll feel better."

"How do you know?" Sarah asked sullenly. "Have you ever chewed tobacco?"

"No, but I've had kids in my class who ate everything from chalk to bugs, and they always felt better once they'd had a chance to rinse the bad stuff out."

Sarah would have argued more, but the truth was, her stomach was starting to rebel again, and it seemed like a smart thing to do. She cupped her hands under the faucet and did as Joan suggested. After a few minutes she straightened, and Joan tossed her a hand towel that smelled pleasantly of detergent and feed-store molasses.

When she'd dried her face, Joan gave her a hopeful smile. "Better?"

Sarah nodded minutely, then threw her a suspicious look. "You can't make me apologize."

"I'm not asking you to," Joan returned. She moved to a nearby stack of grain sacks and sat on top of them. "Besides, your grandfather's already left."

"Good." Sarah said, sticking out her chin. She

plopped on a stool that stood outside one of the stalls. Then tentatively she asked, "Is he mad?"

Joan tilted a glance her way. "What do you think?"

"I hope he is. I hope he hates me and never wants to see me again."

The harsh-sounding words fell into the gloomy silence of the shed. Joan didn't respond for a long time. Then she said, "He seemed like a nice enough old fellow. What did he ever do to you?"

"Nothing. I only met him once before."

"Well, spitting on the poor man's shoes seems a bit over the top, then, don't you think?"

"I wasn't trying to spit on his shoes. I was trying to spit on the floor."

"Oh, that's better," the woman said with a short laugh. When Sarah remained silent, Joan folded her arms and looked at her like a scientist studying a specimen under a microscope. "I don't suppose you want to talk about it?"

"No."

"Your father will find out about this. You know the other day when you told me he'd probably lock you in a tower if you flunked your classes?" She grimaced. "That may be the mildest thing that happens to you when he hears about this."

"I don't care."

Joan slipped off the grain sacks. She went to Sarah, crouching down in front of her as she placed her fingers on the child's bare arm. "I want to help you," she said earnestly. "I really do. But I can't if you won't let me. Whatever it is that's bothering you lately, do you really have to handle it alone?"

"I don't need your help," Sarah said. She lowered her eyes. "I don't need anybody's help."

"Well, sure you do," Joan replied. "Once in a while, we all do. Nothing wrong with that." She lifted a hand and tucked stray blond hairs behind Sarah's ear. Softly she said, "You're a smart girl, Sarah. Maybe you can figure this out all by yourself, but just in case you can't—" she squeezed her arm lightly "—I'm always willing to listen."

Sarah swung her gaze away. All of a sudden she felt like crying again, and she was determined not to. Joan sounded nice. She really might understand. But then, that was her job, wasn't it? To find out what was wrong with loser kids like her and fix them. Sarah clamped her teeth together hard, willing away the temptation to open her mouth and spill her guts.

Eventually Joan sighed and got up. "Just think it over," she said. "And if you can manage to eat something, Merlita should have lunch ready in a few minutes."

What was left of Sunday passed in relatively quiet boredom. Sarah went to bed early that night. Walt limped down to the barns to check on the trio of new calves that had been born during the past few days, this time with no complications. Joan sat on a chaise longue on the *portal,* notebook on her lap, and tried to come up with a way she could keep Cody from packing Sarah off to boarding school. When he heard about this latest fiasco, he was bound to erupt like Mount Saint Helens.

She might be able to dampen Cody's inevitable anger if she could just come up with a reasonable explanation for Sarah's actions. The girl was a puzzle, a fascinating one with a few key pieces missing. And it was frustrating for Joan to accept that she might have to leave here without ever knowing what those pieces were.

She felt annoyed with herself, too, for having failed to accurately interpret the true nature of Cody's relationship with Daphne Ross. There was a lot here she didn't understand. And while some of it was clearly none of her business, anything that might have a bearing on Sarah's current behavior should have been revealed to her.

The fact that it hadn't was as much her fault as anyone's. She knew from experience that families were usually reluctant or unwilling to air their dirty laundry to strangers. She should have pushed.

Looking back, Joan realized that no one in the family, including Merlita, had mentioned anything more than the most basic details about Daphne Ross, and she wondered if the omissions had been deliberate. If the circumstances of Sarah's birth were off-limits as a topic of discussion, it was probably Cody who had put them there.

But why? Because it was too painful to talk about? Because there was still too much anger there? How had Cody ended up raising Sarah alone?

It was all such a mess, Joan decided sadly, crumpling a third sheet of paper from her notebook and tossing it beside the chair. There was only one way she knew to get the answers to these questions. To-

morrow, when Cody returned to Luna D'Oro, she'd
ask him. She just hoped he didn't shut her out as he
had with her queries about that odd character named
Roger.

CHAPTER ELEVEN

THE NEXT DAY Joan was down at the stables, feeding a few carrots to the mare she'd been given to ride, when the summons to Cody's study came. She dusted her hands on her jeans and looked at her watch.

Three-thirty. Right on time. She'd seen the Rover pull into the front drive twenty minutes ago and knew that it wouldn't take long for word of Edward Ross's visit to reach Cody. She wondered where Sarah had escaped to and hoped she stayed there, at least until her father's anger had time to cool a little.

Feeling like a truant child called to the principal's office, Joan followed Merlita back to the house. She stopped only long enough to run a comb through her hair and pick up her notebook.

Cody was behind his desk in the study, looking very businesslike in a suit and tie that made his eyes look darker than usual. He seemed tired. When he saw her, he motioned toward one of the armchairs in front of him. Walt was in the other one, and he lifted his brows and smiled encouragingly at her.

Cody didn't waste time. "I understand you met Sarah's other grandfather yesterday."

"Yes," Joan replied, squaring her shoulders. "He seemed like a very pleasant gentleman."

"Pa's told me that the visit didn't end well. I'd like to hear your version of the story. Particularly your conversation with Ross. Word for word as much as you can remember it, please."

She looked at him curiously. She'd expected him to launch into a tirade about Sarah's unacceptable behavior, but he seemed more interested in what had been said between the adults. His lips were set in firm lines, his posture rigid.

"Well," she began, "we were just chatting, hoping that Sarah would make an appearance—"

"Chatting about what?"

"Nothing, really. The differences between Connecticut and Texas. The fact that his wife had died recently and that he was now retired. He said he was eager to spend more time with Sarah, but that he wasn't sure you'd encourage that."

He stiffened a little. "And you said?"

"I said I doubted that was the case and then made some generalization about children benefiting from a close relationship with their grandparents."

"Why the hell did you say that?" he asked in a sharpened tone.

"Because it's true." She didn't like the way he was looking at her, as if she'd committed some terrible faux pas. "Look," she said firmly. "If there was some script I was supposed to follow when talking to members of your family, you should have furnished me with it. Or stayed home and handled it yourself."

"That son of a bitch is not family," Cody said in a flat voice.

"If he's Sarah's grandfather, he's as much family

as Walt is. I'm not sure I understand what this is all about. I thought we were going to talk about Sarah's little display.''

"We are.''

"Then why am I getting the third degree over the conversation I had with Mr. Ross?''

She couldn't keep annoyance out of her tone. Beside her, Walt stirred in his chair, catching his son's attention.

"You need to tell her, Cody,'' the older man said.

"Pa—''

"No sense in holding back now.''

"Tell me what?'' Joan cut in.

Cody ignored her, continuing to address his father. "It's family business, damn it. It has nothing to do with what I brought her here for. Which was to help Sarah. Not get involved in a war between Ross and me.''

"The war between you and Ross *does* affect Sarah,'' Walt replied in a severe tone Joan had never heard him use before. "And Joan ought to know about him. You're playing this too close to the chest, son. You can trust her. Tell her.''

Cody's hand dismissed his father's suggestion. "You've said enough, Pa.''

The older man stood slowly, inching his way upright with the help of his crutch. "No, I ain't. But I might say too much if I stay here any longer. If anybody wants me, I'll be down at the barns.'' He opened the study door and, before leaving, said, "At least down there, everyone's real clear on what the heck they're doing.''

The room was silent for several seconds. Walt's angry departure had left Joan feeling deflated. If his own father couldn't make Cody see reason, what hope did she have?

With a sigh, she closed her notebook. "I think I've done as much as I can do here, too," she said wearily. "As I told you the other day, I think Sarah has some problems that need to be addressed. I'll write a full report you can take to your doctor. If that's what you decide is best for Sarah."

She stood up.

"Joan, I'd like you to understand—"

"No, you were right," she replied in a reasonable tone. "I think I've accomplished all I can. There's no need to stay here any longer. Would someone be able to take me to the airport tomorrow?"

He was still seated, unbuttoning his collar and sliding the tie off in one agitated movement. "I don't want you to leave."

"That hardly matters."

"Damn it! You said you'd help Sarah."

"I'm trying to help Sarah. But I can't if you won't allow me to understand more about her. And evidently an outsider isn't allowed access to that information." His eyes said as clearly as words that she was wasting her time talking to him. She moved toward the study door. "I'm going to pack."

She was nearly out the door before he stopped her. Not physically, but with words that shocked her into near speechlessness.

"Edward Ross is going to sue me for full custody of Sarah."

She closed the door again and leaned against it. After a long time she asked, "Why would he? How do you know that?"

"His attorneys have been threatening me with it for weeks. And my attorney isn't so sure he won't be able to make a pretty solid case."

"How?" She moved back to the desk. "He's her grandfather, but you're her father. In the eyes of the court, you're still her closest blood relative, whether you married her mother or not. That's always an important factor in custody battles."

"There are extenuating circumstances that may cause a judge to look at me very…unfavorably as a role model for Sarah."

"But obviously you'd never have received custody in the first place if they were so bad. Edward Ross has to accept—"

"I never received custody of Sarah. Not legally."

It was a good thing the armchair was directly behind her. She sank into it, stunned. "What?"

"All I ever did was bring her home as a baby. She never knew her maternal grandfather existed until a few months ago when she met him for the first time."

"I don't understand," Joan said, shaking her head. She repeated Edward Ross's claim that Cody had abandoned his daughter when she was pregnant. That he had refused to marry her. "Is that true?" she asked.

"That's what he chooses to believe, I suppose." He gave her a level glance. "*I* didn't refuse to marry Daphne, *she* refused to marry me. I wanted to bring her back here, raise a whole slew of kids at Luna

D'Oro. But she loved New York—everything about it—and Texas looked like the face of the moon to her.'' He grimaced. ''She didn't want me. She didn't want kids at all. She just wanted her old life back. We argued, and I was here for a few days, tying up the purchase of this place, when a friend of mine called to say Daphne had flown unexpectedly to Europe. Supposedly to stay with a friend in Paris.''

''But that wasn't the truth.''

''Not completely. She planned to visit with friends for a while. After taking care of some unpleasant business first.''

''An abortion?'' Joan guessed.

His expression was suddenly wary, as though he fought an inner battle about how much to tell her. His mouth tightened, but eventually he said, ''Yes. I talked her out of it. I wanted the kid, but she was scared to death her father would cut her off financially if he got wind of it. So I arranged to set her up over there in Paris until the baby was born. Took nearly all the savings I had to do it, but her parents never knew a thing, and I was there for the delivery.''

''Poor Sarah,'' Joan said. ''She idolizes her mother, you know.''

''I'll never willingly tell her the truth,'' he replied with quiet determination in his voice. ''Daphne handed over Sarah without even looking at her. We'd been out of love for a long time before that, and I think she was glad to see the last of both of us. I brought the baby back here. I never heard a word from Daphne, but I figured sooner or later we'd get back together, figure out what to do about legal custody.'' He sighed heavily, tossing the tie that had been bunched in his hand onto the desk. "A couple of weeks later I opened the newspaper and saw that a plane had crashed in the Italian Alps, killing everyone aboard. Daphne's name was on the passenger list.''

"What did you do?''

He gave her a sour grin. "I guess it's more a case of what I *didn't* do. I knew Daphne's parents didn't know about the baby. And frankly, I didn't want to share Sarah with anyone or try to work out some sort of two-family parenting between here and Connecticut. Edward and Margaret never were warm and affectionate with Daphne. I had no reason to think they'd be any better with Sarah, and I definitely didn't want her turning out like her mother, a shallow snob. So I kept my mouth shut.''

"But they were her grandparents. The only surviving link to Daphne.''

"I'm not saying what I did back then was honest or honorable. God knows, I've been waiting twelve years for the other shoe to drop. In some ways, it's a relief to have it out in the open. But I'm not proud of it.''

"How did Ross find out about Sarah?''

"Daphne's friend in Paris had an attack of conscience or some damn thing and called Edward three months ago. All hell broke loose after that. From the very beginning Edward's been making noises about suing for full custody, with the fact that I deliberately tried to keep his grandchild from him as an ace in the hole. We met, and he insisted on coming here to see

her. I've agreed that she can spend time with him in
Connecticut—although I'd rather she didn't—but I'm
not sure that's going to be enough.''

"Does Sarah know any of this?"

"No. And I don't want her to. How would you feel
if you knew that your mother hadn't wanted you? In
fact, that may be the only thing keeping Edward at
bay. The realization that all this would come out in a
custody battle and hurt Sarah."

Joan sat back, thinking about yesterday's conversation with Sarah behind the barn. How adamant
she'd been about not caring whether what she'd done
had upset Edward Ross. But if she'd only met him
once, how could that kind of animosity take hold?
"She told me she hates her grandfather."

"Well, you met him. He's not exactly Mr. Warmth.
I don't think he made any points with her during that
first meeting.''

"But to say she hates him? And that outrageous
stunt she pulled. That seems awfully extreme to me,''
Joan said absently, her mind trying to sort through the
conversation. She couldn't shake the feeling that she
wasn't reading between the lines, that the key to much
of Sarah's behavior lately lay right in front of her
nose, but she just couldn't see it. "Are you *sure* Sarah
doesn't know any of this?" she asked.

While she'd been thinking, Cody had come around
the desk to sit beside her in the second armchair. He
shook his head. "I'm as sure as I can be.''

"Who else knows?"

"Pa. Merlita, maybe, but more likely just that Ross

might want custody. I've told them both that it's not to be discussed with anyone.''

''Which is why neither of them were very forth-coming any time I've asked about Sarah's mother.''

''Yes.''

Well, at least she knew now that Cody wasn't so troubled by memories of a late wife that he couldn't bear to discuss her or have anyone else do so. The thought pleased her somehow. She gave herself a mental shake. *Stay focused on the problem at hand, Joan. Sarah.*

Lost in concentration, she nearly jumped when Cody touched her hand. She turned her head to look at him. Now that he'd told her so much, he seemed more at ease, as if sharing the problem had lessened his burden.

His mouth quirked into a small reluctant smile. ''Please stay, Joan. I know this sounds crazy, but I can only fight on so many fronts at one time. Between the ranch and my investment business and keeping Ross at bay, I don't have much energy left to figure out what to do about Sarah. I need your help right now.''

''I'm not sure I can—''

''If not you, then who? I can't handle Sarah alone. I'm coming to the conclusion that I've spent the past twelve years making nothing but mistakes with her.''

The look he gave her was heart-meltingly direct. She sat for a long time, saying nothing. He sounded so desperate. For a few precious moments Joan al-lowed herself to feel something more for Cody, something that went beyond parenting problems and threats of court battles.

Ever since he'd kissed her on the *portal* that night, her imagination had been completely unleashed, running down fantasy corridors she'd never have thought possible from the normally pragmatic, organized mind of Joan Paxton. He infuriated her. His arrogant opinions tried her patience. But his kiss made her lips burn and her tongue ache. He left her feeling unsteady…and wonderful.

She wanted to stay, not just for his sake, but for Sarah's, too. Still, something told her it would be foolish to let Cody think she had an interest in remaining at Luna D'Oro for any reason other than a professional one. He was watching her very closely, and she took refuge in systematic efficiency.

"You haven't failed with Sarah," she said crisply. "But your parenting skills could stand a little work."

"What?" he asked.

He didn't seem offended. That was a good start. But he had a temper, and as reluctant as he was to hear that Sarah had problems, he'd probably be twice as adverse to hearing about his own failings.

"Well…" She glanced down at her notebook, wondering how much of her findings from the previous week she could safely share with him.

His hand was suddenly under her chin, drawing her eyes upward. His touch made her skin tingle like a cold shower. "Not from one of your damn lists," he said with asperity. Then his hand moved to her heart—only for a moment—but that light contact seemed to burn right through her blouse. "Tell me from here. What's this telling you? You think I'm a poor father?''

Her empathy for him hadn't completely unseated her urge for self-preservation. It took a lot to keep her thoughts coherent, but at least her voice didn't desert her. "I think you need as much behavior modification as your daughter," she said slowly. "Your treatment of Sarah is inconsistent. You let her get away with murder for too long, and then you're ready to tar and feather her. She doesn't know her boundaries with you, because you haven't established them.''

"Is that it?''

"No," she said, deciding that if she was going to get her head handed to her, she might as well lose it for a just cause. "You won't let her grow up. You want to keep her a tomboy, and she knows that. Because she loves you, she won't challenge you, even though she wants to explore being a teenager. And it's time you let her.''

"Now are you finished?''

"Not quite.''

"I didn't think so.''

She looked at him squarely, knowing that his response to her could cut her courage to ribbons. Back in Alexandria, she'd had to show many a parent where their weaknesses lay. Why should it be so hard to tell Cody his?

"You're not home often enough," she said at last. "Sarah spends more time with Walt and Merlita than you. And since this is a home without a mother, it's crucial that you take a more active role as her father.''

"I'm here as much as I can be."

"You sound so much like my father," she retorted, unable to keep irritation out of her tone. "He always had an excuse, too. Only his involved countries, instead of the stock market."

"I'm not offering excuses. I have reasons."

"I'm sure you do," she said.

"Look. For two months I've been putting together a merger for two of my investments clients. It finalized today, but this weekend was touch-and-go. I need the cash this deal brought me." He leaned toward her, stressing his point. "I'm not rich, Joan. We live well, but if I get into a battle with Ross over Sarah, I want to meet him on an equal footing. And that means having the money to afford the best attorneys in the country. I'd hock everything I own to keep Sarah, but I'm hoping that after today, I won't have to."

His eyes captured hers, froze her in place. After a moment she reached out hesitantly across the distance that separated them and laid her hand on Cody's arm. "I'm sorry. That was unfair of me. I shouldn't draw comparisons between you and anyone else. Least of all my own family."

"Apology accepted," he said quietly. He smiled down at her hand on his arm. His free hand came up to stroke her fingers. "Tell you what," he added at last. "Regardless of what Ross does as a result of this weekend's disaster, let me start working on a new approach with Sarah. Help me. There's no place you have to be right away, is there?"

"No. Not right away."

"Then stay a little longer." He clutched her hand

in his, then lifted it to the bold heavy curve of his lips. His brow rose in silent communication, and she thought that with the brutal charm of his lazy Texas drawl and soft voice this man could get anything—anyone—he wanted.

"To help Sarah," she heard herself say softly.

"And me."

"You," she was able to retort as she managed to slide her hand away from those dangerous lips, "might be a little more difficult."

IN THE END Sarah's punishment for what became known in the Matthews household as "the tobacco incident" was to help Merlita scrub and polish every one of the terra-cotta floor tiles in the house. There were a lot of them, and Joan watched with a little apprehension as Sarah took in the details of her penance.

The girl locked stare for stare with her father, then gave a little twitch of her shoulders. She seemed to accept that she'd crossed the line of acceptable behavior. With a great deal of personal flair and stubborn pride, she turned one haughty look on Cody, removed the dangling bucket of soap suds from his hand and proceeded to play a very put-upon Cinderella.

After that, the rest of the week was rather anticlimactic. True to his word, Cody spent more time at home with Sarah. It wasn't all smooth sailing. The girl seemed confused by this sudden increased attention from her father. Cody, impatient and eager to see results from his efforts, became frustrated.

Joan, trying to remain an impartial third party, shepherded them both through the process of learning to deal with each other. She encouraged Sarah in her tentative steps toward becoming a teenager. She coached Cody through the more difficult times, urging him to keep the right balance of ''pushing'' and ''waiting'' with Sarah. There were occasional slammed doors and frazzled looks, but most of the disagreements were minor and easily resolved. No one seemed bent on holding a grudge.

To her knowledge, there was no communication from Edward Ross after his disastrous visit. She knew that Cody continued to worry, but until his attorney indicated a cause for concern, there was nothing he could do but wait.

As for her own relationship with Sarah, Joan felt she made slow but steady headway. Twice the girl had sought her out to ask her opinion about something, and once she even suggested another impromptu concert for the family. But whenever Joan tried to delve deeper into her feelings about her grandfather Ross, she clammed up. Joan was forced to follow the same advice she'd been giving Cody— as tempting as it was to try to question Sarah, she had to let the girl proceed at her own pace.

Saturday came and Joan slept late, having been up long hours the night before writing in her notebook various ways to address the need for structure in Sarah's life. When she got to the dining room, everyone had already been served, and the mood at the table was playful and excited.

''What's on your agenda today, Joan?'' Cody

asked as he dug into a steaming plate full of scrambled eggs.

"I thought I'd call my mother. And maybe write a letter to…a friend." She'd put off responding to Todd's letter, and today seemed like the perfect day to take care of that matter once and for all.

"Do it tonight. Today you're coming with us," he said in that usual commanding way of his.

"Where?"

"Goliath. Today's the day we officially reopen Mission San Benito."

When Joan's blank look indicated she had no idea what he was talking about, Walt jumped in. "That's our own little claim to fame. Mission San Benito was a stop on the Spanish mission trail back in the early 1700s. The place has been a crumbling ruin for a century, but after four years and about a thousand car washes and bake sales, the town's restored it. Goliath is having a big party to celebrate. Lots of food and games." He wiggled his shoulders as if moving to music. "Dancing."

"Sounds like fun, but I—"

Unexpectedly Sarah leaned forward and touched her arm. "You have to come," she insisted. "Merlita's got her chili entered in the cook-off, and she needs all the help we can give her." Her head swung in the direction of her father. "Right, Dad?"

"I think it would please her," he said, and Joan could see in his face that he was just as surprised as she was that Sarah seemed so eager to have her along.

"Then I suppose I have to come."

"Oh, and bring your violin." Walt spoke up.

Joan shook her head uncomprehendingly. "What?"

"Just bring it," Cody said.

Looks were exchanged around the table, as though they all shared some secret, but no one was forthcoming. Deciding it was better not to press the issue, Joan agreed.

Unlike the Alamo, which sat directly in the heart of downtown San Antonio, Mission San Benito was perched on the outskirts of the city on a scrubby bit of land that looked too arid to grow much of anything. Cody parked in the half-full parking lot, followed closely by the ranch pickup, carrying Merlita and Tomas and everything the housekeeper needed to win the chili cook-off. Everyone piled out and stood for a moment staring at the mission ruins, which were surrounded by the town of Goliath's best efforts to entertain its citizens.

Huge striped tents held food and game booths. Bleachers had been set up to accommodate an audience that would later listen to the mayor make a speech about preserving the mission. Under a cluster of live oaks on the property, artisans in Indian costumes from the period displayed their talents. Sheep and horses gave the scene an authentic look, along with actors dressed in the robes of Franciscan friars, doing their best to look as though they didn't feel the heat.

The family staked out a patch of grassy turf under one of the trees, then immediately began to make plans to see and do everything, beginning with a tour of the mission.

"Tour" was perhaps too fancy a word. Even restored to its original form, the mission itself was small
and unremarkable, except for a trio of bell towers, a
short corridor of Romanesque arches off to one side
and a pretty fountain in a courtyard that separated the
mission church from the convent. There were no intricate Renaissance details, no colorful Moorish designs, but it was clear that the town had poured its
heart into repairing the damage that time and nature
had wrought.

The next few hours passed quickly. The game
booths were a big draw for Sarah, who proved to be
better than any of them when it came to tossing rings
over bowling pins or popping balloons with darts.
They ate barbecue and corn dogs and sampled enough
bowls of chili to feed half the state. The mayor made
a short, impassioned speech about the mission's res-
toration. Joan watched in fascination as a tinsmith
hammered and cut designs out of colored tin.

Thirty minutes later, as they sipped lemonade in
the shade, Sarah pushed a small box across the picnic
table until it rested directly in front of Joan.

"I bought you a present," the girl said. Excitement
danced in her eyes, but her smile was oddly uncertain.
"It's no big deal, but I thought you might like it."

Surprised, Joan lifted the lid and discovered a pair
of delicate tin earrings, cut in the shape of clustered
flowers. She lifted one of them, discovering on closer
inspection that the design was really quite intricate.

"They're lovely," Joan said, touched by Sarah's
thoughtfulness.

"They're bluebonnets, the state flower," Sarah explained. "So you'll remember us after you leave."

In the silence that followed, Joan felt a jab of heartache. She'd been so busy the past few days that she hadn't thought much about time running out. But soon—very soon—the time would come when the Matthews family would no longer need her help. She ought to be glad about that, but instead, it left her feeling as if she were made of glass.

Cody sat beside her on the picnic bench, and she could sense him watching her. She reached across the table to give Sarah a playful hug. "Silly girl! Do you think I need anything to remind me of this crazy Matthews clan?"

Everyone laughed a little at that, and the awkward moment passed. Joan removed her stud earrings and replaced them with the dangling bluebonnets, which everyone agreed perfectly matched the peasant blouse and skirt she wore.

A minute later Sarah jumped up from the table. "Dad, it's time," she said. She glanced in the direction of the main tent, where an announcer was haranguing the audience to come closer.

"Time for what?" Joan asked.

Cody gave her a sheepish smile. "I'm afraid you're going to earn those earrings, Joanie. Sarah's got a plan for winning one of the contests today, and it involves you. And your violin. Let's go."

The group trooped over to the tent. Joan couldn't imagine what her contribution to any competition could be, unless it was some sort of talent contest, and they wanted her to go head-to-head with another musician. She was running through her entire repertoire of classical pieces in her head when Sarah slapped a numbered label into her hand.

"We're number three," she said, handing her father a similar label on a string.

"Number three of what?" Joan asked.

"Worm-fiddlers," Cody replied with a grin. He had placed his number over his head and now looped Joan's around her neck. "I'll bet you never do that in Virginia."

"I don't even know what it is."

She found out very quickly.

While Joan watched, square beds of dark, rich earth were placed in different spots under the tent. The audience was informed that three hundred earthworms had been seeded into each bed, far beneath the topsoil. Earthworms liked peace and quiet, and the only way the placid creatures would come to the surface was in protest of any loud, annoying noise—created by "fiddlers," contestants who could use any raucous means they wished to entice them out of their beds. Once exposed, the worms would be scooped from the soil and placed into buckets by "pluckers" on the team. One fiddler and two pluckers were allowed to enter the contest, with the winning team being the one that was able to lure the most earthworms to the top in a set time. Digging for the worms—the announcer told everyone gravely—was grounds for disqualification.

The pluckers began lining up to collect buckets for scooping worms. The fiddlers began unpacking their instruments. To Joan's surprise, very few of them

were true musical instruments. They varied from saw
and hammers to bongo drums to metal pipes rigged
to look like a xylophone. There was a great deal of
laughter and heckling comments made by the surrounding crowd over these bizarre pieces of equip-
ment, and a surprisingly sharp thrill of anticipation in
the warm air under the tent.

Joan shook her head. "No way. I got roped into
playing for a cow, but I draw the line at playing for
earthworms."

"You have to!" Sarah cried in a plaintive tone.
"We already paid the entry fee!"

Behind her, Cody was busy inspecting his bucket
and avoiding eye contact. Joan narrowed a glance at
him. "You put her up to this," she accused. "You
really do hate the violin, don't you?"

He looked up and grinned at her. "Actually it's
starting to grow on me."

Walt pointed toward one of the other contestants.
"That guy with the washboard looks like your best
competition."

Sarah frowned at the contestant, then swung back
to Joan. "We can beat him, Joan. You know we can.
You play, and Dad and I scoop. It's easy."

"Oh, no!" Joan said, smacking her forehead in
mock horror. "I forgot my worm music."

"Worms probably aren't any more discriminating
than cows," Cody offered the opinion. "Wing it."

"Show 'em what you can do, gal," Walt encouraged. "I'll bet half this crowd ain't never heard fiddle
music the way you play it. Not to mention the
worms."

Joan heaved a huge sigh, knowing she was outnumbered. Sarah was so excited now she was practically bouncing up and down. Joan eyed the guy with the washboard, who caught her looking at him and flashed her a thumbs-up victory sign. He and his teammates seemed very cocky. "What's the grand prize?" she asked.

"A hundred dollars," Sarah piped up.

"Cash?"

"Uh-huh."

She drew in a deep, determined breath. "Let's go get some worms."

CHAPTER TWELVE

"TEAM NUMBER THREE—Go!"

The starter's shout bounced off the tent walls, bringing a loud eruption from the crowd and impelling Joan into frantic action. She mentally raced through her repertoire of music— First, "At the Hunt," then "Bahn Frei," then "Circus Renz" by Peter, maybe go right into— Oh, hell, what was she thinking? Earthworms wouldn't know Strauss from Straub, would they? She launched into a frenzied "Buffalo Gal" just to give this Texas audience a crowd pleaser. No sense making them as mad as the worms.

The tent reverberated with the sound of their encouragement. Tipping her violin down, she tilted a look to the side and saw Walt with his head thrown back, howling like a coyote.

"Faster!" she heard Sarah shout.

"Go, Joan!" Cody's voice came to her out of the din. "Don't stop!"

She found her teammates, saw them standing by with buckets and gloved hands, ready to pounce, their eyes glued to the dark soil. Not a single wormy head had made an appearance yet. She panicked, inhaled sharply and switched to just sawing blindly back and forth in the highest whine she could manage. Cody caught her eye and gave her a thumbs-up.

It seemed as if they might be doomed to failure, but suddenly up the worms popped, angry, wriggling creatures with evidently very little tolerance for noise. Cody and Sarah moved into action, jumping around the perimeter of the soil bed, sometimes scooping, sometimes bumping into each other as they raced crazily back and forth.

"There, Sarah!" Cody called, pointing to one of the far corners of the soil bed. Then another. "Over there, too! I've got three here!"

"I've got him! I've got him!" Sarah shouted over the noise. "Don't let that one get away, Dad!"

Joan just kept playing, thinking that at any moment her arm was going to give out—where the heck was the one-minute warning buzzer they'd been promised, anyway? Pretty soon she went on automatic pilot and started thinking that it was nice to see Cody able to act silly with his daughter. Nice to see him having fun with her. He really wasn't like Joan's father at all.

For just a few moments there was a lull in the number of worms enticed to the surface, just enough for Sarah to scoop quickly by herself. Cody stood off to the side, waiting to be called upon. His eyes met Joan's, and he gave her a wink that said he knew how ridiculous this all was, but—what the hell—Sarah was having a ball, wasn't she? *So I must be doing something right for a change,* his look seemed to say.

It was all so clear in that moment, as though he'd

spoken the words aloud. A person could really care about a man like this, Joan thought.

One hour later it was over. Joan stared down at the purple ribbon the worm-fiddling judge had just placed across her palm. The wording said it all with humiliatingly forthright humor: DEAD LAST.

Walt came up to her, shaking his head. "Man! Fourteenth place out of fourteen. I didn't expect you guys to do *that* badly."

Beside her, Cody was lightly shaking his bucket, inspecting the knot of worms that writhed within. "I think our worms were sedated. Look at them. They're not even moving."

"That was embarrassing," Sarah complained, although she didn't sound too disappointed that only sixty-four worms had popped to the surface of the soil. "We didn't even need a third bucket."

"Sorry, guys," Joan said. "I did my best. Should have brought a washboard, I guess."

They all glanced toward the washboard team, three college-age fellows doing victory laps around the tent while being cheered on by the crowd, which had proved to be remarkably fickle.

"That's okay, Joan," Sarah said. "We know you tried."

"Well, I learned something very valuable today," Joan said as she snapped the lid of her violin case shut.

"What's that?" Cody asked with a grin.

"Losing stinks."

They all agreed it certainly did.

"Who wants a soda before we see how Merlita's

doing?'' Cody offered, peeling off the plastic gloves he'd worn to scoop up worms. ''I'm buying.''

The heat of the day seemed trapped under the tent, and everyone spoke up. Cody took orders and then nudged his way through the crowd. Walt gathered up the buckets and headed toward the announcer's table to return them.

''Might as well wear our failure proudly,'' Joan said, indicating the ribbons the three of them had been given.

Sarah pushed out her chest, and Joan attached the ribbon to the girl's blouse.

''Do you think they have stuff like this in Connecticut?'' Sarah asked.

''You mean worm-fiddling? Or celebrations in general? I wouldn't think worm-fiddling's a big draw in Connecticut. But they have lots of historic places, and I'm sure they have lots of celebrations.'' Joan looked at Sarah closely. It was the first time since the tobacco incident that the girl seemed willing to discuss her maternal grandfather. ''Are you thinking about when you visit your grandfather Ross?''

''I looked up Connecticut in the school library. I don't want to live there. It's an awful small state.''

''Well, everything's small compared to Texas. But I'm sure it'll be fun. A totally new experience for you.'' She frowned at the girl. ''Who said anything about living there?''

Sarah was staring sullenly at her feet. Joan tapped her arm with one of the ribbons. ''Now me,'' she said, touching the edge of her own blouse.

She bent her knees so that Sarah could attach the

ribbon, placing her fingers between her blouse and her skin to make sure Sarah didn't skewer her. Even as she did so, the pin slipped behind the ribbon, and Joan felt a sharp stabbing pain in one of her fingers.

"Ouch!" she yelped, and her hand flew out from under her blouse.

Sarah looked horrified. "I'm sorry. Are you okay?"

As if she could chase away the pain, Joan shook her hand back and forth. "It's all right. I know you didn't mean it. Let's see what the damage is."

She held her hand out, and they both stared down at it. The pin had scraped along the edge of her index finger, opening up the skin in a long slice. It wasn't deep, but blood welled from the cut, making Sarah gasp.

"There goes my worm-fiddling career," Joan said lightly to reassure Sarah that she really was all right, but also to keep her mind off the way her stomach rolled at the sight of blood.

"Use this," Sarah said, pulling off the pretty scarf she'd used to tie her hair in a ponytail. She wrapped it quickly around Joan's hand, making the injured finger hurt even more. "You need a bandage. There's a first-aid station over by the mission."

The girl started to go, and Joan grabbed her. If she was going to faint, she didn't want to do it around Sarah and all these people. "No, you stay here," she told her. "I'll get a bandage and be back before you know it."

At the first-aid tent, a rather harried nurse was applying ointment to the scraped knee of a little boy who sat wailing in a lounge chair. She looked up as Joan entered.

"I just need a bandage," Joan said quickly. She averted her eyes from the sight of the boy's bloodied shin.

"Help yourself," the nurse replied, indicating with a toss of her head the medical supplies that lay on a nearby table.

Joan snatched one up, as well as an antiseptic swab, and left the tent. She got as far as the mission when she decided to check her wound. It had surely stopped bleeding by now.

But when she unwrapped her hand, beads of blood immediately made a bright red trail along the cut. Her head started to swim. She sat on one of the stairs leading to the mission's bell tower and tilted her head against the wall. The stucco felt cool and smooth against her cheek. Joan closed her eyes, letting her pulse settle, trying to keep her mind off the stinging of her hand.

It was very peaceful; there was no one else around. In the distance she could hear an announcer encouraging everyone to get a final taste of their favorite chili before the judging took place.

She should get up and join the others to cheer Merlita on to victory. But the air felt so wonderful, flowing down the stairwell to cool the back of her neck, and her legs wouldn't respond to her commands. In a minute, she thought. Just one more minute.

The breeze from the stairwell kissed her cheek, and she smiled at the feel of it, a soft, warm sensation that almost felt like a caress. It occurred to her that previously the breeze had not been warm at all, but cool, and she opened her eyes to discover Cody kneeling in front of her, the backs of his fingers brushing lightly against the side of her face.

"You all right?" he asked her.

"Yes."

"Sarah told me she got you with the pin." He lifted her hand and began unwinding the scarf. "Let me see. Shut your eyes again."

She did as he told her. He manipulated her fingers—he had the gentlest touch for a man.

"For pity's sake—"

Her eyes flew open. "What? Is it worse than I thought?"

"Hell, no," he said with a little laugh. "Here I am, thinking Sarah stabbed you badly enough to warrant a trip to the emergency room, and it's actually no more than a scratch. I've had paper cuts that bled more than this."

She pulled her hand back against her breast. "I never said it was bad."

"It's that faint-at-the-sight-of-blood-thing, isn't it? You're as white as a sheet."

Exasperated, she plucked the scarf out of his hand and rewrapped it quickly around her finger. "If you aren't going to help, then go away."

He spotted the bandage and antiseptic packet in her other hand and grabbed them. "Sit still. And don't look at it."

He sat next to her on the stairs, took her hand again and began cleaning the cut. Joan kept her eyes averted.

"Guess you're not as tough as you pretend to be," he remarked with a shake of his head.

"I don't pretend. I *am* tough. Ow!" The antiseptic stung as it seeped into the cut, and her hand jerked in protest.

"Yeah, you're the woman of steel, all right," Cody said. "We'll let this air-dry for a minute before I put on the bandage. Just relax. Think of something else."

She sat quietly, trying to focus on anything but the disturbing, distracting influence of the man beside her. She stared at the mission fountain, with its gentle, laughing cascade of water. She listened to the far-off sounds of musicians playing "Turkey in the Straw." She inhaled the scents of the day: chili and corn and the sweet, sweet smell of cotton candy. And when a long minute had passed, all she could think about was what a wonderful mouth Cody Matthews had.

"Are you having fun today?" He broke her concentration.

"Very much."

He gave her a skeptical look. "Do you mean that?"

"Why wouldn't I?"

"The mission's not exactly the grand palaces of Europe you're probably used to. Even the best celebration that Goliath has to offer must seem pretty corny to you."

"Yes, it is," she murmured, half to herself. She sighed. "But it's wonderful. And best of all, I really sense that Sarah has relaxed her defensiveness a little. You can feel that, too, can't you?"

"Yes," he admitted. A rush of heat rippled through her at the expression in his eyes. "That's your influence, you know? You've been good for the two of us.''

She looked away, not trusting herself to say anything more. When she left here, would Cody miss her? Her heart ached at the thought that he might not.

''What are you thinking?'' he asked as he wound the bandage around her finger and smoothed it into place.

''I'm thinking that when I leave here I'll be taking the most wonderful set of memories with me. This mission. The kinds of sunsets you get from the back of Luna D'Oro. Not to mention playing the violin for a pregnant cow and a bunch of worms.''

''And us?''

She smiled at him. He still had her hand, and for a moment she lifted her other one to the tin earring dangling from her earlobe, thinking how touched she'd been by Sarah's gesture. ''Of course. As I told Sarah, I'm not likely to forget the Matthews clan.''

''I wasn't talking about the family as a whole,'' he said softly. He reached for the earring, rubbing it lightly between two fingers. She felt the heat of his hand against her neck, a gentle presence. ''Not far from the ranch there's a valley that's covered in bluebonnets in the spring. So many it looks like a lake. I'd like to take you to see them someday.''

She sat still, calm, thinking how much she was going to miss this man. It seemed impossible, but there was a chemistry between them. She knew the danger she was slipping toward, and it frightened her. She shook her head at him. ''I won't be here come spring.''

"You could be."

"I've stayed too long already."

"Ah, Joanie," he said with a rueful twist of his mouth. "I'm beginning to think a hundred years with you wouldn't be long enough."

His fingers slipped underneath her hair to slide to the back of her head. They kneaded gently for a few moments while his eyes met hers, questioning, wanting. She tried to think sensibly, tried to remind herself about romantic fools and summer flings and where they always led. But the truth must have been in her face, the embarrassing impossible truth. That she wanted all the memories she could have of a man with eyes the color of Texas bluebonnets.

Impulsively she turned her head, so that her lips came against the base of his wrist. She regarded him mutely for a timeless moment, and then his mouth met hers. His kiss was cool and yet feverish, fiercely arousing, asking a response from her that made Joan feel as if something inside her had suddenly snapped. She answered with a swift recklessness that took her breath away, opening her mouth, letting her tongue meet the smooth, hot persuasion of his.

Her arms rose to bring his body closer, already resenting the delay. She felt the heat of him: hard male muscle pressed against her breasts. Cody ended their kiss at last, only to make her gasp as his mouth moved along the side of her neck, then along her collarbone. The thin peasant blouse was no defense against his touch, but she wished she could dissolve it at will, until his hand stroked her flesh. As though hearing that unspoken demand, he slipped the elastic collar down, then her bra strap, just far enough to tease one nipple out of hiding, to cup his hand around the full-ness of her breast. She pushed against him, crying out softly as he lowered his lips to where his hand had stroked, creating a swollen, sensitive spot. She was so eager for his touch, so robbed of movement or speech. All of Goliath could have marched past this dimly lit alcove, and she wouldn't have cared.

Unexpectedly it was Cody who brought back sanity.

In the distance there was a sudden high cheer from the crowd, followed by applause. He stilled his move-ments, then lifted his head to find her eyes. His mouth was tilted in wry regret. "Something tells me we missed Merlita's big moment." He tugged her blouse back into place. "And that probably means we've had all the privacy we're going to get."

Somehow Joan managed to put her body back to-gether, though it was a trembling hand she raked through her disheveled hair as she nodded. "We should go. Find out if she won."

"Yes," Cody agreed. "And then let's go home." Tenderly he caressed the damp wisps of hair off her forehead. "It's been a full day, don't you think?"

She smiled, and when he took her hand and led her out of the alcove to find the others, she didn't pull away.

MERLITA HADN'T WON the chili cook-off, after all. She'd come in second. There were muttered com-plaints from Walt and sulky looks from Sarah, but the housekeeper seemed completely unperturbed by the outcome, only offering the dire prediction that the winner had better look out next year. By the time they'd helped collect her chili fixings and piled everything into the back of the ranch truck, it was nearly dusk.

The ride home in the Rover seemed to take forever. The atmosphere was subdued—Walt and Sarah were half-asleep in the back, but in the front seat the air seemed charged with anticipation. With every mile, Joan could feel her pulse quickening, and when she chanced a glance Cody's way, she knew he felt the same. His hands gripped the wheel so tightly, the knuckles were white. Her attempts at casual conversation were met with absentminded agreement.

She suspected that his private thoughts closely matched her own. When everyone had gone to bed and Luna D'Oro was settled in for the night, she and Cody would make love. They hadn't discussed it, but she knew that it was going to happen.

The Rover bumped onto the driveway. In the setting sun the house looked red, as though on fire.

"We've got a visitor," Cody remarked, and he sounded annoyed.

Joan saw a nondescript sedan parked in front of the house. Its dark-tinted windows gave no clue to the presence of a driver. Cody pulled the Rover to a stop, and everyone piled out slowly. As Joan rounded the back end of the vehicle, the occupant of the other car got out and walked toward them.

It was Todd.

JOAN CLOSED the study door behind her and turned to face her ex-fiancé. Cody had been pleasant through the introductions, had probably seen the tension on her face, and made the suggestion that Joan use his study.

It would have been flattering to think that Todd had missed her so much that she'd be able to see it in his eyes and in the lines of his face, but she couldn't. He looked no different than the last day she'd seen him. Eyes the color of soft rain. Hair so blond it was like sun on frost. Todd had always had a certain fluid grace, but he moved around the room restlessly now, obviously finding nothing of interest.

She realized in that moment that he was tense and gathered together like a cat ready to spring. His eyes traveled around their surroundings quickly, disparagingly. "Study?" he remarked. "This looks more like a bargain basement. I'm surprised the guy can find anything in here."

She didn't respond. It was true, of course. Cody's study was hopelessly disorganized, off-limits to Merlita's tidy regimen. But oddly enough, it had ceased to bother her. She tried to keep a pleasant, nonconfrontational look on her face. "Do you want to sit down, Todd?"

"No. I want to know why you left Alexandria— left me—for this."

"I left because I'd been hired to come here to do a job."

He frowned and gestured at her clothes. "What kind of job calls for a getup like that?"

"Todd, if you've come here to pick a fight…"

He pursed his lips, his expression contrite. "Look,

I'm sorry. I'm hot, and I guess I've run out of patience. My plane was late, it took me forever to find this place, and I've been out in the car for three hours, waiting for someone to come back to this...this fortress.''

"You shouldn't have come."

"That's what your mother said when I made her tell me where you were. But I had to see you, Joan."

"Why?"

"You didn't answer my letter. Or call me."

She drew a deep breath, then let it slowly out again. "I didn't have anything new to say."

"I don't believe that." He made a sweeping motion with his hand. "This isn't where someone like you belongs."

She took a step in his direction. "How would you know, Todd?" she asked him. "In all the years I've known you, I don't think you've ever bothered to find out who I am."

He flushed a little at the mild accusation, and in that moment, she almost felt sorry for him. He was so clearly uncomprehending.

He came to her, touching her face lightly, his eyes full of uncertainty. "I know who you are, Joan. You're the woman I love."

She took his hand away. "No, I'm not, Todd," she said gently. "Our relationship was built on dreams we had when we were very young. When we both thought we needed each other to make those dreams come true. But we're very strong and competent people now, and neither one of us needs the other to feel complete. You're an excellent teacher, and one day

you're going to get your school. But it can't be with
me, because that's not *my* dream.''

He rubbed the bridge of his nose tiredly, and when
he looked at her again, she saw annoyance on his
face, as if she was a wayward child who refused to
listen. ''This is ridiculous. You can't tell me that
you've suddenly discovered that *this* is your life's
dream—to live on a ranch with virtual strangers. You
don't even have a home of your own.''

She was losing patience. ''I don't know what my
dream is. But I know what it *isn't*. It isn't to spend
year after year knowing that there's very little I can
do to help the children I'm working with because the
parents can't or won't take the time to get one-on-
one help. I'm not making a difference in their lives.
I'm only getting them through to the next grade
level.''

He made an attempt to protest, but she cut him off
with a raised hand. ''And something else that's not
my dream—to be in a relationship that only exists
because it's easy and convenient. We've grown apart,
Todd. And neither of us has had the courage to admit
that we weren't happy. But I'm doing that now. I'm
sorry.''

''You're not making any sense.''

She stared at him, unable to find anything in his
face resembling agreement with what she'd said.
Frustrated, she walked away.

It took years of practiced self-control to remain
calm and unmoved in his presence, but taking a deep
fortifying breath, she turned to face him once more.
''I'm making sense for the first time in months. I like

the way I feel when I get up in the morning now. Here I really see the difference I can make with a child. I think I've helped the young girl in this family. And her father.''

There was a short silence. Then Todd laughed suddenly. The sound had an unpleasant edge to it, and when he spoke his tone was thick with fury. "My God. The kid's father—you're in love with him, aren't you?''

"No," she said, though even to her own ears the denial came too quickly.

In love with Cody Matthews? It seemed impossible, but it was suddenly as if all the emotions in her had been stripped to reveal this clear inevitable essence.

She swung away from Todd's cynical gaze and moved to the door with brisk efficiency. "I'd like you to leave now," she said in a cool voice. "We don't have anything further to discuss.''

For a moment his face darkened with anger, but eventually he came toward her. She avoided his eyes, staring off into the middle distance of the room, but she knew his features would be sullen and brutally contemptuous. When he made no further attempt at conversation before stalking out of the room, relief was the only thing she felt.

She struggled to compose herself, struggled to find some way back to the buoyant, joyful mood she'd known only an hour ago. But the argument with Todd had left her feeling flayed and unsteady, and his accusation seemed burned into her brain.

She left the study, eager for the safety of her bedroom, knowing that for the rest of the evening she couldn't be with the Matthews family. As for what she had hoped for later with Cody…that seemed impossible now.

Her hand was on the doorknob when she became aware of another presence in the hallway. She turned her head to find Cody watching her. He leaned against the doorjamb of his own room, arms folded across his chest. The light from the hallway emphasized his cheekbones and lent blue fire to his hair, but she couldn't read his expression.

"Everything all right?" he asked softly.

"Yes," she managed to articulate.

He came to stand at her side, and when she lifted her eyes to his, she saw the tender concern in his eyes. "You look tired," he said.

"I am. It's been a long day." Unconsciously she retreated a couple of steps, until she could feel the doorknob pressing into her back. "I think I'll skip dinner, if you don't mind. All I really feel like right now is a good night's sleep."

"Of course," he said, giving her a small, understanding smile. Then he leaned forward suddenly and touched his lips to hers in a kiss so gentle that her heart reeled with the sweetness of it. "Sleep well."

She nodded and escaped into her room. The mirror over her dresser revealed a woman with deep color in her cheeks and eyes as bright as shallow water. She ran a distracted hand through her hair, as she tried to make sense of her emotions.

In love with Cody Matthews? Impossible. Attracted, absolutely. But *love?* No. She mistrusted that impulse completely.

Annoyed with herself, she jerked away from the mirror. There was no way to think about it without touching something frightening.

I am not in love with Cody Matthews. I am not.

Feeling suddenly desperate, she ripped a blank page out of her notebook, then settled at the small desk, ready to write. She worked on the list for over an hour. Approached it from every possible angle. She thought she'd create a hundred lists if she had to, all Cody's faults, all his failings, and when she'd finished, the very suggestion of loving him would be out of her head, out of her thoughts. She felt better already, knowing she could manage this.

But in the end, she went to bed exhausted and disappointed. For the first time ever, her tried-and-true method of relieving stress had deserted her. All she was left with was a sizable wad of discarded paper on the corner of the desk and a hand that ached from writing.

Taking deep, unsteady breaths, Joan lay in bed and stared up at the shadowy ceiling. It seemed that when it came to matters of the heart, no list could begin to capture her feelings for Cody Matthews.

CHAPTER THIRTEEN

HE HAD WANTED to make love to her last night.

Flush with the excitement and fun of the day's event, thankful to Joan for showing him that he and Sarah could regain what they'd once shared, Cody had been ready to admit it—he wanted Joan Paxton.

She'd welcome him, too. It was the kind of truth you felt in your bones. He knew women well enough to recognize the signs, to know that somewhere in the past week or so they'd both made the leap to something else, something more. Not a business relationship. Not even friendship, really. Pure, unadulterated lust between a very attractive woman and a man who'd been away from the game far too long.

But that had been before the damn boyfriend had made his appearance. Before the private conversation between Joan and Todd, whatever it had been, had put the wariness back in her eyes. Cody had sensed her withdrawal immediately. He hadn't been able to resist kissing her just to make sure, and—who was he kidding?—just to touch her again. But he'd been smart enough not to push.

What *had* transpired in the study between Joan and that immaculate, stiff-necked SOB? Was she still in love with the guy? Cody's conversation with Joan's friend at the school had indicated their break had been unexpected after so many years together. Had Todd Ingles's trip here made her realize just how much she missed him? How much she regretted that decision? Hell's half acre, Cody thought. How could she be mooning after that ass when she was supposed to be wanting *him?*

He told himself he should let her sort it out herself. But in midafternoon he came up from the barns and onto the *portal* and saw Joan curled in the shade on a lounge chair, that inevitable notebook of hers lying across her lap. He was hot and tired after spending the morning trying to make a bunch of ornery cattle stand still long enough for Doc Swain to examine them.

It didn't help that the Texas summer had finally landed with a thud, and that she had on one of the shorts outfits she'd bought since coming here. He felt his heart jolt at the sight of her. Too bad she wasn't wearing one of those throat-choking outfits she'd arrived in. The sight of her shapely legs and slim bare arms was almost more than he could bear.

She glanced up as he covered the distance between them, and he would have given anything to take the misery out of her eyes.

"You the only one braving the heat?" he asked, trying to keep his tone neutral and nonchalant. He sat on the edge of the lounger as she moved her legs aside.

Closing her notebook, she nodded. "Walt's still worn-out from yesterday, I think. He's watching television in his room. I'm not sure where Sarah's gone."

"To the movies in Goliath. One of her friends from school called this morning and invited her. She won't be back until supper."

"I'm surprised she has the energy for it in this heat."

"Welcome to Texas," he replied sympathetically. "So what are you up to?"

She looked down at her notebook, then shook her head. "Just trying to get my thoughts in order, I suppose."

"More lists? Are they really that helpful?"

"Definitely," she said in a firm voice, then frowned. "But not so much today, it seems."

He studied his clasped hands, which hung loosely between his knees. She sounded so listless and sad. If only he could take that away from her, he thought. If only Todd Ingles had never come here.

He raised his head as a thought occurred to him. "Tell you what," he began. "I might have a solution for us both. How about a nice, cool swim? Do you have a bathing suit here?"

"No."

He scraped a hand across his chin. "Well, leave that to me. Grab a towel and meet me in the foyer in thirty minutes."

PUNCTUAL AS EVER she was in the foyer in twenty-five minutes, a beach bag and sunscreen borrowed from Merlita in one hand and her notebook in the other. She had no idea what Cody was up to. Maybe he planned to take her to a community or country-club pool in the area. Anyplace cool would be nice, she thought.

Unexpectedly the front door opened behind her. It was Cody, rushing in as if he thought he was late, bringing a blast of air with him from the outside that felt like someone had opened the door of a smelting furnace.

He grinned when he saw her. "Come on, let's go."

He led her to the Rover, which was still running. As he pulled away, he jerked his head toward the rear of the vehicle. "Check out the back seat."

She swiveled and a short investigation revealed a large folded blanket, Cody's own towel and a small plastic bag, the kind discount stores provided. "What's in the bag?" she asked.

"That's your swimsuit. Hope it fits. I got it at the trading post nearest to the ranch, and the selection stank."

She brought the bag to the front seat and removed a bathing suit. It was a one-piece neon-pink thing with high-cut legs, but a modest neckline. Flipping the tag over, she saw that it was close enough to her size. Unfortunately it also had a rather embarrassing catch-phrase printed across the bodice in bold, black letters: EVERYTHING'S BIGGER IN TEXAS.

"Not bad," she said. She cocked a wry look his way as she tapped lightly on the lettering. "Can't say I care much for the sentiment, though."

He tossed her a grin. "Hey, it could have been worse. It was either this one or a lime-green thong, and I figured if I brought that back, you'd just throw it in my face."

"Wise choice," she agreed with a laugh, and realized that she was feeling oddly exhilarated. "So where are we going?"

"You'll see."

"Are we still on Luna D'Oro land?"

"Yep."

In a few minutes he pulled off the road, cutting along a grassy double-ribboned path of pasture land that wasn't nearly as sparse as the landscape that she'd become used to around the ranch. They bumped along for about a mile, down ravines and then up again, past lazy cattle and two-hundred-year-old live oaks.

Cody cut the ignition. "We're here," he proclaimed.

Joan looked around her. "We're where? I don't see anything but pasture and cows and—"

"The best swimming hole for a hundred miles." He pointed over the steering wheel, toward a squat, cylinder-shaped object that sat on high stilt legs under a canopy of tall trees.

"What are you talking about? It's a tower."

"A *water* tower, Joanie. Holding the prettiest, coolest water you'll ever see. Part of the irrigation system we use runs through it before it gets distributed. We come here all the time when the days get too hot. Even Pa makes the trip up the ladder. Come on," he coaxed, and already he was sliding out of the truck, turning away from her to pull off his clothes. "Get into your suit. I won't look."

In no time Cody had stripped to his suit and was urging her to hurry into hers while he kept his back turned. The suit he had picked out for her fit reasonably well, although she was chagrined to realize that for all its simplicity in the front—that embarrassing logo notwithstanding—the back was cut nearly to the last knob of her spine. So much for modesty.

Cody, damn him, didn't pretend not to notice. She came around the front of the Rover, and his brows lifted. And when she had to turn to pull her beach bag off the seat, he emitted a low whistle. "Wow! I'm going to have to shop at that trading post more often."

He carried the blanket and their towels. Near the tower, under the highest tree, he spread the blanket on grass so dry it crackled underfoot, then placed their things on top of it.

She watched him covertly; it was the first time she'd had a real glimpse of his chest. Black hair fanned out across healthy bronzed muscles that moved with such fluid energy she yearned to reach out and touch. The desire was so strong that she turned aside, toeing off her shoes so that her mind and body had something harmless to focus on.

He did likewise, and then he took her hand and led her to an iron ladder that went straight up the side of the tower. She eyed the rungs warily.

"You go first," he said. "When you get to the top, there's another ladder on the inside if you want to climb down slowly, but we usually just throw ourselves into the water at that point. It's deep enough to dive."

"Cody, it's…awfully high."

"It just looks that way because we're under it.

Don't worry, I'll be right behind you." His brow
puckered suddenly. "You don't have a thing about
heights like you do about blood, do you?"

"No, but..."

"Not fancy enough for your tastes?" he asked.

Instead of answering him, she grabbed the closest
rung and started up. She set such a slow pace that the
heat of the sun began to feel uncomfortable on her
back, but Cody didn't press her to go faster.

When she reached the top and the interior of the
wooden tower came into view, she could see that
there really was water inside. Six feet from the top
lip, an inviting, still pool lay placidly waiting. It made
her think of the country swimming hole she'd once
enjoyed at camp years ago.

"How's it look?" Cody called up to her.

"Like heaven," she had to admit.

"Then jump."

She couldn't quite bring herself to do that, but the
inside ladder was right there, so she swung one leg
over the side and then the other, making a slow de-
scent. As she expected, the water was so cold it
caused goose bumps, but that was preferable to the
sticky feeling of perspiration. She was halfway into
the pool when there was a whoop from above and
then a splash that sent a spray of water over her. Cody
hadn't waited.

She turned on the ladder, noting that it continued
far beneath the surface, probably all the way down to
the base of the structure. The tower was wider than
it had looked from down on the ground, about fifty
feet across. She waited for Cody to emerge. Beneath

the water she could see the pale wavering image of his body, churning across the distance with deep, powerful strokes. He touched the opposite wall, kicked off and swam back to her, then headed across the distance again without resurfacing.

Only when he'd completed a third lap, when she thought he must surely be out of air, did he reappear directly in front of her. He expelled a pent-up breath and grinned at her, shaking water out of his eyes with one quick flick of his head.

"Come on, Joanie," he cajoled her, the walls causing his words to bounce in hollow echoes. "Don't keep hanging there like a scared landlubber. You can swim, can't you?"

"Yes, but I like a slower approach."

"To what? Having fun? Let go, girl. Just jump in with both feet and see what happens."

"I *am* in," she protested, but she did so with a smile, because he was so persuasive, and the pool and the confined wooden walls of the tower seemed more and more like a summer idyll created solely for the two of them.

She let go of the ladder and treaded water. Then she struck out for the opposite side of the pool, using even strokes she had learned in years of swim classes. Cody was beside her, in front, then all around her, like a playful otter. Deciding to ignore him, she closed her eyes and swam.

Back and forth she kept at it, until her arms felt heavy and her lungs began to burn. Even Cody had given up trying to keep pace or distract her. When she finally came up against one side of the ladder, she found him on the other, only a foot away, watching her with an amused and puzzled smile on his lips.

She scraped water and hair away from her face, then asked, "What's the matter?"

"That's your idea of letting go?" he returned. "I thought I was watching a swim meet in slow motion. You are one uptight methodical lady, Miz Paxton."

She didn't take offense. How could she when the sun bouncing off the water made his eyes look like polished turquoise? "Just because I don't act like a goofy schoolboy turned loose from his mom and dad for the first time—"

"Race you to the other side and back!" he challenged, pushing away from the wall.

She tore off after him, knowing she couldn't beat him since he'd had a full second's head start. No *honest* way, at least.

He reached the opposite side, turned and was just passing her when she propelled her body upward and landed almost fully on top of him. She knew he wasn't expecting such deceit from her, and sure enough, he went under. An instant later she brought her feet up to his broad back and used them to push him farther beneath the surface. The heck with touching the opposite side, she thought, and struck out for the ladder.

She almost made it. Her fingers stretched for a rung when suddenly she felt his hand clamp around her ankle, yanking her backward. She gulped air frantically before she slid beneath the surface. She kicked with her free foot, hard, but got nothing for her efforts. Then she felt Cody's arm slip around her waist and under her breasts, levering her up and out of the water as their bodies came together, slick and cold and as clumsily playful as adolescents coupling in some lovers' lane.

Gasping and laughing, she struggled to pull his hand from around her, digging through the water with her other one to make for the ladder again. But he had superior strength, of course, and held her just out of reach.

She splashed about for a few moments in pure frustration and determination, but then through the chill that the water brought to her body, she felt something else, something warm and thrilling to her insides.

Cody was dragging her slowly toward the ladder, and she stopped struggling. Her cheek was pressed against the wet satin of his chest; his heart pounded in her ear. Her legs continued to scissor, and every so often they collided with his. His every move carried the water back and forth between them in a strong current, so that it seemed as if his body caressed her flesh. It was a heady, delightful sensation.

Finally, laughing, both out of breath from their exertions, they clung to the side of the ladder. Joan opened her eyes, grinning foolishly and ready to berate him for cheating.

The words died on her tongue, and her heart stuttered in her chest. Something in Cody's face told her the teasing time was over. His lips still smiled, but there was such intensity in his gaze that her own smile froze.

There was a moment or two of silence, where the only sound was their breathing. He was one rung above her, and before she realized what he intended, his arm reached out and hauled her upward against his chest. His fingers dug into her wet hair, pulling her head back so that he could kiss her—a passionate invasion that left her gasping when it ended.

He turned her loose, and she was so stunned that she had to make a grab for the ladder rung to keep from sinking beneath the surface of the water.

"That's how to let yourself go, Joanie," he said.

Then he was moving up the ladder, and in another moment he was lost to her in the blinding glare of the summer sun.

THEY LAY ON the blanket in the dappled sunlight and let the water steam from their bodies. The worst heat of the day was over, and with the afternoon winding down, there was a pleasant breeze. The warmth felt restorative to their numbed flesh.

Neither of them said a thing about that kiss in the tower. Joan wasn't going to bring up the topic. That quick intimate gesture had unsettled her, reminding her of just how easy it was to backslide in her efforts to resist Cody's magnetism. As for him, he probably thought nothing of it.

Joan turned her head to look at him. He lay on his back beside her, his eyes closed, hands behind his head, long legs crossed at the ankles. He didn't appear to have a care in the world.

She stopped studying him because every inch of his honey-toned flesh seemed to bring a revelation: the ropy muscle of his thighs, the subtle flex of bone and muscle in his arms, the soft curling hair that arrowed from that strong chest to the waistband of his suit...and beyond.

She squinted into the sun, trying to take her thoughts someplace else, and when that failed, she ran a thumb along the edge of her notebook pages, thinking maybe she ought to try putting her thoughts down on paper.

"You know, Joan," Cody said suddenly, "you're the only woman I've ever known who doesn't know how to relax."

How can I, she wanted to ask, *when all I want to do is lean over and kiss you?* Instead of voicing that, she searched for something safe to say.

"That's not true." Denial was the best she could do.

"Then put that damn notebook away and talk to me. Tell me about life in Alexandria. How does it compare to Texas?"

She laughed. "This is about as far away from Alexandria, Virginia, as a person can get."

He rolled onto his side, tucking one hand against his head so that he could look at her. "Why did you really quit your job?" he asked. "Your friend at the school told me it was an argument with your headmaster, but all the pieces didn't seem to fit."

She could have told him that it was none of his business, but she suddenly found herself eager to know what he thought. Would he see her actions against Mueller as the foolish protestations of the too-prissy schoolmarm he had once accused her of being? Or would he agree with Todd—that she had somehow brought that unpleasantness on herself?

He listened quietly while she gave him an abbreviated version of the story. Telling it, she could almost feel her hand sting again with the force of the slap she'd given Mueller. She ended the narrative with a sigh. It seemed so long ago somehow, and so pointless.

"Well," Cody remarked after a short silence, "I think you made a mistake."

Her blood chilled in spite of the heat. She turned to look at him sharply.

The lazy stretch of his arm captured her hand where it lay on the blanket. "I think you should have sued the bastard. No woman should have to put up with that."

A kind of relieved wonder flooded her veins as she stared at him. Even if she hadn't been half in love with him already, she felt it in that moment.

She was in love with Cody Matthews.

With a sudden laugh, he sat up, then leaned back on one arm. "Sam Houston's whiskers! *That's* why you were so mad at me that day in the hotel lobby when I got out of line. You were still smarting from a run-in with that randy old goat."

"Nooo. I was mad at you because you were rude and overbearing and I'd come to the interview hoping you wouldn't be like every other man in my life at the time."

He looked at her strangely. "Does that include Ingles?"

She mused on that, then said, "Todd and I didn't see the problem with Mueller the same way. We were…going through a difficult time on the day I met you.''

"And then you split up.''

"The relationship wasn't working.''

"And now?''

"Nothing's changed.''

"Do you want it to?''

"No," she said quickly. She frowned at him. "Why would you think that?''

Cody shrugged. "The man came a long way to see you. That says something.''

She grimaced. "It says I'm destined to associate with men who don't know how to take no for an answer.''

He straightened, so that she had to turn her head to meet his gaze. His hand ran tenderly up her arm, cupping her bare shoulder. Her heated flesh felt suddenly charged with fire. "Does that include me, Joan?'' He moved her sun-dried hair aside, kissing the back of her neck lightly. More fire. "Do you want *me* to take no for an answer?''

The reflection of her own yearning was there in his eyes. No use pretending it wasn't. She dragged in a breath. "I don't think I'm capable of saying no to you, Cody. And I don't want to. All I want is for you to kiss me.''

His smile ignited again. He trapped her shoulders in his hands and coaxed her closer, until he could bring her fully into his warm embrace. "Why didn't you say so sooner?'' he said softly. "I never like to keep a lady waiting.''

Their swimsuits were cast aside in moments. Joan

was too filled with joy to be proficient, but it didn't matter. Cody seemed to have such knowledge of her and how to arouse her. He moved with inflaming expertise, touching her everywhere, tongue playing tag, working his hips against hers in slow, grinding circles until she felt sure they had been forged into one. She squeezed her eyes shut. She heard herself crying out for him to hurry, the words harsh and frantic, her body rising to welcome him.

He resisted her speed. "Open your eyes, Joanie," Cody murmured against her ear, feathering kisses along the side of her face.

Somehow she obeyed. "Don't make me wait," she gasped, hardly recognizing her voice.

"Easy, sweetheart," he said softly. "I want to go slow. Show you how many ways I can make your body respond."

He stroked her until her breathing became less hurried and her heart no longer seemed to be trying to pound its way out of her breast. She smiled at him and pulled him closer. "Do you think I haven't already imagined those ways? That's all I've been able to think about for days."

"You always look so serious. I'd never have guessed."

She took his face in her hands, touching her lips to his brow. "These beautiful eyes. One look can make me feel hot and cold at the same time." Her teeth nipped lightly at his lips. "This mouth—with kisses like warm honey." She ducked her head to his torso, letting her tongue slide languorously around one hard, dark nipple, sucking, worrying it between her teeth.

"This chest—making my breasts ache for your touch."

His body twitched. He chuckled low in his throat and then buried his hands in her hair to drag her head up to his. "You and your damn lists," he whispered thickly.

CHAPTER FOURTEEN

CODY LEANED BACK on his elbows and watched Joan dress. He'd already done so, but she seemed to be having difficulty.

"Need help?" he asked as she struggled to hook her bra. He had to resist a smile. She had modestly turned her back to him, and that action didn't fit at all with his memories of how wantonly she'd behaved only an hour ago.

"I've got it," she replied.

He rose, anyway, pushed her hands away and finished the job. Unable to resist, he laid a trio of kisses across the sun-blushed smoothness of her shoulders.

She looked back at him. "We have to go, Cody. It'll be dark soon."

"I know," he said with a sigh, wishing he could control the earth's rotation. But already the straight white dart of light that had been today's sun had bled into the horizon. A gold-and-pink-and-lavender sunset gave the air a wondrous trancelike quality.

He watched her pull on her blouse and then rescue the rippling fall of her hair from beneath the collar. Her breasts lifted with every breath. She started tugging on her sneakers, and his hands itched to run along the strong, shapely length of her legs. *God help me,* he thought. He was so infatuated with her no move she made seemed innocent anymore.

She turned her head, favoring him with a pretty frown. "You're making me very self-conscious, sitting there watching me like that."

"I don't want to *watch,*" he said, his tone rich with meaning.

He reached out to twitch apart the top button of her blouse. His finger slid along the space between her breasts until it touched the top of her bra.

She slapped his hand away. "Behave. We have to go home. I want to walk Sarah through some stress-coping strategies tonight, and I'm not sure how she'll react."

He knew that look on her face. "She'll do fine, Joan. You'll see."

"I'm sure you're right. I just worry." She thumped him playfully on the chest. "She's so stubborn. It's easy to see where she gets that streak."

His heart jerked in his chest. He looked at her, letting his mind make patterns he'd never dared before. Joan wasn't like any woman he'd ever known. She fought hard for what she believed in. Cared deeply about people. Most of all, she was bringing Sarah back to him, little by little. Didn't she deserve to know the truth?

"What is it?" she asked, her smile fading.

For too many years he'd kept the secret. Not even Pa knew. But now it came bearing down on Cody like a runaway mustang—Joan was someone he could trust. Someone he *wanted* to trust.

He gave her a plain, hard stare. "Well, that's the

funny thing about it, Joan. Sarah *doesn't* get her stubborn streak or anything else from me. Because I'm not her father.''

By the look on her face he'd shocked her, just as he'd known he would. She was silent for a while, then, in a voice that was barely audible, she asked, ''What do you mean, you're not Sarah's father?''

He settled back on the blanket, one hand resting on one cocked knee. Where to begin? he wondered. He'd never told the story to anyone, so he had no way of knowing how it would be received. The beginning, he supposed. Wasn't that always the best way?

''It's ridiculous how clichéd the truth really is,'' he said. ''Daphne didn't get pregnant by me. When she wasn't sleeping in my bed, it turns out she was working her charms on the gardener. He worked on the family estate the last summer Daphne and I were together. Sarah's father is Roger Gleason.''

Joan gasped. ''The man who stopped me on the street that day.''

''Yes.''

''But Daphne told you the child was yours?''

''I guess I looked like the lesser of two evils. Gleason didn't have a cent to his name. And she probably thought telling her father I'd gotten her pregnant was easier than telling him she'd been sneaking off to the gardener's cottage when I wasn't in town.''

Her hand seemed to unconsciously find his as she gave him a sympathetic glance. ''How did you find out the truth?''

''Gleason showed up at the ranch years ago. He threatened to tell Edward Ross everything.'' Cody grimaced, remembering that day. "I suppose I could have lived with the truth coming out then, but he went too far, threatened to tell Sarah, as well. I was ready to take him apart for that." He shook his head. "But in the end..."

"You gave him money," she finished for him.

"I'd have given him half the ranch to keep that kind of filth from touching Sarah," he said. "But it turns out he didn't have very high aspirations. I had a private investigator do a little digging. He was out of work, a heavy drinker. All he said he wanted was enough money to make a fresh start in California. I gave him that."

"But it wasn't enough, was it? That's why he came here to see you. That's what he meant about your having something you hadn't finished paying for. Sarah."

"Yes. He shows up every couple of years, and we go through the same routine."

"Is it possible he's lying about being Sarah's father?"

"No." He dismissed the suggestion with a flip of his hand. "He has all the times and dates right. And, without being crude, let's just say Gleason knows things about Daphne that only a man who's been intimate with her would know." He released a long sigh, then continued in a matter-of-fact voice, "Even if I wanted to deny it, you have only to look at Sarah to see the resemblance to him. She's got that bastard's eyes and mouth, not Daphne's."

"That man is Sarah's father," she said with a disbelieving shake of her head. "It seems so impossible. He'll never really go away, will he?"

"Probably not of his own free will. Last time I checked up on him, he was so far into the bottle that he hardly knew his own name. He's killing himself."

She winced. "Oh, God. What a mess. Poor Sarah."

Cody straightened. "Sarah will be fine. She's my kid in every real sense of the word."

"Who else knows?" she asked.

"Just you. I've never even told Pa. It seems simpler that way. Less chance of it ever coming out."

"Will you ever tell her?"

He raked his hand through his hair. "I don't know. Maybe a cleaned-up version someday. The whole truth is just too sordid. Finding out that your mother wanted to abort you would be hard enough, but then to discover that your father was a man like Gleason? There are just some truths too painful to ever be revealed."

She looked at him gravely. "So why did you tell me?"

"Because I..." He stopped, took a breath, then started on a fresh tack. "You've been so good for Sarah." He reached out to run the back of his fingers gently along her cheek. "And for me. When you said what you did about Sarah's stubborn streak, it was on the tip of my tongue to make some glib remark, but I looked at your face and all I saw was integrity and caring and trust, and I couldn't do it. I guess I just don't want any lies between us."

Joan said nothing for a long moment. Her gaze roved over him as though she was seeing him for the first time. And then she came up onto her knees and leaned toward him, locking her arms around him as if he was drowning. The stricken look in her eyes astounded him, made his breath catch in his chest.

"I'm sorry, Cody," she said softly, taking his head in her hands as she touched her mouth to his lightly, over and over again. "I'm so sorry."

They drove home slowly. There were no street-lights to guide them, no neon billboards to point the way. Inside the vehicle, the only illumination was the eerie green light from the dash reflecting off their faces.

"What about Ross?" Joan asked. "Have you heard from him since his visit?"

"No. I wish I thought that was a good sign."

"Perhaps it is. He didn't strike me as the sort of man who was completely unreasonable. Just concerned about his granddaughter."

"I hope that's true. Maybe it's time to give him that visit from Sarah—now that she's doing so well. Show him that she's not a hellion."

"She's dreading it, you know. Yesterday when we were talking, she gave me the impression that she doesn't even like the state of Connecticut, much less her grandfather."

Cody snorted. "That sounds like her."

Joan suddenly turned in the seat, grabbing his arm. "Cody, Sarah thinks she's going to have to *live* with her grandfather."

"What are you talking about? Why would she think that?"

"We were talking yesterday, and I said she might

like visiting. And she said—how did she put it?—'I don't want to live there.' Those were her words exactly. *Live*. Not visit.''

Cody scowled, shaking his head. ''That's not possible. I've never given her the slightest reason to think that.''

''You have to talk to her,'' Joan insisted. ''Find out. It makes sense if you think about it. Her behavior started to deteriorate after Edward Ross's first visit, didn't it? It's almost as if she's trying to punish you for something she thinks you've done. And she definitely has fears of abandonment. Please talk to her.''

She was so agitated that he nodded agreement. He didn't see how that could be the problem, but by the time they reached Luna D'Oro, he'd promised to talk to Sarah that night.

But once home, Merlita met them with the news that Sarah had gone to bed early without supper, claiming that she'd eaten too much candy at the movies and didn't feel well. And just as troubling, Walt hobbled out to the foyer to inform him that Cody's attorney had phoned and wanted a return call as soon as possible.

Seeing Cody's scowl, Joan spoke up. ''Go call your attorney. I'll check on Sarah.''

He nodded with a grateful smile, then hurried to the study, his heart hammering in his chest.

JOAN FOUND SARAH in her bed, the glow from a night-light painting inky shadows along the bedroom walls. She looked up sleepily as Joan came into the room.

"You feeling all right?" Joan asked, touching her forehead.

"Uh-huh."

She gave the girl a knowing look. "No mysterious fevers?"

Sarah made a chagrined face. "Nothing like that. Just too many candy bars, I guess. Grandpa Walt gave me some tablets to chew." Her gaze flickered toward the door. "Where's Daddy?"

"He'll be in to check on you soon. Do you need anything?"

"No. Grandpa said you went for a swim at the water tower today. Did you like it?"

Oh, yes. She didn't have the words to describe just how much. And certainly nothing she could share with a twelve-year-old. "I had a wonderful time," she said with a smile. She tucked the covers around Sarah. "Tomorrow I'll tell you all about it, and you can tell me about how your day went. Good night, Sarah."

She was about to pull the bedroom door closed when Sarah's voice stopped her. "Joan?"

"Yes?"

"I'm glad you came to Luna D'Oro."

"Me, too." She managed to keep the delight out of her voice.

She went to her own room, took a bath and hung the neon-pink bathing suit over the shower rail to finish drying. She hardly recognized her own face in the mirror over the sink. Her skin was lightly tanned, her hair tangled and streaked with golden highlights. It had been years since she'd seen herself this way—

looking as carefree and reckless as a teenager after a long day at the beach.

She touched her lips, finding them sensitive and slightly swollen. Cody's kisses had done that. Hot. Demanding. Wonderful.

She closed her eyes and thought of him again, broad and strong, and yet so gentle and skilled a lover that her blood blazed with fresh urgency just imagining his hands on her flesh. What was she going to do? How could she construct a life anywhere else now that she knew what could be found right here? But as beautiful as today had been, no declarations had been whispered, no commitments made. With Sarah's improved behavior, there was nothing to keep her at Luna D'Oro.

She picked up her brush and ran it ruthlessly through her hair. She wouldn't think about that right now. There were other things to worry about, such as the significance of the after-hours telephone call from Cody's attorney.

The study door was still closed when she passed it. Walt was reading in the family room and told her that Merlita had gone out for the evening and left dinner for them warming in the oven. Their eyes met as she thanked him, and without a word, she knew he was just as worried.

She went into the kitchen. The room was dimly lit by only the light over the stove, but scrupulously clean. A short investigation revealed chicken in the oven and side dishes in the fridge. Joan pulled silverware out of a drawer, wondering if she should fix a plate for Cody. Surely he'd be finished with the phone call soon. The fact that he hadn't made an appearance yet seemed like a bad omen. Her stomach knotted.

Planning to eat in the kitchen, she had just set a place mat on the small table when she turned around and saw Cody standing in the doorway. She met his gaze squarely and offered a small smile. Her heart clenched when he didn't return it. Bad news, then.

Trying to appear undaunted, she motioned toward the table. "Merlita left us a dish of chicken. There's potato salad and baked beans, as well. Do you want some?"

"No."

She watched him stride across the kitchen, open the refrigerator door and pull out a cold beer. His lips were clamped in a thin line.

"Was it bad news?" she asked.

He twisted off the cap and threw it toward the trash can a few feet away. "Just about as bad as it can get," he said in cold, measured words. "Ross's attorneys have notified mine that they'll be filing for custody this week."

"Oh, no, Cody."

"It gets even better. They've found out about Sarah's real father."

Her nerves fluttered. She sank onto one of the kitchen chairs, her lips parted in shock. "How?"

He took a long swallow of beer, then thumped it on the counter. He leaned back against the ceramic-tile top, crossing his arms over his chest. His eyes, when they met hers, were bleak. "My attorney said something about an investigation and a report that

Ross received this week. I'm sure I'll have all the gory details soon enough. Hell, considering Edward's financial status, it may even make the tabloids.''

"I can't believe he'd take the chance of hurting Sarah that way. He wouldn't be so cruel.''

"Edward was never afraid to go after something he really wanted. And he'll certainly have enough to impress a judge with what a bad influence I am on Sarah. What a failure I am as a father.''

"A failure?'' she repeated with a frown. "He doesn't stand a chance of making a judge believe that.''

"As a matter of fact, he does. My attorney thinks Ross has someone who can offer a pretty powerful testimony in court.''

She couldn't resist a skeptical look. "Who?''

He snorted in disgust. Picking up the beer bottle, he lobbed it into the trash. It landed so hard she heard the glass shatter. He gave her a hard stare. "You.''

That statement brought her to her feet. "What?''

"You're going to be Ross's star witness against me.''

"He's out of his mind. What could he possibly be basing that on?''

She watched him as he stared down at the floor a long time, as if trying to find command of his temper. The light made the lines in his face look deeper than they were. At last he said quietly, "He's basing it on the conversation he had with you during his visit. He says you stated quite plainly that I was…in over my head raising Sarah. That she has needs I can't handle. That I put business first, before family.'' He lifted his eyes to her, and the look in them was so fierce she flinched. "Any of that sound familiar?"

"No!" The words clawed at her heart. Her memory stretched to remember that afternoon exactly as it had happened. She could feel her face flooding with heat. "Yes! But he's completely twisting my words."

"Is he?"

The question, simply stated, hurt almost beyond bearing. "Do you think I would betray you that way?"

"When we talked about what I should be doing to help Sarah, I seem to recall those same complaints."

Her senses swam with panic and loss, but she wouldn't allow him to judge her this way. She tossed her silverware back in the drawer, her appetite gone. "A frank discussion with a parent involving my professional opinion is not something I share with just anyone. He can try to make it whatever he wants, but that doesn't make it true."

She stood directly opposite him, seeing in that stare of his that he couldn't, or wouldn't, accept that. Softly she added, "You don't believe me, do you?"

"It doesn't matter what I believe," he said, jerking away to bang shut a cupboard door that had canted open. "What I *know* is that I'm about to go into the toughest fight of my life, and one of the people I thought would be in my corner is going to be used against me."

"I won't let him use me that way."

"Whether you end up being a hostile witness or not doesn't matter. His side will make sure your comments get heard. The damage will be done."

"Cody, how can I—"

He swung back to face her. "Let's drop it for now, all right? I'm tired. I have a lot to think about. Frankly, more than anything else I'm worried about this business with Roger Gleason coming out." He sighed heavily, rubbing a weary hand across his chin. "I don't want Sarah hurt by it."

"There has to be something we can do," she said, desperately trying to figure out what that might be.

He strode across the kitchen. "I'm going to my attorney's office first thing in the morning. Don't look for me at breakfast."

"Cody—"

He glanced back over his shoulder at her. In a tired, unmetered voice, he said, "I think the best thing you could do right now is stay out of it."

SARAH WAS DREAMING. Familiar images where she was on Ladybug in the far pastures, surrounded by a herd of beautiful stallions that were swift and eager to run for the sheer joy of it. Her father was beside her on his own black mount. She smiled at him, and with a deep laugh he coaxed his horse into a gallop, pulling away. Her hand flew out to stop him, but already she had lost sight of him, hearing only the sound of hoofbeats pounding in the distance....

The dream bled away, as it always did, and Sarah opened her eyes. The well-known touchstones of her bedroom were revealed, hazy and golden in the early-morning light streaming through her window.

With a sigh she turned on her side—and saw her father.

He was seated on her desk chair beside her bed, bending forward, staring at his hands. They held *Stable Buddies,* the statue she'd glued back together. She was disappointed to see that he was dressed for travel, she knew what that meant—but he looked so tired she didn't have the heart to be mad at him.

"Daddy?"

His gaze lifted. He smiled. "Good morning, buttercup. You were asleep when I came in last night. How do you feel?"

"Okay. Is something wrong?"

"No," he said quickly. "Not a thing. I just wanted to check on you."

"Before you go."

He grimaced. "I have to drive into San Antonio this morning. I don't want to. I'd rather spend the day with you."

"Honest?"

"Do you really think I'd rather sit in a stuffy office with a bunch of old coots with too much money and not enough sense when I could be here with you, swimming in the water tower or chasing jackrabbits on horseback?"

She giggled. "You're being silly."

"No, honey, I'm being serious." He lifted the statue. "This is how I see us, Sarah. Two buddies. Maybe a little patched together in some places, but inseparable. Don't you?"

"I used to." She swallowed, hoping she didn't sound as sulky as she felt.

He reached out to tuck a strand of hair behind her ear. "I know I haven't been around as much as I should have lately. I've been trying to change that. But some things take time to work out. Do you understand?''

Her stomach knotted. Her father never talked to her like this. Never looked so sad. It scared her. "I guess," she mumbled.

"Let's talk about your grandfather Ross for just a minute. He wants to know you better. Even after that little stunt you pulled." He held out a forestalling hand when she moved fretfully and started to speak. "I know, I know—you don't like him."

"I hate him."

"Why, Sarah? You hardly know him."

Her heart went wild in her chest, like a bird tangled in wire. Was today the day she'd be packed off to Connecticut? She felt so vulnerable in that moment, and completely terrified. Unable to speak for the lump of fear in her throat, she only shrugged.

He cocked his head at her curiously. "Joan says you think you're going to have to live with him. Is that true?''

She turned her face away, because tears had begun to star her vision.

He took hold of her forearm, giving it a little stroke. "Sarah, talk to me." His tone didn't sound angry, only frustrated. "I can't fix things if you won't tell me what's wrong."

She swallowed again. If she really was going to get shipped off today, he should at least know that she'd known for a long time, that he hadn't fooled her one bit. She turned back to face him. "I heard you and

Grandpa Walt talking after he left. About sending me to Connecticut.''

''For a visit. That's all.''

''That's not what you said.''

''What do you think I said?''

''You said Grandfather Ross should raise me.''

He leaned forward and knuckled away tears that she hadn't even known were running down her cheeks. ''Sarah, honey,'' he said with a shake of his head, ''that wasn't quite the way it was. Your grandfather Ross doesn't think I...''

Her father paused as though trying to figure out how to say what he had to say. ''He questioned the way I've raised you. You know how mad I can get. So when I was talking to your Grandpa Walt later, I said he should have to raise you and find out how hard it is. How hard it is for *any* single dad to keep up with a growing young girl who's as much a handful as you are.''

''I don't think I'm a handful,'' she protested. ''At least, not too much.''

He grinned. ''You *are* a handful. But I like that. You're smart, so I have to keep on my toes around you, and your jokes make me laugh, and when the day's been tough at the office or the cattle won't cooperate, I know you'll be here to make me feel good. What would I do with a timid, silly rabbit for a daughter who just did whatever I said and never had an opinion of her own?''

''You haven't been so happy with me lately,'' she pointed out.

''Yeah, but mostly that's my fault, because I didn't

know how to help you. But we're going to work on that."

"So I don't have to go to Connecticut?"

He set the statue back on her desk. With his chin resting on his clasped hands, he looked down at the floor. "Sarah, I'd like you to believe me when I say this," he said at last. "I love you. I would never abandon you, and there isn't anything or anybody in the world strong enough to keep me out of your life. But there are other people who love you and want to be a part of your life, too. Your mother's father is one of them."

"But I don't know him."

"He has no family now, and he's very lonely. Would it be so bad to get to know him better? To let him see that you turned out just as wonderful and loving as his own daughter?"

"Why don't you just tell him?"

"Your mother would probably like to think that the two of you were friends."

Sarah blinked, hard. Her father never talked about her mother. If she did what he asked, got to know her grandfather Ross better, would she find out more about her mother, too? "I guess it wouldn't be so bad. I don't really hate him. I just…don't want to lose you. I love you, Daddy."

He tilted in the chair until his mouth touched her forehead. "Sarah, my sweet girl, you'll never lose me. I'll always be a part of your life."

She couldn't help it. Her eyes were full of tears. He saw them and pulled her into his arms, into a hug that seemed like it would crush her bones. But it felt good, too. Like there was nothing to be afraid of anymore. Like all the months she'd been thinking he didn't want her had just been part of a big ugly dream that now vanished in the morning light.

CHAPTER FIFTEEN

BY NOON Joan was on a plane to Connecticut.

She stared down at her lap, going over the list she'd created last night during the long hours when sleep hadn't come. *Ways to Persuade Edward Ross to Drop the Custody Suit.* It was a pitifully short list, and she wasn't sure what it would accomplish, if anything. But she had to try.

This morning Cody had left Luna D'Oro for San Antonio, and she hoped that the meeting with his attorney went well. But she couldn't do as he asked, just stay on the sidelines praying for a miracle. She had an emotional investment in the Matthews family now. And she had a professional viewpoint to offer. She couldn't just sit by and see all the progress they'd made with Sarah destroyed. So an hour after Cody's departure, she'd told a surprisingly calm Sarah that she had an errand to attend to and would be back at Luna D'Oro by dinnertime. Then she called the airlines for the first flight out.

Walt had been hard to convince. Needing Edward Ross's home address, she'd been forced to tell him her intentions and then swear him to secrecy. Even as he made the arrangements to have Tomas drive her to the airport, he'd done nothing but scowl and mutter, voicing the opinion that she should wait for Cody to come home. Together they could work out a game plan, he'd told her.

But could they? Joan wondered as she gazed out the window of the plane. Walt didn't know how cold and abrupt Cody had been last night in the kitchen. How shocked he'd been to discover that the woman he'd made love to only hours ago, the person with whom he'd shared the deepest secrets of his heart, was the same woman he now suspected of betraying him. How could they work together on *anything*— including a personal relationship—with that kind of suspicion between them?

She sighed. *One problem at a time, Joan,* she told herself. When she'd done what she could to sway Ross, then she could concentrate on what she should do next about Cody.

The cab ride from the airport took her to Edward Ross's home in no time. The house—big and sprawling across several acres—was unexpectedly approachable and unpretentious. Five minutes after her arrival, Joan was sitting in a small, delightfully bright sunroom, prepared to face Sarah's maternal grandfather.

He didn't keep her waiting. When he appeared, she stood and held out her hand. He took it in a friendly enough manner, but there wasn't a flicker of what he was thinking on his lined face. He was dressed severely in a dark business suit.

"I apologize for not calling first," Joan said quickly. "But frankly, I wasn't sure you'd see me otherwise."

"My quarrel isn't with you, Miss Paxton."

"No, it's not. But I am involved. You've brought me into this struggle between you and Cody."

"I'm afraid it couldn't be helped," he said in a very precise way. "If the purpose of this visit is to talk me out of using your testimony in court, I'm afraid you've wasted your time."

She held out a forestalling hand. "Mr. Ross, please. Just hear me out. I haven't come all this way for myself, or for Cody. I've come because of Sarah."

His chin notched up slightly. Finally he said, "Go on."

"I'm not sure how much you know about my involvement with the Matthews family. Cody asked me to come to his ranch to evaluate his daughter."

"Evaluate Sarah for what?"

"Attention deficit disorder. It's not all that unusual in this day and age. I'm sure you've heard of it."

"Of course. You think Sarah suffers from it?"

"No."

He shifted, as though losing interest. "What does this have to do with the custody suit?"

"Please bear with me. I'd like you to understand that I have had a great deal of experience with children undergoing stressful changes in their lives." She gave him an abbreviated version of her credentials as a therapist and teacher. "I don't tell you these things to impress you. I only want you to understand that I'm a professional who has spent some time with Sarah. Normally I wouldn't share my findings with anyone other than the parents, but considering the circumstances, I think you should be aware that the problems I've seen in Sarah are emotional, not a result of ADD.''

Ross turned away from her, crossing to the wall of windows where sunlight made pretty patterns on a bank of potted plants. Ruthlessly he pinched off the drooping head of a dead bloom. He looked back at her, as though suddenly remembering her presence. ''All the more reason for me to have custody of the child. I have resources up here that Cody never dreamed of. If Sarah needs help, I can get it for her.''

She moved toward him. ''Forgive me for saying this, but you're wrong. The kind of help Sarah needs doesn't involve money. What she needs is the stable, secure environment that Cody is building for her at Luna D'Oro. I'm sure you love her and only want the best for her. But I've spent a great deal of time watching the two of them, and what's best for Sarah right now is to stay with her father, not be pulled into a court battle that can only hurt and confuse her more.''

''The child runs wild down there,'' he snapped with a contemptuous movement of his hand. ''You can't deny what happened during my visit.''

''No, but I think I can explain it.''

He turned to listen, and she told him of her suspicions about Sarah's feelings about him, the reason her behavior had been so outrageous that day.

He obviously didn't like what he was hearing. White lines of tension bracketed his mouth. ''If the child hates me, it's because Cody's planted that idea in her head.''

''I don't believe that. My conversations with Sarah

have never indicated that kind of manipulative behavior from Cody."

"Then perhaps you were too protective of her father to see it."

She knew what the man implied. Although her face felt warm, she met his gaze squarely, refusing to acknowledge the insinuation. "I'm trained not to miss signs like that. I'm convinced that much of Sarah's recent behavioral problems stem from a misunderstanding she has about what role you want to play in her life. Cody and I spoke just yesterday about trying to get to the bottom of it with her."

Ross looked only slightly less annoyed. "You said yourself that he was overwhelmed by the task of raising Sarah."

She bit her lip, trying to find the right words. "I've thought a lot about that conversation we had, and I can see now that my comments were inappropriate. They could be easily…misunderstood, particularly by someone who only wants the best for Sarah. I'm embarrassed to admit it, but I failed that day to pick up on your distress and the reasons behind it."

"Don't be too hard on yourself, Miss Paxton. I think you're a very bright woman. That's one of the reasons why I'll be delighted to see you testify."

She stiffened. "Mr. Ross, your lawyers will certainly ask if I said the things I did to you, and I'll have to tell the truth. I did. But you might want to think about how much benefit you'll get out of my testimony, because Cody's attorney will have an opportunity to question me, as well, and I don't intend to do him any harm."

Ross came closer, and his eyes seemed as cold and hard as ever. "I'm amazed you can defend the man. He's deprived me of my granddaughter for twelve years."

She knew that was true, but she couldn't indicate she was aware of that fact. "I can't speak for Cody about that matter," she hedged. "But I understand that you were once friends and business associates. Surely you're able to put your differences aside long enough to get to the truth of what happened back then."

He shook his head. "You give the man too much credit."

"No, I don't believe I do," she countered quickly. "But am I giving you too much credit, Mr. Ross?"

"What is that supposed to mean?" he snapped, eyes flashing now.

"I would like to honestly believe you want what's best for Sarah. Not what would give you some satisfactory revenge for what you think he did in the past."

He jerked visibly. "I will not stand here and be insulted in my own home—"

"Please," Joan implored. "All I'd like you to think about is your motivation for pursuing this custody battle. Do you really think that uprooting Sarah—at a very crucial time of her life—is really what she needs? Everything she knows and loves is in Texas. I don't think you could do more harm to Cody than taking his daughter away from him, but you won't gain Sarah's love by doing it." Edward Ross continued to stare at her, suddenly looking like a weary old man. But there was no gentle way of stating this. She added in a softer voice, ''And you may get Sarah, but she's not your daughter. It won't give Daphne back to you.''

The silence in that peaceful sunlit room was unbearable. Then Ross moved toward the double glass doors, clearly indicating their meeting was over.

In a firm, uncompromising tone, he said, ''I don't believe we have anything further to discuss. Good day, Miss Paxton. My housekeeper will see you out.''

THE TWENTIETH-FLOOR conference room at the offices of Chapman, Grainger and Whitaker was everything Cody hated about big-city legal firms. Cold, slick and impersonal. He sat on one side of the firm's mahogany conference table, across from Edward Ross and two of his attorneys, one of whom had been introduced as Grainger, the number-two man on the firm's letterhead.

Cody could feel the hot fingers of a headache reaching into his skull. Since flying up to Hartford to meet with Edward—against his own attorney's advice—Cody had done nothing but spend the past hour being battered by these two legal sharks, while Edward Ross sat quietly by and watched. Cody felt he had held his own, but it was clear that what he had hoped for from this meeting wasn't going to happen.

Ross was not going to drop the suit.

Even worse, there was a chance that he would go for full custody, with no visitation rights for Cody, based on the fact that Sarah wasn't really his child. That thought left him with blood and blind rage pounding behind his eyes, but he knew he couldn't give in to the temptation to reach across the table and throttle the life out of the old man and his two smarmy hitmen.

Tired of this endless confrontation, he rubbed his eyes. He couldn't imagine his life without Sarah in it. But did that give him the right to air all this dirty laundry, knowing how much Sarah would be hurt by it?

In the end, Cody walked out. Not because he'd gained the upper hand or had a snowball's chance in hell of changing anything, but because he needed to think very carefully about his next move.

He said as much to Edward's two legal boys. The attorneys sputtered a protest in almost comical unison. Edward only narrowed his eyes and stilled their complaints with one raised hand.

"Take all the time you want," the old man said calmly. "As long as you're back in this office at nine tomorrow morning, ready to capitulate."

Cody checked into a nearby hotel and sequestered himself at the writing desk in his room. He made only two telephone calls, one to his attorney and one to Sarah, reassuring her that he would be home soon. He did not speak to his father or Joan. There seemed to be no point. What could he tell them that they wouldn't find unbearably upsetting?

Unwilling to lose the time, he did not go out for dinner, and over the course of the evening and beyond, he laid out every conceivable argument he could use against Edward's claim. He listed every significant contact he'd made over the years, anyone who might be able to speak on his behalf, every person of power who owed him a favor.

Somewhere around two in the morning Cody accepted the fact that he had very little to draw upon. Not a single thing of substance, really. He looked at all the hastily scribbled notes, the balled-up pieces of paper that had missed the trash can and laughed grimly.

It was funny, wasn't it? Sometime in the past couple of weeks he'd picked up Joan's habit of list making.

The next day, at nine o'clock precisely, he was back at Chapman, Grainger and Whitaker's mahogany conference table. He hadn't slept, hadn't been able to swallow the coffee he'd bought from a street vendor. Edward and his two lackeys looked as fresh and crisp as newly minted coins.

He drew a deep breath. "Look," he said to Grainger, "I know what you boys want from me. We can hash this out in front of a judge if that's the way it has to be." He slid his gaze toward Edward Ross. "But all I really want right now is to talk to Edward—alone."

"We don't advise that—" Grainger began.

Ross held up a hand, his eyes never leaving Cody. "Leave us alone for a few minutes."

Grainger and his associate looked ready to argue, but one glance from the old man silenced them. The two men departed, leaving Cody and Ross with only dead quiet. Not even the soft, muted bustle of the outer office intruded.

Cody met the older man's stony countenance. "I

don't want to fight you in court,'' he said simply. ''But I won't give her to you willingly.''

Edward Ross picked up a photograph from the file in front of him. It was a picture of Roger Gleason coming out of a bar. It had to be a recent one. The man looked as if he'd rolled out of bed, bleary-eyed and still drunk, no different than he had the day Cody had gone to his Wigwam Motel room.

Edward tossed it across the table until it slid directly in front of Cody. ''She's not really yours to give, is she?''

''Gleason's already made his interest in Sarah quite clear.''

''He's still her father.''

Cody snorted. ''Don't try to play that card with me. You don't give a damn about Gleason, and you're not planning to bring him into Sarah's life. We both know it.''

''Can you really be sure of that?'' Ross asked, flicking a small bit of lint from his coat jacket. His eyes found Cody's again. ''You could have saved yourself the last payment, you know. According to my sources, after Gleason left Texas and you, he made it as far as Louisiana. The man's in a New Orleans hospital right now, probably in the last stages of liver disease. He won't really be an issue. Unless you continue to fight this.''

The news that Roger Gleason might be close to death didn't really surprise Cody. He'd been shocked by the man's appearance during their last meeting. There'd been no sign of the fair-haired boy Daphne had lusted after, and looking into those bloodshot eyes, seeing those shaking hands, Cody had almost been able to feel sorry for him.

But right now, he couldn't think about Roger Gleason. He looked at Edward Ross. "Do you expect me just to turn Sarah over to you?" he asked. "To never see her again?"

"Should I consider your feelings? Did you consider mine the past twelve years?"

Over the tightness in his chest, Cody shot his chair back and stalked to the windows. In the street far below, people were going about their day-to-day existence, while up here, he felt as though he was fighting a battle for his life.

"No," he admitted, "I didn't."

"You were never so selfish in the old days, Cody."

"I never had a kid before," he said softly, his hands pressed against the warm glass. "Never anything as precious as Sarah."

"Was that what you wanted from Daphne all along? A broodmare with good genes? I find the way you concealed my daughter's pregnancy unbearable to even think about. I treated you like family. Like a son. You repaid me by persuading my daughter to give up her child."

Cody swung around. "For God's sake, Edward, think about it. Did you ever know Daphne to have one maternal bone in her body? Maybe you were too wrapped up in business to notice, but your daughter thought having children was the biggest inconvenience a woman could have forced upon her. When she found out she was pregnant, she didn't come to me. She didn't go to Gleason. She went to Europe.

And if I hadn't tracked her down, she would have had—'' He stopped abruptly, unwilling to completely destroy this man's memories of his daughter. "She wouldn't have kept the baby, Edward. And you'd have been none the wiser. That was the way she wanted it.''

After a long silence, Edward said, "That doesn't excuse what you did next.''

"No, I suppose it doesn't,'' Cody replied in a tired voice. He knew what he had to do now. There was no stopping Ross any other way.

He returned to the conference table, reaching across the smooth expanse to gather all the ammunition the lawyers planned to use against him—pictures, affidavits, investigation reports—into one big pile in front of him.

"Here's what I'm willing to do. You destroy this,'' he said, pinning the top picture of Roger Gleason with one finger. "You never let one word of it get any farther than those two rottweilers you have working for you. Sarah never gets called to a witness stand. She never has a meeting in some judge's chamber to ask her who she wants to live with. I give you full custody without a fight.''

Edward Ross stared at Cody. "And what do you get?''

"I get to be a part of her life. You don't cut me out completely. Sarah's got some tough years ahead of her, and she needs to know I still love her, no matter where she's living.''

"You won't stick to an agreement like that.''

"Have your guys draw it up. I'll sign it in blood,

if that's what you want. Just accept the offer. I'll find a way to explain it to Sarah.''

"Why would you concede so easily?"

"Easily!" Cody struggled to get himself under control. He looked down at his hands, realized that they were clenched, then mindfully unclenched them. Through gritted teeth he said, "My gut has been tied in knots from the day I found out you knew about Sarah. I've done nothing but think about ways to fight you if the worst happened. To the detriment of my entire family, including Sarah. But you hold all the aces, Edward. I won't let Sarah think her mother didn't want her, and I sure as hell won't let her learn who and what her father really is. She can't handle it right now. I love her too much to put her through something like this." He sighed, raking a hand through his hair, then shoved the file toward the older man. "So you win."

Edward Ross sat silently for several long minutes, evidently considering the offer. Cody didn't say a word. He wasn't sure he *could* have said any more. His heart felt like one large ache, and a grayness had settled around him like a shroud. Losing Sarah. How would he ever live without her? Could he possibly feel any deader in his grave than he did in this office right now?

Finally Edward rose slowly and went to the mahogany sideboard, where glasses and assorted refreshments sat waiting for clients. From a crystal decanter, he poured two glasses of whiskey, kept one and set the other in front of Cody.

"Drink it," he commanded. "It's early, but you look like hell, Matthews."

Cody couldn't argue that, but he didn't drink.

"I'm sorry it's come to this," the older man said after a while, and for the first time Cody thought he heard regret in Edward's tone. "I meant what I said earlier, about thinking of you like a son. When I found out about Sarah's existence, I didn't really believe it at first."

Cody sat staring at the whiskey glass. He couldn't drink it. Grief had split him in two.

He heard Edward sigh heavily. "I've been very lonely since Margaret died. Retirement isn't all it's cracked up to be."

"No," Cody heard himself say. "I suppose retirement's too tame for an old tiger like you."

There was a long silence. The air-conditioning kicked on with a slight hiss, making the room feel colder.

There was a soft clink as the ice cubes in Edward's glass rattled together. "Sarah has her mother's looks, don't you think?"

"Yes. All the best parts. She's a great kid, Edward."

"It's unfortunate that she dislikes me so much."

Cody swung a glance his way. "I'll persuade her to think otherwise."

Edward finished off his whiskey and poured more. Facing Cody again, he said, "Your Miss Paxton doesn't think it will be that easy. Did you know that she came to see me yesterday? I was on my way to this office when she showed up at my house."

Cody frowned, not certain he'd heard correctly. "What? Why would Joan come here? I told her to stay out of this."

"Yes, well…" Edward cleared his throat. "She doesn't strike me as the sort of woman who lets a man boss her around. In fact, she was quite assertive with me over the conversation she and I had the day I visited your ranch."

"Did she want to persuade you not to call her to testify?"

"Not really. She seemed more concerned with persuading me to leave Sarah right where she is. With you." He downed the whiskey and set the glass on the sideboard. "She seems to think you're a wonderful father."

"I didn't send her to plead my case, if that's what you're thinking."

"It crossed my mind, but I believe what really motivated her was something else entirely. She's in love with you."

Cody stared at Edward, transfixed by those words. Through the gray, gritty hopelessness of it all, his heart flickered to life. "She told you that?"

"Of course not. But I haven't gotten where I am without being able to size up my opponents. She's in love, and she seems like a very capable, very compassionate young woman. What do you intend to do about it?"

Cody didn't know what to think. Or do. His senses felt dulled. Could Joan really be in love with him? It didn't seem possible. Remembering their last unpleasant hour together, Cody had been sure he'd forever destroyed the harmony between them.

"Listen," he said in a dead-level tone to Edward, "I can't think this through right now. All I want to do is go home. Call your guys in here and let's get this over with."

Edward didn't say anything, evidently too pleased with his coup to care how Cody handled this aspect of his personal life. After a moment he reached to the center of the table and punched the intercom button that summoned a secretary.

When the woman acknowledged him, he said shortly, "Could you ask Mr. Grainger to come in, please?"

JOAN HAD COME to a painful decision of her own. It was time to leave Luna D'Oro.

She'd thought about it long and hard on the flight back from Connecticut, and there really was no other choice. She didn't know if her meeting with Edward Ross had made the situation better or worse. She supposed she'd find out eventually if she got a call from his attorneys. Regardless, Sarah was doing much better. As for Joan's personal relationship with Cody, that appeared to be over. Staying here, hoping for more, would only bring humiliation.

If she had any doubts about her decision, it was settled for her when the mail arrived that morning. In the middle of the four-poster bed lay a letter that Merlita had delivered. It had been forwarded by her mother, and the envelope's return address was that of the school she'd applied to before coming here. The Bristol Academy in Portland, Oregon.

Joan slit it open. It was an invitation to come for an interview with the governing body of the school. In stiff, formal wording, they asked if she could call them so that a suitable time could be arranged.

Even the fates, it seemed, were determined to see her away from here.

Skipping breakfast and the prospect of facing any of the Matthews family, she spent the morning packing. The first available flight out wasn't until the afternoon. In the meantime she'd have to come up with a way to make parting as painless as possible.

She sat in the chair in her bedroom and came to the realization that it would be difficult no matter what she did. She'd come to care about this family—all of them—too much to just walk away.

The sounds of piano music reached her. Probably Sarah practicing. She supposed she ought to see how the girl was faring. See if she was handling her father's absence better than Joan was. Maybe, she thought, she should start laying the groundwork for her departure, as well. With a huge sigh, she left her bedroom.

But when Joan reached the living room, she was surprised to discover that it wasn't Sarah at the piano.

It was Cody.

He was perched on the edge of the bench, picking out a one-fingered version of "Buffalo Gal." Badly. She would have backed out of the room, but he lifted his head and saw her.

He beckoned her toward him and gave her that wonderful smile that always made her stomach take an unexpected leap. "Come over here and help me," he said in a petulant voice. "Sarah's been working with me on this, but now she's deserted me for the stables, and I'm lost."

She walked over to the piano. His hand rested on the keyboard, and she stared down at it, remembering how well those fingers had played over her body. Around a hard swallow she said, "You're in the wrong place."

"Show me," he replied, and tugged her hand until she was positioned on the bench beside him.

He seemed oblivious to her presence, fingers picking out random notes. She, however, was aware of nothing but the scent of him, the warmth of his body next to hers. She shifted a little on the bench, eager to escape. "Cody—"

"I know, I know," he said, stopping to look at her. "You want to know how it went." He sighed heavily. "Frankly, it was hell."

Her heart sank. "Then your attorney doesn't think you have much of a case?"

"I don't know what he thinks. I fired him and went up to Hartford to speak to Edward myself. We spent hours in a conference room hashing it out. I didn't get home until just a few minutes ago."

She saw now that he looked completely beat. Dark circles under his eyes. A day-old growth of stubble on his cheeks and chin. "And?" she asked. Her heart rate doubled. "I know it's really none of my business, but I have to know."

"Edward got what he wanted."

She pressed her fingers to her lips, horrified. "Oh, God," she whispered.

"So did I."

"What?"

His mouth lifted in a small smile. "You were right about Edward. He's not really cruel or unreasonable. Mostly he's just a lonely old man who wants to know his granddaughter better. I've agreed to bring Sarah up to visit with him later this summer. He's coming down here for the holidays. We'll work it out, but I keep full custody."

"Oh, Cody, that's wonderful!" she cried, barely able to resist the temptation to hug him. "I'm so relieved he changed his mind."

Cody seemed very calm, continuing to move his hands idly across the piano keys. "I wonder if he would have if you hadn't pointed out a few things to him." His head was low, listening to the notes, and he tilted his gaze to her. "Weren't you going to tell me about your little visit?"

"I don't know," she said hesitantly. "I suppose I wanted to see what came of it."

"Only good things, it seems." He motioned toward her own hands, which were curled in her lap. "Pick out 'Buffalo Gal' for me. I want to surprise Sarah with it tonight."

She did as he asked, going slowly through the song while he matched her movement for movement a few octaves down the piano. She didn't really want to, but Cody seemed determined to learn it. Was it just his way of avoiding an in-depth discussion?

"Let's see now," he said at last, as he frowned down at the keys. "Okay, I think I have it." He made a few false starts, then settled into the tune. To help himself maintain the beat, he sang softly, "'Buffalo Gal, won't you come out tonight? Come out tonight. Come out tonight. Buffalo Gal, won't you come out tonight, and—'" he turned his head to look at her "—marry me?"

She stared back at him, stunned. "What?"

"You know. Marry. Man and woman pledge undying love and devotion to each other before a minister. Have kids. Live happily ever after."

"Don't joke like this."

"Who said anything about a joke?" His eyes looked straight into hers, as though trying to read what was in her heart.

"I can't."

"Sure you can." He straightened to search the top of the piano, where sheet music and lesson books lay scattered. "I even made a list. *Ten Reasons Joan Paxton Should Marry Cody Matthews.* See what a good influence you've been on me?" He scowled. "Now, where the heck did I put it?"

She grabbed his arm to draw his attention. "Cody, I'm leaving today. I have a job interview in Oregon the day after tomorrow."

"Call them and tell them you're not interested."

"Why?"

"Because we need you here."

"No, you don't. Sarah's going to be fine. You said so yourself."

"Well, when have I ever been right? And what about me?" he asked, pulling a face. "I'm hopelessly in need of help."

She shook her head. "You don't need me, Cody."

He captured her chin lightly between two fingers. His eyes were locked with hers, tender and loving. "For once you're not so smart, Miss Paxton. You're wrong. I need you in so many ways I could fill two of your notebooks. I'm a hotheaded cuss who most of the time is too stubborn to admit when he's done something wrong and too blind to recognize when he's done something right. But not about this." His fingers moved to the side of her face, caressing her cheek. "I love you, Joan. And I think you love me. Isn't that the truth?"

She bit her lip, wanting to say no because it would be so much simpler than anything she could ever hope for with this man. Life with Cody Matthews would never be calm or mundane or safe. But just looking at him, something widened in her heart, forever. "Yes," she murmured. "I really do love you."

His smile stretched into a wicked grin. "Then why would you want to go to a place where it rains all the time? Where the kids you teach change every year and the men probably don't ever take their women on worm-fiddling dates? Stay here. Teach me to like the violin. Let me show you that meadow of bluebonnets. We could be swimming in the water tower tomorrow, Joanie. Naked."

He kissed her then, his firm mouth scalding all her blood vessels with intense desire. He pulled her into his embrace, and when awareness of the outside world finally came back, she was against his chest, listening to the hard, steady beat of his heart.

"Leaving does sound rather foolish when you put it that way," she said, wondering if anyone had ever made love on a piano bench.

"Good. Now you're starting to make sense. Everyone will be so relieved."

"They will?"

He kissed the top of her head. "Before I made Pa

and Sarah get lost, I floated the idea of asking you to marry me past them.''

''What did they say?''

''Pa gave me hell for not asking you sooner. He thinks I need even more help than Sarah.''

She smiled at that. Then said worriedly, ''And Sarah?''

''Sarah wants to know if you'll show her how to put on makeup.''

Joan straightened. Was he being serious? She could see in his eyes that indeed he was, that everything really would be all right. Her heart expanded so she could hardly draw breath.

''That list with the reasons I should marry you,'' she asked with a suspicious, playful smile of her own. ''You didn't really come up with ten, did you?''

''Sure did. Where is it?'' he muttered, again sifting through the paper on top of the piano. After a moment or two, he pulled it out. ''Ah, here we go.'' Clearing his throat, he read aloud in a serious voice, '' 'Reason number one—I love her. Reason number two—I'm crazy about her. Reason number three—I adore her. Reason number four—' ''

She didn't find out what reason number four was. By the time Cody got to it, Joan was kissing him again, and the list fluttered to the floor, forgotten.

Presenting...

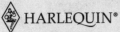

HARLEQUIN®

PRESCRIPTION RX ROMANCE

Get swept away by
these warmhearted romances
featuring dedicated doctors
and nurses.

LOVE IS JUST
A HEARTBEAT AWAY!

Available in December
at your favorite retail outlet:

SEVENTH DAUGHTER
by Gill Sanderson
A MILLENNIUM MIRACLE
by Josie Metcalfe
BACHELOR CURE
by Marion Lennox
HER PASSION FOR DR. JONES
by Lillian Darcy

Look for more
Prescription Romances
coming in April 2001.

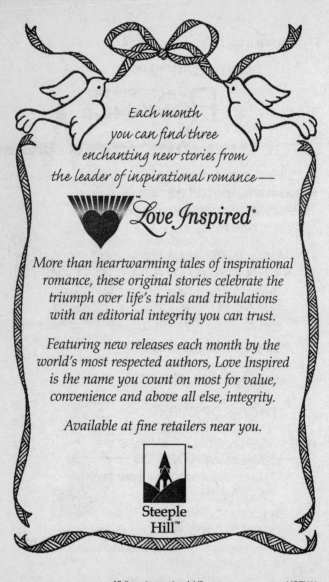

Each month
you can find three
enchanting new stories from
the leader of inspirational romance—

Love Inspired®

More than heartwarming tales of inspirational
romance, these original stories celebrate the
triumph over life's trials and tribulations
with an editorial integrity you can trust.

Featuring new releases each month by the
world's most respected authors, Love Inspired
is the name you count on most for value,
convenience and above all else, integrity.

Available at fine retailers near you.

Steeple
Hill™

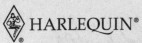
HARLEQUIN®

makes any time special—online...

eHARLEQUIN.com

your romantic escapes

—Indulgences—

- ♥ Monthly guides to indulging yourself, such as:
  - ★ Tub Time: A guide for bathing beauties
  - ★ Magic Massages: A treat for tired feet

—Horoscopes—

- ♥ Find your daily Passionscope, weekly Lovescopes and Erotiscopes

- ♥ Try our compatibility game

—Reel Love—

- ♥ Read all the latest romantic movie reviews

—Royal Romance—

- ♥ Get the latest scoop on your favorite royal romances

—Romantic Travel—

- ♥ For the most romantic destinations, hotels and travel activities

Tyler Brides

It happened one weekend...

Quinn and Molly Spencer are delighted to accept three
bookings for their newly opened B&B, Breakfast Inn Bed,
located in America's favorite hometown, Tyler, Wisconsin.

But Gina Santori is anything but thrilled to discover her
best friend has tricked her into sharing a room with
the man who broke her heart eight years ago....

And Delia Mayhew can hardly believe that she's
gotten herself locked in the Breakfast Inn Bed
basement with the sexiest man in America.

Then there's Rebecca Salter. She's turned up at the
Inn in her wedding gown. Minus her groom.

*Come home to Tyler for three delightful novellas
by three of your favorite authors: Kristine Rolofson,
Heather MacAllister and Jacqueline Diamond.*

HARLEQUIN®
Makes any time special ™

PHTB

HARLEQUIN®
AMERICAN ◆ ROMANCE®

and **Muriel Jensen**
present

WHO'S THE DADDY?

$\mathcal{A}$t a festive costume ball, three identical
sisters meet three masked bachelors.

$\mathcal{E}$ach couple has a taste of true love behind
the anonymity of their costumes—but
only one will become parents
in nine months!

Find out who it will be!

November 2000
FATHER FEVER #858

January 2001
FATHER FORMULA #855

March 2001
FATHER FOUND #866

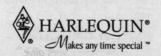

◆ HARLEQUIN®
Makes any time special ™

#1 *New York Times* bestselling author

NORA ROBERTS

brings you more of the loyal and loving,
tempestuous and tantalizing Stanislaski family.

Coming in February 2001

The Stanislaski Sisters

Natasha and Rachel

Though raised in the Old World traditions of their
family, fiery Natasha Stanislaski and cool, classy
Rachel Stanislaski are ready for a *new* world of love....

*And also available in February 2001 from
Silhouette Special Edition, the newest book in the
heartwarming Stanislaski saga*

CONSIDERING KATE

Natasha and Spencer Kimball's daughter Kate turns her
back on old dreams and returns to her hometown, where
she finds the *man* of her dreams.

Available at your favorite retail outlet.

Where love comes alive™

TEXAS
CONFIDENTIAL

Penny Archer has always been the
dependable and hardworking executive
assistant for Texas Confidential, a secret
agency of Texas lawmen. But her daring
heart yearned to be the heroine of her
own adventure—and to find a love
that would last a lifetime.

And this time...
THE SECRETARY GETS HER MAN
by Mindy Neff

Coming in January 2001 from

 HARLEQUIN®

AMERICAN *Romance*